Dogs of War

Ixan Legacy Book 3

Scott Bartlett

Mirth Publishing
St. John's

DOGS OF WAR

© Scott Bartlett 2018

Cover art by: Tom Edwards (tomedwardsdesign.com)

This work is licensed under the Creative Commons Attribution-NonCommercial-ShareAlike 4.0 License. To view a copy of this license, visit creativecommons.org/licenses/by-nc-sa/4.0 or send a letter to Creative Commons, 171 2nd Street, Suite 300, San Francisco, California 94105, USA.

This novel is a work of fiction. All of the characters, places, and events are fictitious. Any resemblance to actual persons living or dead, locales, businesses, or events is entirely coincidental.

Library and Archives Canada Cataloguing in Publication

Bartlett, Scott

Dogs of War / Scott Bartlett ; illustrations by Tom Edwards.

ISBN 978-1-988380-13-1

To those who endure.

PROLOGUE

Other Husher
21 Years Ago

"Riesling," Captain Vin Husher said, "I want constant active scans of the area around the *Firedrake* as we approach the far side of the system."

"Yes, sir," the sensor operator said, still sounding a little shaken from the recent battle.

Wicks was in sick bay, expected to make a full recovery. Chief Hernandez had been bumped from second watch up to first. Lieutenant Myers would never be returning to the CIC again, and Ensign Volkov had taken her place.

The *Firedrake* was deep down Pirate's Path. They'd been sent here by Admiral Carrow, to find out what had the Winger pirates so worked up. At last, after the most recent attack, he had his answer: stealth tech. They'd used it to latch onto his corvette's hull undetected. Then they'd cut through her, coming out into a bunkroom full of sleeping marines.

Those marines had all died. Husher had paid the Wingers back in kind, though the ship's pilot had escaped with the stealth ship.

They're hiding something in this system. They had to be—else, why would they resort to such a desperate attack?

The Wingers had also struck just before the *Firedrake* had entered this system. Husher shuddered as he remembered how it had felt to use wormholes in battle for the first time. Enabled by dark tech, the wormholes could be engineered to allow only the *Firedrake*'s ordnance through. They'd fired on the pirate ships without fear of retaliation. They'd slaughtered them.

As they combed the section of the asteroid belt where they expected to find a pirate base, Husher compiled a full report on the recent incursion into his ship. When he was finished, he transmitted it to Admiral Carrow via the micronet—another dark tech-enabled innovation that allowed instantaneous communication.

It didn't take long for a reply to come, in the form of a single line of text: "Contact me the moment you find something."

And so, Husher and his crew kept searching. They found nothing on the first day, nor on the second. On the third, Husher began to doubt, even though all the evidence pointed toward *something* being concealed in this part of the system.

At last, they found it: a hollowed-out asteroid, with barely anything to indicate it was different from any other, except for the light that bounced off a partially concealed airlock. If they hadn't approached the asteroid from just the right angle, they could easily have missed it.

Husher sent a shuttle of marines aboard to inspect the installation, and they found it empty, with all the relevant data taken or destroyed. But it was already clear what the structure was: a shipbuilding facility, large enough to produce two vessels at a time, of a size with the one that had latched onto *Firedrake*'s hull.

Who knows how many of these they might have hidden in random locations along Pirate's Path. The Path was long, and largely uninhabited, other than the Kaithe. There were plenty of hiding places, where an installation like this might go unnoticed for years.

Husher got in touch with Admiral Carrow as soon as the marines returned with their findings. He patched the connection through to the CIC, so that the admiral's gaunt face appeared on the main viewscreen.

"Destroy it," Carrow said once he heard what they'd found.

Husher turned to Volkov and nodded. "Four Banshees should do it."

With the admiral occupying the main screen, Husher opened a visual on his console, as well as a tactical display, which he used to track the missiles' progress.

The asteroid blossomed with flame, flinging pieces of rock and metal in every direction.

"It's done, Admiral," Husher said.

"Very good. Unfortunately, you're *not* done, Captain. You've uncovered quite an infestation, and I want it burned out. Entirely. I want you to continue—"

Husher noticed Riesling tense up at his console. "Sir," the sensor operator said, "I'm sorry to interrupt, but we just detected an engine burn consistent with a vessel the size of the one that attacked us."

Husher frowned. "Do you think it could be the same one?"

"I doubt it. Its trajectory suggests it came from the facility we just destroyed."

"It's a stealth ship, then? How did we detect it?"

"It's hard for me to say, without knowing how stealth tech functions. It's possible they were waiting until an asteroid drifted into place so that they could conceal their engine burn, but they made a miscalculation. We only saw a glimmer, so they nearly had it right, but I can confirm without a doubt that it was indeed an engine firing."

"Can you project their position based on the burn?"

"I can tell you their trajectory, and I can also estimate their position within a fairly tight range of possibilities. But one thing's certain: they're within firing range, and if we shoot along their exact trajectory, we'll hit them. They would have to perform another engine burn to evade our ordnance, which would reveal their exact position to us."

"I want that ship destroyed, Husher," Carrow said.

Some of the CIC officers glanced at their captain, and others kept their gazes fixed on their consoles. Husher noticed Riesling's head jerk a little, and Tucker's shoulders rose and fell with deepening breaths.

As Husher stared down at the tactical display on his console—at the region of space he imagined the stealth ship would be—he remembered the rumors that Darkstream, the company built on dark tech, had Admiral Carrow in their pocket. Darkstream wanted war, people said, no matter the reason. No matter the cost. It was the company's business model.

"Sir, if we can hit them with a missile, then we can definitely reach them with a transmission request," Husher said at last.

"What's your point?" Carrow asked, narrowing his eyes.

"Maybe we can secure their surrender."

"Why in Sol would we want to do that?"

Husher lifted his gaze to meet the Admiral's. "Because they haven't fired on us. They should be given the chance to surrender peacefully. Isn't that what we're supposed to do, under the ROIs?"

"You're out in the middle of nowhere, Captain," Carrow growled. "And that ship just came directly from a pirate base. We're not going to have any trouble firing on that ship. Are we?"

But Husher pressed on: "If we apprehend them, we could reverse engineer their stealth tech. We could build stealth ships of our own. At the very least, we could find out exactly what we're dealing with."

But either there were factors at play that Carrow wasn't sharing, or he just didn't like having his orders questioned. Whatever the case, Husher could see the resolve in his eyes, even before he opened his mouth to double down: "We *are* going to send a message to these pirate scumbags today, Captain, but it's not going to be a transmission request. We're going to show them that even stealth tech won't save them from the might of the Human Commonwealth. *We* say what goes and what doesn't in this galaxy. We *are* the moral high ground. Now, Captain, I hope I won't have to say this again: *take that ship out*."

"I'm sorry, Admiral. I can't."

"Excuse me?"

"I can't continue shooting beings in the back from an unassailable position. I could fire on that ship, and if it performed an engine burn to evade, I could open a wormhole behind it and blast it from space. But this isn't even warfare anymore. It's butchery. I won't fire on that ship—not without at least offering them the chance to surrender."

Carrow's eyes were wide, and his face achieved a darker shade of red than Husher had ever seen from him. "What if I told you that if you don't follow my order, then I plan to personally ensure you're stripped of command?"

Husher met the admiral's stare for several long seconds. He could feel the gaze of his CIC crew on him.

The right choice shone before him, like a beacon. *It's your career or your principles.* He didn't have a family to support, so he didn't have that pressure to preserve his military career by compromising his morals. But being a starship captain had always been his dream, and he was one of the youngest officers to serve as one since humans first took to the stars. *Am I really going to throw that away?*

The Commonwealth called the pirates terrorists. Maybe they were right. Maybe the Wingers didn't deserve the chance to surrender, or a fair trial.

Husher lowered his eyes, very aware of his CIC crew all around him. "Tactical, fire on the stealth ship with a round of kinetic impactors."

Chief Tucker turned toward him, eyes wide with shock and disappointment.

"Do it," Husher said, his voice hardening.

"I can't continue shooting beings in the back from an unassailable position. I could fire on that ship, and if it performed an engine burn to evade, I could open a wormhole behind it and blast it from space. But this isn't even warfare anymore. It's butchery. I won't fire on that ship—not without at least offering them the chance to surrender."

Carrow's eyes were wide, and his face achieved a darker shade of red than Husher had ever seen from him. "What if I told you that if you don't follow my order, then I plan to personally ensure you're stripped of command?"

Husher met the admiral's stare for several long seconds. He could feel the gaze of his CIC crew on him.

The right choice shone before him, like a beacon. *It's your career or your principles.* He didn't have a family to support, so he didn't have that pressure to preserve his military career by compromising his morals. But being a starship captain had always been his dream, and he was one of the youngest officers to serve as one since humans first took to the stars. *Am I really going to throw that away?*

The Commonwealth called the pirates terrorists. Maybe they were right. Maybe the Wingers didn't deserve the chance to surrender, or a fair trial.

Husher lowered his eyes, very aware of his CIC crew all around him. "Tactical, fire on the stealth ship with a round of kinetic impactors."

Chief Tucker turned toward him, eyes wide with shock and disappointment.

"Do it," Husher said, his voice hardening.

"Sir, if we can hit them with a missile, then we can definitely reach them with a transmission request," Husher said at last.

"What's your point?" Carrow asked, narrowing his eyes.

"Maybe we can secure their surrender."

"Why in Sol would we want to do that?"

Husher lifted his gaze to meet the Admiral's. "Because they haven't fired on us. They should be given the chance to surrender peacefully. Isn't that what we're supposed to do, under the ROIs?"

"You're out in the middle of nowhere, Captain," Carrow growled. "And that ship just came directly from a pirate base. We're not going to have any trouble firing on that ship. Are we?"

But Husher pressed on: "If we apprehend them, we could reverse engineer their stealth tech. We could build stealth ships of our own. At the very least, we could find out exactly what we're dealing with."

But either there were factors at play that Carrow wasn't sharing, or he just didn't like having his orders questioned. Whatever the case, Husher could see the resolve in his eyes, even before he opened his mouth to double down: "We *are* going to send a message to these pirate scumbags today, Captain, but it's not going to be a transmission request. We're going to show them that even stealth tech won't save them from the might of the Human Commonwealth. *We* say what goes and what doesn't in this galaxy. We *are* the moral high ground. Now, Captain, I hope I won't have to say this again: *take that ship out.*"

"I'm sorry, Admiral. I can't."

"Excuse me?"

"Yes, sir."

On the main viewscreen, Carrow nodded, the scarlet slowly draining from his face. "You can have a bright career with the UHF, Husher. I've rarely seen a young officer with your potential, so I'm willing to overlook today's transgression. But if you ever *hint* at defying my orders again, I *will* arrange that court martial. Is that clear?"

"Yes, Admiral."

CHAPTER 1

Not a Request

Fesky stared at the CIC's main display, unable to process what she was seeing. The display showed her best friend's face—Captain Vin Husher's face. But it wasn't really her friend. It couldn't be. This Husher had a scar running from temple to chin, and he was glaring at her with murder in his eyes.

"Unknown vessel, identify yourself at once or prepare to be attacked," he said.

Fesky tried to speak, but couldn't at first. Then, finally, she managed it: "*Husher?*"

He narrowed his eyes, though otherwise he didn't react. Fesky sensed the coldness that exuded from him—as though he was ready to kill her without a glimmer of remorse. For her, that was the most jarring thing of all.

"How do you know my name?" he said.

When Fesky had agreed to captain the *Spire*, the IGF's first interdimensional vessel, she'd assumed she was in for some bizarre experiences. But nothing could have prepared her for this.

"I asked you a question," Husher said. "Two questions, technically. Who are you? And how do you know my name?"

She glanced at the tactical display on her console and estimated that the other ship would enter firing range within ten minutes. *We should transition out of this universe.* But Husher—the Husher she'd known for decades; the one who didn't act like he wanted to kill her—had sent her to the Progenitors' home dimension to gather intel for the IGF. Intel they could use to end the war.

There was plenty about this place she didn't understand. Why did the Progenitors occupy a system whose layout matched Sol? And why was there a gigantic forcefield surrounding the entire system, suspended just beyond what could only be the Kuiper Belt?

Why is my best friend captaining a Progenitor ship?

Fesky's own ship, the *Spire*, sat just inside that Kuiper Belt. She needed to use the ten minutes before the opposing ship entered firing range to find out anything she could. And right now, this warped version of Husher was her primary source of intel.

"Last chance," he said. "Who—"

"I'm Commander Fesky of the Integrated Galactic Fleet," she said. "I've known you for twenty years, and I served as your XO for seventeen of them. I'm also your best friend."

"Liar. I'd never befriend a Winger."

Fesky's beak snapped shut. It felt like she'd been slapped. "Why not?" she said at last.

"Because you belong to an inferior species. Which is why you were wiped out."

"But we weren't wiped out. I'm right here."

Husher frowned. "Prove it to me. Prove that you know me."

"Okay," Fesky said, and drew a shaky breath. "Your greatest hero was Leonard Keyes."

Husher laughed loudly. "That couldn't be farther from the truth. I'm not sure how you knew Keyes, but I was no *admirer* of his." He lifted a finger to his face, running it along the puckered line that crossed it. "Keyes was the one who gave me this."

"We served together, you and I," Fesky said, fighting through her shock at Husher's words. "On the *Providence*."

"Wrong again. Absurdly wrong. Are you delusional, Winger?"

"Your father is Warren Husher, a starship captain before you. Your mother is Cassandra. She raised you in a bungalow on Venus."

That seemed to give Husher pause. "So you do know some personal details about me," he said. Nodding as though to himself, he went on: "I'd like to discuss this further, face-to-face. I'm interested to hear how you came by your information, but I'm much more concerned about how you made it to this system in the first place."

"I'm afraid that discussion isn't going to happen," Fesky said. The other ship was drawing too near, for her liking, and it was time for the *Spire* to leave. This other Husher hadn't been very forthcoming, but her sensor operator had had plenty of time to collect data—on the thousands of ships in this system, as well as on its layout. *We have to get back with what we have.* She turned to her Nav officer.

"Oh, it wasn't a request," Husher broke in before she could give an order.

"Ma'am," her sensor operator said, sounding panicked, "there's a change with several asteroids along a wide arc off our stern. Parts of them are opening up, revealing mounted weapons. They're firing on us."

"Nav, get us out of this universe!" Fesky yelled.

Chief Devar bent over her console to enter the necessary command, but it was too late. Ordnance connected with the *Spire*'s hull, and an explosion rocked the ship, then another.

"Yvan, what was that?" she snapped.

"Our starboard and port main capacitor banks," the sensor operator said. "They're both blown."

Devar turned to Fesky, and when she spoke, her voice was soft. "We no longer have the charge necessary to transition out of this universe, ma'am. We're stuck."

With creeping horror, Fesky returned her gaze to the tactical display, where the Progenitor ship was about to enter firing range.

She remembered the cold stare this version of Husher had directed at her, and part of her wanted to order an attack, in the hopes of forcing him to destroy the *Spire*. She had no desire to meet him in person, or to give him access to whatever information there was to be gleaned from her ship or her crew.

But she had a duty to that crew. She couldn't just sacrifice their lives on a whim.

"Coms," she said softly, "send the approaching ship a transmission request. Tell them we surrender."

CHAPTER 2

The Cavern

Husher adjusted the cuffs of his midnight Darkstream military uniform as he walked toward the shuttle that would take him and his prisoner to Ragnarok Station, in high Earth orbit.

He found her inside, strapped into a crash seat, arms and wings bound together.

"I'm told you didn't resist capture," he said. "You're pliant. Just like a Winger."

She cursed him, and he sat in the crash seat opposite her, fixing her with his gaze. A pair of marines filed into the shuttle, taking seats on either side of the Winger.

He'd taken several prisoners from the strange vessel that had appeared on the system's outskirts, but he didn't want them all crowded in the shuttle with him during the trip to the space station. They would all end up there before the day was out, but he didn't want to have to look at them.

He didn't particularly want to look at the Winger, either. But since she'd been in command, he expected her to be the most valuable source of information.

Information he intended to extract quickly.

"I'm taking you into the Cavern," he told her. "The difference between you and everyone else I've ever taken there is that they knew where they were headed. You're much calmer than they were."

"I won't tell you anything," the Winger said.

"Of course you will. Wingers always put on a show at first, always so eager to demonstrate their loyalty and obedience to their masters. But I'm going to hurt you, Winger, in just the right ways. I'm going to dismantle your psyche, and then I'll rebuild it to serve a new master. Me. You'll be just as eager to obey."

"I won't tell you anything," the Winger repeated.

"We'll see."

The shuttle passed through an exterior airlock and into one of Ragnarok's massive landing bays, setting down near a hatch leading into the station. Husher nodded to the two marines, and they seized the Winger, dragging her from her seat and through the shuttle's airlock. That done, they fell in behind Husher as he led the way through the labyrinthine station.

At last, they arrived at the Cavern, situated in the center of the station. Husher punched in his access code, and the hatch slid open to admit them. "Put her in the chair," he ordered the marines. They shoved the Winger through the hatch.

Husher followed at a leisurely pace, hands clasped behind his back, enjoying the vastness of the Cavern. The ceiling hung far overheard, hidden by the chamber's murk. When you stood in the center, the bulkheads weren't visible either—only the floor was lit, by a light source none could see. At Husher's request, one of the AIs had been instructed to work out how to make oxygen molecules low-hanging and phosphorescent.

He felt powerful, here—more powerful even than sitting in the command seat of his destroyer. Here, he commanded the universe, and the universe obeyed.

The marines had finished strapping the Winger securely into the chair. "Go," he told them, and they left.

"Welcome to the Cavern," Husher said, turning to his subject after watching the marines exit. "I'm sure even your dim wits can discern what's about to happen." He smiled. "I make no promises about what will happen after the pain stops, but I can tell you that there's only one way to make it stop completely: by giving me what I want. I want to know how you reached this solar system—this universe—and from where. I'll start with the second part. A small bit of data you might offer me, to smooth relations between us. Are you from the Milky Way? The one situated in the universe we're in the process of conquering?"

The bird remained silent.

"You can spare yourself any pain at all by giving me the information I need right away," he said.

"We're best friends," the Winger said. "We've been best friends for twenty years."

"Well, if you're not going to talk, I'm afraid today may strain the friendship." He took a step forward. "I think you are from the Milky Way, which means I must know how you got here, and whether the IU has the means to get here as well. Trust me, I will find out. I've tortured thousands of beings, including plenty of Wingers. You may think it distasteful for the commander of system defense to moonlight as a torturer, but the truth is, I've come to enjoy it. Besides, no one else is as good at it as I am. Keep in mind, bird, that I'm not restricted by the sort of interstellar conventions they have in the IU. I have full reign to use absolutely any method I wish, and if you die in the process, I won't face any consequences." Husher turned, gesturing at the murky void created by the Cavern. "I requested this room's construction myself, after developing a theory of what sort of environments would best facilitate the infliction of pain. I was given exactly what I wanted. Don't you think it perfectly emulates the empty hopelessness of space?"

"You can't do this to me," the Winger rasped. "Vin Husher would never be able to bring himself to do such a thing."

"Anyone can bring themselves to do such a thing. Anyone is capable of this. If you haven't realized that yet, you haven't been paying attention. You should know, bird, that continuing to resist me will guarantee permanent disfigurement, of the sort your society's iatric nanobots simply cannot repair. That's in case you're harboring hope of escape or rescue. If that were to happen, which it won't, you'd never be able to look upon your peers again without them seeing how you've been diminished.

Husher approached the chair, directing both hands toward it and shaping it with midair gestures. The top half of the chair twisted toward him, offering the Winger's face for him to backhand. He did so, and she cried out, her face snapping sideways.

"You'll feel like you're deteriorating," he went on, "like you're being removed from yourself, piece by piece. That's because you *will* be deteriorating."

He snapped his fingers, and twin syringes extended from opposite sides of the chair, affixed to the ends of spindly, articulated metal arms. They were programmed to identify the species of the subject and seek a usable vein, which they did now, jabbing the Winger in the neck and arm.

The Winger's beak snapped shut, and her head lifted from the chair's headrest as she strained against the straps keeping her down.

"You've just been injected with methamphetamine," Husher explained. "It will help keep you conscious, and once you've developed a dependence on the drug and I start denying you it, the withdrawal symptoms will serve as additional threads in your tapestry of pain."

Sliding a vertical hand through the air, he opened a compartment built into the deck underneath the chair, from which he extracted a pair of leather, steel-studded gloves. His fist crashed into the side of the Winger's face.

An hour later, he stood over a battered, bleeding Winger, whose beak was cracked and whose wide eyes jerked back and forth.

Still, she refused to give him the information he needed.

A memory gripped him, then—from the last time he'd underestimated an enemy.

Captain Leonard Keyes had locked eyes with him the moment he'd exited the shuttle. They were cold eyes, and they never left Husher's as the marines forced the rogue captain to cross the flight deck.

"Nine years," Husher said when the marines brought Keyes within earshot. "Nine years I've hunted you while you played the downtrodden revolutionary. And now my marines find you in an incompetently hidden base on a forsaken rock deep inside the Bastion Sector. I suppose it's fitting."

"The Bastion Sector won't exist for much longer if your masters are allowed to continue, Darkstream dog."

Husher chuckled. "Who's going to stop them? And why would anyone want to? Humanity rules the galaxy. We've achieved something our ancestors couldn't have even dreamed—"

"The galaxy won't exist either," Keyes said. "Dark tech is ripping this universe apart."

"We have contingency plans," Husher said. "The AIs—"

Keyes tore himself from the marines' grasp, a blade extending from his uniform's sleeve. His arm swung upward in a wide arc, and Husher raised his hands to block—too late. Keyes dragged the blade across Husher's face, and he staggered backward, blinking through a curtain of blood.

Husher palmed the wetness from his face and saw that the marines had seized Keyes again, though the man's bunched sleeve was still clutched in his fingers, to give the blade stability.

Husher drew his sidearm and shot Keyes in the face at point-blank range. The marines released him, then, and the rebel captain slumped backward onto the deck. Striding forward, Husher emptied the clip into his torso.

The Winger coughed, pulling him back to the present. He realized he'd been standing there in silence for at least a minute, completely still.

Without another word, he yanked off the scarlet-covered gloves by the fingertips, dropping them to the floor. Then he strode toward the exit hatch.

Out in the corridor, he yanked his com from its holster to contact his boss.

"Captain Husher," Tennyson Steele said. "Have you extracted the relevant information from the subject?"

"No. I intend to, but for now, she's holding out. I don't think we should underestimate the significance of that. The fact she's so determined not to talk suggests she possesses some very valuable intel."

"Like the IU having discovered interdimensional travel."

"Yes. I don't know how, but the bird's presence makes it a near-certainty. Sooner or later, more ships will follow."

"How do you think we should respond to this revelation?"

Husher drew a deep breath. "We need to begin prioritizing speed over efficiency. It's time to begin the invasion."

CHAPTER 3

Laying Waste

The day after Husher defended Thessaly with the help of Captain Norberg and the battle group led by Captain Harding, the Progenitors struck again. This time, the target was the next system over: the Caprice System, home to the galactic capital, Abdera.

Despite that the *Vesta* was still limping after the previous day's battle—one of her main capacitors had been blown out completely—Husher was left with no choice: he ordered the *Vesta* to respond.

"The Progenitor ships are reacting to our approach, sir," Winterton said, mostly successful in keeping the fatigue out of his voice.

We're all exhausted. They'd just finished fighting back-to-back battles against the IU and then the Progenitors, and now the Progenitors were pressing the attack again. "Reacting in what way, Winterton?" Husher could already see how the enemy was reacting, but he needed the sensor operator to say it, so that every CIC officer was on the same page.

"They appear to be abandoning their attack on Abdera completely. Their ships are vanishing from the universe, one by one."

"I don't trust that for a second," Husher said. "Coms, order Commander Ayam to launch the Air Group, and tell Captain Harding that she and the other captains should expect an attack at any moment. They need to be ready to adopt lateral evasive maneuvers, in the event the Progenitors target them with particle beams."

"Aye, sir."

"Tremaine, ready the primary laser, along with two Hydra broadsides. If they form a sphere around us again, I don't plan to leave it intact for very long."

"Yes, Captain."

"Ships appearing off our bow, sir," Winterton said, which confirmed Husher's suspicions about the Progenitors' supposed retreat. *They just wanted to engage us away from Abdera's defense platforms.* "Looks like a curved wall formation, one that's fairly dispersed," the ensign continued, then he winced. "One of the UHF-model ships just went down."

Damn it. Husher's warning about the particle beam clearly hadn't arrived in time. He opened a direct channel to his CAG. "Commander Ayam, do you read me?"

"Loud and clear, Captain."

"I need you to pressure those vessels now, or they're going to start knocking down the rest of our warships. Are your subspace pilots ready?"

"They are. We can start savaging the nearest destroyer within five minutes."

Husher hiked an eyebrow at the Winger's colorful description, but decided now wasn't the time to remark on it. "Deploy the rest of your pilots as you see fit, then transition to subspace at once, Commander."

"Will do, Captain."

The tactical display Husher had ordered his Oculenses to project onto the main display showed that the enemy formation had almost finished appearing. By opting not to surround the *Vesta* as they had yesterday, they'd once again anticipated Husher's tactics. The enemy's formation meant the Hydra broadsides he'd prepared were next to useless.

But maybe not completely useless. "Helm, I want you to increase power to engines by twenty-five percent. In the meantime, Tactical, I want you to reprogram the starboard-side Hydras. Once we've outstripped our allied ships, I want them to launch from their tubes and follow a dispersed arc that blankets the left side of the enemy formation with warheads. That should keep them busy as our Pythons get into position."

"I'm on it, sir," Tremaine said, tapping his console furiously as he updated the telemetry.

The sensor operator turned toward Husher. "Progenitor ships are still appearing, Captain. More than were originally attacking Abdera."

Husher resisted an urge to put a hand to his forehead and massage his taut brow. "They see an opportunity to take us down," he said. "If they manage that, they'll return to Abdera and finish penetrating her defenses." He shifted his gaze to Chief Noni. "Nav, set a course for the Larkspur-Caprice darkgate under reverse thrust. Tell the other captains to do the same, Coms. After that, I want you to launch a drone with a message requesting aid from Captain Norberg and her remaining battle group ships. They should still be in orbit over Thessaly."

"Aye, sir," both officers answered.

Ek shifted in the XO's seat, peering at him through the water-filled helmet of her exoskeleton. As she spoke, her suit's AI translated the sound waves traveling through the fluid and projected her words clearly through a speaker: "Something seems amiss here, Captain Husher. The *Vesta* may not, in fact, be the Progenitor's primary target this day."

"Right. But whether their true aim is the galactic capital or my ship doesn't really matter. Either way, we can't let a Progenitor force of that size remain at large in one of the core systems."

"Yes, sir," the Fin said, turning to face the main display once more.

Husher narrowed his eyes. "Is there something you're withholding, Commander?"

"I have given you my analysis based on the data available to me at this time. If I reach further conclusions, I will let you know at once."

"Very good."

"Enemy ships are launching Ravagers in enormous numbers, sir," Winterton said. "Thousands are in play already, leaving very little room for our Pythons to maneuver."

A sigh escaped Husher's lips. "Coms, tell our fighters to abandon the attack on the enemy vessels and focus instead on cutting down that Ravager barrage. Squadrons that manage to cut a swath big enough, however, should follow through on my original orders and try to get in an alpha strike."

On the tactical display, Husher saw defensive missiles already streaming forth from the old UHF ships, without him having to request them. *That's nice.* The *Vesta*'s only remaining battle group ship—the *Knight*, a destroyer—did the same, and the sole Quatro ship added its own missiles to the barrage as well. The Quatro missiles were more or less conventional, except for the salvage function, which Husher doubted they'd have an opportunity to use today.

That didn't bother him, so long as they lost no further ships, and he was willing to risk overcommitting to defense if it meant preventing that. The UHF-model ships were all twenty years outdated at least, but along with the *Knight* and the Quatro ship, they were the only battle group the *Vesta* had now, and he doubted he'd get another.

His force danced backward, using missiles and Pythons as a shield against the unending onslaught of Ravagers while keeping up lateral propulsion to ensure hulls weren't exposed to particle beams for too long.

At last, as they neared the darkgate, the *Eos* burst out of it. Four warships trailed her, which were all that remained of the combined battle groups of two capital starships: the *Eos* and the felled *Promedon*.

They moved to bolster Husher's ranks, lasers lancing out, all tightly focused on the same Progenitor destroyer. Under normal circumstances, Husher would have called that overkill, but given the Progenitors' tendency of vanishing whenever pressured, it made sense to destroy targets as rapidly as possible.

Indeed, the moment the destroyer went down, the Progenitor force disappeared as one, leaving only a tide of missile-robots for the allied ships to clean up.

"Thank you, Captain Norberg," Husher said once he had her on the main display. On the tactical display, he watched the assembled warships continue to inch backward toward the darkgate, using mostly kinetic impactors to mow down the incoming Ravagers. "I owe you one."

Norberg nodded briskly. "Think you can handle the rest of these Ravagers? I need to get back to Thessaly. The colony's undefended right now, other than the orbital defense platforms, and it's missing one of those after yesterday."

Husher glanced again at the tactical display. "We can handle things here, Captain."

"Very good." Norberg terminated the conversation, not bothering with formalities. Things were still a little prickly between them—they *had* been fighting each other right before the battle over Thessaly, after all.

Minutes after Norberg's departure through the Caprice-Larkspur darkgate, a com drone emerged from it. The Coms officer tapped her console, no doubt accessing the message, and a few seconds later her face turned white.

"What is it, Ensign?" Husher asked.

"It's a message from Captain Norberg, sir. The *Eos* returned to Larkspur and found the Progenitors already laying waste to Thessaly."

CHAPTER 4

Spread Too Thin

Husher sat on his bunk with head in hands.

There's nothing to be done.

By the time Norberg and her ships reached Thessaly, the Progenitors had finished their work and vanished again. As soon as the government on Abdera got the news, they ordered the *Vesta* and her battle group to maintain orbit around the capital, along with Norberg and her remaining battle group ships.

Quatro vessels had been called from elsewhere to protect what was left of the IU's presence in Larkspur, and more had come to bolster the defenses around Abdera. President Chiba had decided that losing the galactic capital would prove crippling to the war effort.

I'm sure that's true. But Husher also wagered Chiba's presence on Abdera might have had something to do with the decision.

Husher had given the necessary orders to array the *Vesta* and the other ships around Abdera in proper defensive formation, and then he completed his watch. After, he'd retreated to his chamber, to mourn the people of Thessaly, and to berate himself for letting the Progenitors bait him enough to leave the colony exposed.

Thessaly was a major colony—a mainly human colony. Why hadn't the admiralty allocated more defenders to it?

He swept aside such conspiratorial thoughts. *The IU is just too big, and our forces are spread too thinly.* The Progenitors were exploiting that situation viciously.

Where are you, Fesky? He'd expected her back by now. Surely, the recon mission he'd given her wouldn't have had her lingering in the Progenitor's home dimension for this long. *Something went wrong.* He told himself he was leaping to that conclusion too quickly, but it felt true in his gut.

The com buzzed on the bunk beside him, and he snatched it up. Major Gamble was contacting him.

"Go ahead, Major."

"Sir, the sheriff in Cybele just informed me we have a new round of unrest brewing over there. Said he wanted to let me know, in case you wanted to put some soldiers on standby."

"What level of unrest?"

"Loud but peaceful demonstrating, so far. But some Sapient Brotherhood members have been spotted gathering nearby, and they're staying strangely quiet. I know you threw out all the people caught rioting, but..."

"We can't be too careful," Husher said. "I'm heading over there myself to check it out."

"Sir, if you're doing that, I have to insist on sending an escort to meet you."

"Fine. I'll take two marines with me, Major. *Two.* Beyond that, I can handle myself. Have them meet me just inside the hatch into Cybele."

"Yes, sir," Gamble said, sounding resigned. If Husher knew the man, he'd have at least two platoons waiting somewhere nearby, ready to deploy until Husher reentered the ship's crew section safe and sound.

The pair of marines he'd authorized to accompany him saluted when he approached, and together, they ventured out of the crew section, into the great hold that held the city. They found the protesters outside the Epicenter, which was a domed building that always reminded Husher of half a golf ball. It was meant to serve as a social hub for the community, but mostly people used it as a place to house their bodies as they entered digital spaces.

He estimated there were a couple hundred demonstrators, whose chants became more distinct as they approached. Just before Husher and his marines reached the group, the chanting trailed off as a woman got up to speak.

Penelope Snyder.

"There haven't been very many times in my life when..." she began, but then stopped. Her eyes were locked on Husher. "I see we have a visitor."

The sea of faces turned toward him, a great tide following Snyder's gaze.

"Captain Husher," Snyder went on. "Do you know what we're protesting here today?"

He shook his head.

"I might have guessed. Well, let me fill you in. We're protesting the way Thessaly's evacuation was handled."

Husher pressed his lips together. *That anyone managed to escape the colony at all is a near-miracle.* From the vids he'd seen, the Progenitors had done a pretty thorough job of scouring the planet's towns and cities. A few loners living out in the wilderness had survived, but that was about it.

"The colony's wealthy elite were grossly overrepresented among the evacuees," Snyder said. "The Progenitor attack was tragic enough, but the fact that the underprivileged were left to burn makes yesterday a grotesque travesty. Do you have anything you'd care to comment about that, Captain?"

He cleared his throat, preparing to project his voice across the crowd. "I agree that yesterday was a tragedy *and* a travesty," he said. "But I would point out to you that the colony's wealthy were also the ones who owned the ships capable of going off-world. And many of those shipowners packed their vessels with their fellow citizens before departing. True, some didn't—some of them had no time, and others let fear override their nobler impulses. But most did."

Snyder was shaking her head. "You said it yourself, Captain: *some didn't.* You're minimizing that point. This is what happens when beings are allowed to lord their privilege over others, racking up riches and influence. Monsters are created."

"There are monsters among every segment of society," Husher said.

"*This* monstrosity is without equal," Snyder shot back. "The fact remains, the poor died yesterday in droves, while the rich largely survived. Frankly, I find your defense of the situation disgusting."

With that, the crowd broke into angry jeering. Husher waited for them to finish, but soon realized they didn't intend to—not until he left.

And what could he do about that? No one was turning violent. They were following the laws he so firmly stood by. The fact that Snyder was taking advantage of a crisis to push her agenda of leveling out society was nauseating, but not illegal.

Not for the first time, he turned and walked out of Cybele, having accomplished nothing.

He'd spent the last twenty years fighting to make galactic society formidable enough to take on the Progenitors when they came. Never had it been so clear how thoroughly he'd failed.

Does society even deserve to survive?

But he quickly swept aside that thought, shocked at how much it made him sound like Teth.

CHAPTER 5

Iris

As he reentered the *Vesta*'s crew section, his com buzzed with a text transmission from Ensign Amy Fry: "Just a head's up, sir: your ex-wife has arrived on a shuttle from Feverfew. She's on Flight Deck Omicron right now, and she's looking to speak with you."

Husher sighed, though at the same time he felt a measure of gratitude toward Fry. *My crew has my back.* No matter what happened next in this war, he knew that wouldn't change, and that held a lot of value for him.

He messaged back: "Have her shown to my office, and please contact my daughter to join us there as well. I'll need another chair."

Other than Maeve, Husher couldn't think of anything else Sera would want to discuss with him. And if they were going to talk about their daughter's situation, then he wanted her to be present. She deserved to be.

Ten minutes later, he sat in the chair behind his desk, contemplating the awkward silence that had descended when Sera entered to find Maeve already present.

"I asked to speak to you, Vin," Sera said at last. "You alone."

"What can you possibly have to say to me that our daughter can't hear? Or that she *shouldn't* hear?"

Sera grimaced.

"Is there anything other than Maeve's situation you care to discuss with me?" he asked.

"No."

"I see. Well, if you wanted to talk about Maeve without her present, I can only conclude one thing. Since you don't want her to remain aboard the *Vesta*, you must have been hoping to convince me to talk her into leaving."

Sera's tightening lips told him everything he needed to know about whether he was right. For her part, Maeve looked at her mother with an unreadable expression.

"Please, sweetheart," Sera said. "I've been torn apart with worry ever since you left Zakros. This ship has almost been destroyed so many times since then. Why do you need to do this to your mother?"

For reasons that weren't clear to him, Sera's words sent Husher back to his childhood, when he'd been nine. His own mother had come across him on the playground having a conflict with another boy he often spent time with—a conflict that was quickly escalating to a fight.

He hadn't realized it at the time, but her reaction that day was one of the things that made her so extraordinary. She didn't separate him from the other boy. She didn't even say anything. Instead, his mother walked on as if she hadn't noticed, and Husher and the other boy had had their tussle. After that, their differences sorted out, they'd become even better friends.

"Are you going to make me beg?" Sera went on, gaze locked on her daughter's face.

Husher cleared his throat. "I hate to say it, but the *Vesta* may be the safest place for Maeve, now." He wasn't sure he believed that, but his ex-wife had to be placated somehow, and besides, it might even be true. "The rest of the galaxy is in turmoil, Sera. Colonies with full complements of orbital defense platforms are getting destroyed. Who's to say she'd be any more secure on one of them than on a capital starship?"

Sera glared, which told him exactly how well that gambit had paid off. Softening her gaze, she returned it to their daughter. "Maeve, please—"

"I've decided not to go by Maeve anymore," she said.

Husher's eyes widened, and Sera recoiled as if slapped. "*What?*" she said.

"I'm going back to my birth name. The name you *both* gave me. I want to be Iris again." She stood and embraced her mother. "I love you, Mom. I really do. But you should go back to Zakros. I've made up my mind. I'm staying on the *Vesta*."

With that, Iris left Husher's office.

CHAPTER 6

Cast Low

Sera didn't have much to say after Iris left, and Husher didn't want to lord their daughter's decision over her, so he let her return to her shuttle without further comment.

He left his office soon after her, heading for sick bay. It was the first chance he'd had to visit Jake Price since he'd been shot.

When he drew back the curtain surrounding Price's bed, he was surprised to find Maeve—Iris—already sitting beside it. *She must have come straight here from my office.*

"Iris," he said, glad he hadn't used the wrong name out loud.

"Hi, Dad."

He took the seat next to her. "Did Bancroft mention how he's doing?" he asked, nodding at Price. Despite that Doctor Bancroft had helped Kaboh have Husher temporarily stripped of command, Husher hadn't made any move to get her off his ship. She was a good doctor, and he didn't want to lose her. He had her number, now, and that would have to be enough.

"She's worried about damage to his prefrontal cortex," Iris said. "Iatric nanobots repaired his skull, but the bullet caused his meninges to swell, which put a lot of pressure on the brain. Still, there's a good chance he'll make a full recovery."

"That wouldn't be true, if you hadn't done what you did."

She shrugged. "I didn't really think about it. I saw what Sato was doing, and I just acted."

"Others would have let shock hold them back. Or fear. If you'd hesitated for even a fraction of a second, Price would be dead."

Iris shrugged again.

They both fell silent, watching the rise and fall of Price's chest, listening to the beeping machines all around them.

Then, Iris looked at him. "I hope you don't think changing my name means I'm siding with you."

He raised his eyebrows. "I don't think there are sides. At least, there shouldn't be. Not when it comes to family."

"What family?" She gave a bitter chuckle, which sent a stab of remorse through his heart, even though he'd had nothing to do with splitting their family apart. "There *are* sides, Dad. You know there are. There's the side that wants to wrap society in a protective bubble, and there's the side that believes it's impossible to protect anything completely."

"Okay. Which side are you on, then?"

She shook her head. "Both, I think." Frowning, she continued: "I was at the protest earlier, you know. I heard what you said."

"That's fine. I wouldn't try to hide it from you."

"Don't you think it's awful that when disaster strikes, it's the poor that get screwed?"

"I do think it's awful. I think it's awful that anyone was killed by the Progenitors."

Iris shook her head. "That's a dodge. You're avoiding the heart of it: we can't go on like this, letting the poor get wiped out every time a crisis comes."

"Again, I'd rather no one got wiped out. I think that's a valid thing to say, and a valid thing to strive for. But I don't think it's what Snyder is striving for. She's laying the problem at the feet of the wealthy, when it should be laid at the Progenitors' feet, and the solution she's agitating for is to cast the wealthy low."

"People who leave behind their neighbors to die *should* be cast low."

"I agree with you. But many packed their ships full with evacuees. Should they be punished, too? Because that's how wide a net Snyder wants to cast. She wants to remove wealth from the equation altogether—make it so there are no more rich people. That's a very stupid thing to try to accomplish. We should be doing everything in our power to make it so that if people work hard and produce things society needs, there's a reasonable expectation of becoming wealthy. If we level things out completely, we'll remove most of the incentive to contribute. Goodwill alone doesn't keep a society going, sadly."

But Iris was shaking her head. "So you want to keep letting the chips fall where they may. Let the strong prosper and the weak perish."

"That's not what I said. I think it's fine to help people—to raise a tide that lifts everyone. But Snyder wants to make people equal by bringing the successful down, not by lifting the unfortunate up. It's poison."

His daughter had stopped listening. He followed her gaze to the bed, where Jake's eyes were open, and his brow furrowed.

He was staring straight at Iris.

"Who are you?" he said.

CHAPTER 7

Accelerate the Plan

Chiba, the President of the Interstellar Union, leaned back in his chair and gazed wearily at the seventeen documents his Oculenses now displayed in midair over his desk.

"I need sleep," he muttered to himself.

His job had always been taxing, but nothing could have prepared him for the way this war was testing him. Billions of lives hung on every decision he made, and on top of all that, the Quatro seemed uninterested in speaking with anyone except the President of the Union when it came to diplomatic and military matters. Or any matter, really. He supposed it was a reflection of their top-heavy style of governance, but whatever the reason, the Elders appeared to consider it beneath them to talk with any functionary except the president.

His office door's heavy, brass knobs turned, and the Quatro Eldest barreled through, sending both doors flying against the wall.

Speaking of which...

The doors closed behind the Quatro leader of their own accord, or so it would appear to an uninformed observer. Evolution had granted the Quatro brains laced with superconducting fullerenes, allowing them to manipulate metals at will. The warm temperature Chiba kept his office at dampened the power considerably, but the Eldest's superconducting capacity seemed stronger than his fellows. Enough that he could make the large, oaken doors fly open and closed with ease, anyway.

"Eldest," Chiba said. "To what do I owe the pleasure?"

He wasn't an expert in Quatro body language, but the alien didn't seem happy. It stalked across the office and came to a stop in front of the desk, lips peeled back in a silent snarl. Chiba fought to conceal his reaction. Normally, the Eldest sat on his haunches during their meetings.

"The Quatro are deeply disappointed with your recent actions, President Chiba," the alien growled.

"You'll have to be a little more specific," Chiba said, letting some of his annoyance come out in his voice. "I've been taking thousands of actions a day, lately. Today, I'm mostly trying to prevent what happened to Thessaly from happening elsewhere. With hundreds of colonized star systems, almost half of them accessible only by warp travel, that's proving very difficult."

"I refer to your continued willingness to work with Captain Vin Husher, who refused to turn over to us the Quatro criminal he harbors aboard his ship. And now, he flies with a ship full of such criminals. As I told you when we formed this alliance, we reserve the right to discipline wayward Quatro. They *must* be folded back into the drift."

Chiba shook his head, causing the muscular tail that hung from it to switch back and forth against his chair. "Husher is a man of the moment. As I told *you,* Eldest, right now we need him. But he's a tool whose utility will expire the day the war is won. It goes without saying that he gained his position because of privilege he never earned, and that will be his undoing, in the end. But until then, he has demonstrated his willingness to do battle to prevent those Quatro from being handed over. We can't afford to lose any more ships, Eldest. Or any more captains."

The Quatro reared up, planting his massive paws on Chiba's desk and lowering his head toward him, as though intending to strike.

Chiba recoiled—he couldn't help it. But the Quatro came to a stop within inches of his face.

"Your hollow ploys fail to impress," the Eldest growled. "We have grown weary of them. You need our military might, Kaithian, and we are prepared to withdraw it if we are not satisfied."

In spite of himself, Chiba quivered where he sat. "I d-don't know what I can do," he managed. "I'm at an impasse, Eldest. I w-wish—"

"*Silence,*" the Eldest hissed, and Chiba complied. "We need a gesture from you, something that indicates you are committed to cleansing your society of the toxicity that continues to pervade it. We will not maintain an alliance with an ally who is not willing to spurn toxic individuals."

"You want to accelerate the plan," Chiba said, hopeful for a way out of this conversation—from a diplomatic perspective and also from a bodily harm perspective.

The Quatro pulled away, so that Chiba no longer felt hot, moist breath on his face. "This is the perfect opportunity to do so," the Eldest said. "After the war, your people will be less susceptible. But right now, when they are at their most vulnerable, we can show them that our way is the only way forward."

"Yes," Chiba said, aware he was nodding a little too vigorously. "I completely agree. Let's iron out the details right now. Shall we?"

"We shall," the Eldest said, his orange eyes locked onto Chiba's.

CHAPTER 8

The Target Universe

Near the center of Ragnarok Station sat the office of Tennyson Steele, CEO of humanity. It doubled as a fully loaded panic room, designed to float in space for a week in the unlikely event of the station's destruction, providing full subsistence and amenities to its occupant.

A silky voice came from somewhere to Husher's left, where he sat in a plush leather armchair in the waiting room outside:

"Come in, Captain."

Husher stood in time for the office door to slide open, and he stepped through.

The CEO gestured toward the waiting chair before his desk, which caused his multiple jowls to wobble dynamically. He could have afforded all manner of cosmetic surgery to rid himself of the weight and to recapture a youthful appearance, but for some reason the CEO chose to keep his bulk. Husher knew that during certain times in human history, girth had been seen as a measure of status. *Maybe Steele is of the same mind.*

He sat, and the CEO wasted no time. Folding his hands on his desk and leaning forward slightly, he said, "I don't often get personal visits from you, Captain. To what do I owe the honor? If you're here to inquire about ramping up the invasion, I assure you it's well underway."

Husher nodded slightly. "That's why I'm here—that is, the fact I had to come here to get an update about the status of the invasion, even one as vague as you just gave me."

Steele narrowed his eyes. "This star system is your domain, Captain. Your jobs include inspecting the resources our AIs send us, making sure warships are ready for deployment, and maintaining our defenses in case we're ever attacked. *This* is your domain, just as the rest of the galaxy was, before it was swallowed whole. As for the target dimension, that's Teth's domain. And personally, I'm pleased with the job he's doing, despite the setbacks."

"I understand that," Husher said. "And I understand the reasoning for it. But with the things I'm learning from interrogating the Winger, I'm shocked by just how in the dark you've kept me. Why didn't you tell me my double is prominent in the Milky Way's defense?"

Steele tilted his head to one side. "You must have known there was a strong possibility you were alive in that universe, in some capacity."

"All I know is what you told me: that I went against Darkstream in that universe. I assumed that would have disadvantaged me, but now I learn the opposite: I'm prominent there, too! Look, I know my double's behavior has led you to distrust me, at least on some level. I'd feel the same way, in your position. But if he's playing a role in coordinating the Milky Way's defense, then I can guarantee you, you have bigger problems than you think you do."

A smile sprouted across Steele's red, chubby face. "I appreciate your faith in yourself."

"It isn't faith. It's certainty. I can help you, Steele. I'm not asking you to send me to the target universe. I know how cautious you are about letting me leave this star system, and again, I understand that. I have no desire to leave. But if you start letting me in on the intel you're getting from the Milky Way, I can help you anticipate my double's moves. I can help you counter them." He laid a hand on the desk, fingers curled upward, and Steele glanced at it before lifting his gaze once more. Drawing a deep breath, Husher added: "Withholding information was what got us in the situation we're in."

Steele's smile faded a little, at that. "We're in a *good* situation. What situation are you referring to, Captain?"

Husher waved at the surrounding walls. "I'm referring to our universe collapsing around us. I've always served Darkstream faithfully, but I'm also going to call things as I see them. The company's disinformation campaigns kept the public from seeing the truth about dark tech until it was too late. Now, we're forced to huddle in Sol while we fight to claim another universe for ourselves."

Steele's smile had vanished completely, replaced by a sneer. "I had no idea you took such a dim view of the results of Darkstream's actions, Captain. If this universe hadn't collapsed, wouldn't our enemies here still be alive? And would we have been able to consolidate power over our species as we have? Would we ever have had any reason to develop interdimensional travel, or to build AIs that could subvert the very history of another universe?"

Husher blinked. "I suppose not."

"Instead of one Winger, you'd have a whole species of them to contend with. The same goes for the Gok and the Kaithe, both who tried to defeat us in the end. If it hadn't been for the collapse, we might not have beaten the Kaithe. We weren't strong enough, then."

Husher's eyes fell to the desktop. "I understand your point of view. And it makes sense." He lifted his eyes once more. "But my argument still stands. Letting me in on more intel would bring benefit."

With a sigh, Steele said, "There's a lot of sensitive information kicking around the target universe; information I have no desire to let our public in on. Like the fact that my own double was killed by Captain Keyes, over there."

At that, Husher's eyebrows shot up.

"Yes," Steele went on, nodding. "Something else you don't know: Darkstream was exiled from their galaxy twenty years ago, for the crime of subverting democracy, and now the company's all but destroyed."

"The Milky Way has a democracy?"

"You see? These aren't things the people need to know—not until our hold on the target universe has been cemented, at the very least. But you'll note that I'm telling them to you."

"You're going to start letting me in on more intel."

"Indeed. I recognize the wisdom in what you've said. Which leaves me with the question of how to convey the relevant information to you in the most effective, efficient manner."

"Teth," Husher said. "I'd like to speak with Teth."

Steele smiled. "I'll arrange for you two to meet."

CHAPTER 9

Not Meant for Mechs

As he approached, Andy studied the marine guarding the hatch into Hangar Bay Zeta. The man held an R-57 assault rifle at the ready, and he studied Andy back.

"Hey man," Andy said once he reached the hatch. "Can I get through?"

The marine frowned at him. "I'm not supposed to let any Oneiri member access the mechs until we figure out why Sato attacked Price. Captain's orders."

"Right," Andy said letting his face fall. Then he lifted his gaze back to the marine's. "I get that, but listen, I want to ask if you'd do me a solid and bend the rules for just a minute." The marine opened his mouth, probably to say no, but Andy raised a hand to forestall him. "I know, I know. I'm asking you to do exactly what you were ordered not to. The thing is, I left my com inside my MIMAS, and I'm totally useless without it. I don't have any Oculenses, and my implant's connection to the ship's narrownet is routed through my com. If Gamble finds out I let myself get separated from it, I'm gonna be in big shit."

The marine sighed, then took a hand off his gun to put two fingers near his eyes and then direct them at Andy. "I'll be watching you the entire time. You make one move to get into that mech, and I *will* shoot you. Got that?"

A chill spread through Andy's chest. But he grinned through it. "Of course, man. I want you to know I really appreciate this."

The marine stepped aside, slapping the control panel behind him to open the hatch.

Andy slipped his hands into his pockets as he crossed the hangar bay, and his forefinger brushed up against the sedative he'd put there—the sedative that would grant him access to the mech dream.

When he neared his MIMAS, he glanced back at the hatch, where the marine was standing inside the hangar bay, watching him.

"It's inside the mech," Andy called. "Just need to lower the ramp and grab it."

The marine hesitated, then nodded.

Andy sent the command using his implant, and the back of the MIMAS popped out, lowering for him to climb. Without glancing to his right at the marine, he popped the pill into his mouth, clambered up the ramp, and slipped into the waiting cocoon.

"Hey!" the marine yelled. The sound of rapid footfalls echoed through the hangar bay, followed by gunfire. Bullets glanced off the ascending ramp, but none hit Andy.

Idiot.

He awoke inside the mech dream, and the MIMAS became his body. Turning, he retracted his fingers so that they lay flat against his wrists, revealing the twin rotary autocannons built into his forearms.

The marine had almost reached the mech, and the point-blank high-velocity rounds tore him to shreds. He fell backward against the deck, a bloody, motionless heap.

Andy wavered for a moment. It dawned on him that he'd just crossed the point of no return, without giving it much thought at all.

Well, there certainly wasn't time to dwell on it now. The shooting would draw more marines to him in short order.

He sprinted across the hangar bay, and he had to duck through the hatch to get through. On the other side, there was barely enough room to stand at full height, and the bulkheads on either side felt way too close. Unlike the hold that contained Cybele, the *Vesta*'s crew section was designed the way warships had been back when atmosphere had to be hauled up from a planet's gravity well: as cramped as possible. The atmosphere problem no longer limited size, but there were plenty of other advantages to conserving space in…well, space.

The corridors weren't meant for mechs, in other words, meaning Andy would enjoy virtually no cover as he made his way through them. Not only that, but he didn't come close to Gamble's marines in training or skill.

On the other hand, he *was* piloting a MIMAS.

I'll be fine.

He started down the corridor at a leisurely jog. Ahead, a crewmember emerged from a side hatch. Zooming in on the insignia, Andy identified her as Engineering.

"Get out of the way," he boomed through amplifiers built into the mech's exterior. "If you comply, you won't be harmed."

The woman didn't comply. Instead, she drew her standard-issue sidearm and started firing.

Wow. He hadn't expected to have to kill any noncombat personnel. Nevertheless, his autocannons spun up again, and the unarmored woman was tossed backward, where she crumpled to the floor. Andy tried to avoid stepping on her as he ran past, but his metal foot came down on her wrist all the same, which emitted a dry crunch.

Damn it. Now he felt even more conflicted about what he was doing. He'd never been fully resolved in the first place, which was why he hadn't spent much time considering the decision. If he'd done that, he probably would have chickened out.

I can't let them put Lisa in a cell for the rest of her life. If she tried to kill Price, she must have had a damned good reason. Hell, he'd wanted to kill Price on a few occasions.

A pair of flashing muzzles appeared ahead—marines with R-57s, firing at him from two hatches opposite each other. Clearly, word of Andy's actions had spread quickly.

He charged, managing to neutralize one of them right away, but the other ducked behind cover before Andy could target him. When he reached the hatch, he ducked low and spotted the surprised-looking marine, who was crouched against the metal frame. Clearly, he hadn't expected Andy to come right up to him.

They still aren't used to fighting mechs. Andy extended his left bayonet and stabbed the marine with enough force to pierce his para-aramid body armor—and then his torso.

It took him ten minutes and seven more kills to reach the brig. The guards there gave him little trouble. Once he'd pumped them both full of lead, he ducked through the hatch they'd been guarding and strode between the cells.

Lisa occupied the second-last one to the left. She was already at her bars, tight body pressed against them. Her jumpsuit was pulled taut, accentuating her curves and making Andy's heart race. *That's what I'm fighting for, right there.*

"I knew you'd come for me," she said.

From deep inside the mech dream, he grinned, even though the expression wouldn't register on his MIMAS' face.

Stepping forward, he bent down and gripped two adjacent bars of her cell. With a quick wrench, the bars parted as though made from cheap aluminum. That made him feel powerful, even though it was the mech doing the actual work. *I am the mech.*

He stepped back to make room, and Lisa turned sideways to squeeze herself between the crooked bars, emerging into the corridor between the cells.

"Where next?" she asked.

"Follow me. We're getting your MIMAS, and we're getting out of here."

CHAPTER 10

A Grim Logic

Jake woke from a nightmare of gunfire and screaming to discover it wasn't a nightmare.

He heard a rhythmic pounding from somewhere in the corridors outside sick bay—and he *felt* it, too, as vibrations that reached him through his bed from the deck. The pounding stopped, and the harsh staccato of a heavy gun followed. He'd recognize that sound anywhere: a MIMAS' rotary autocannon.

A deep, disorienting ache gripped his skull like a vise, which had been the case ever since he'd woken to find Husher sitting at his bedside, with a young woman who turned out to be his daughter.

I need to concentrate. His first thought was that someone had figured out how to infiltrate and control one of the mechs, which would involve learning how to navigate the mech dream.

That seemed unlikely. More likely, he realized, was that this was a member of Oneiri Team. It wouldn't surprise him to learn Lisa was the perpetrator, if she'd managed to escape the brig somehow. Lisa had been his friend, but Jake had noticed her acting weirdly since before they'd left the Steele System. No one had believed him. Not until she tried to kill him.

The pounding outside sick bay receded, which meant the attacker was moving away. *Isn't the brig in that direction?* That didn't make much sense, but ultimately, it didn't make any difference to his actions. No matter who was piloting that MIMAS, Jake needed to reach his own mech to stop them.

His legs felt like lead weights as he swung them over the side of the bed and planted them on the deck. When he tried to stand, he staggered forward instead, careening through the curtain surrounding his bed. Gripping it, he yanked it from the rod it was suspended from, so that it barely slowed his fall. Next, a narrow metal table in the next enclosure crashed to the floor, and he stumbled over it, catching himself on the next bed over, which shifted with his weight. Thankfully, the bed was unoccupied.

"Seaman Price," a harsh voice said from somewhere to his right. "What in Sol are you doing?"

"Saving the *Vesta*," he muttered, scrabbling against the deck with his feet and pushing down against the bed with an immense effort of will, till he'd reached a standing position.

A wave of dizziness washed over him, and he planted his hands on the bed once more to steady himself.

"You're in no condition to save anything," Doctor Bancroft said. "What's more, you're disrupting my sick bay."

"Once I reach my mech, I'll be fine. I need to get to my mech."

"You need to get back into bed. There's no way I'm letting you leave. Look, if you go any farther you'll pull out your IV tubes."

His gaze followed the tubes protruding from his arms to a tall, wheeled rack. *I can use that to keep my balance.* Fighting the dizziness, which continued to intensify until he worried he might faint, he stumbled back across the divide and clutched the IV rack like a drowning man would clutch a floating log. The bags of liquid hanging from the crossbar at the top wobbled with the effort.

"Seaman!" Bancroft said.

Price turned, hobbling toward the foot of the bed—toward Bancroft. The rack tipped forward dangerously, and for a moment he worried he was going to go crashing with it to the floor.

Jake drew a shaky breath. "I need to reach my mech, Doctor. Someone's rampaging through the *Vesta*, and that puts us all in danger. Major Gamble may not even know about the threat yet, or his people may be out of position to do anything about it. But my mech is in Hangar Bay Zeta, which is pretty close. I can make it there. And maybe I can end this."

She said nothing, her lips a firm, whitening line. But he could tell she was coming around to the realization that he was leaving this sick bay, one way or another.

"Unless you plan to wrestle a gunshot victim back into his bed, I suggest you move out of the way, Doctor," Jake said.

Shaking her head and sighing heavily, Bancroft moved off to the side, crossing her arms.

"Thank you."

He pushed the rack forward then stumbled after it. Push, stumble. Push, stumble. All the way across the sick bay. By the time he reached the hatch, he felt more tired than he ever had in his life. His eyelids felt like they held too much Ocharium, and a yawn stretched his mouth wide. All he wanted to do was crawl back into his sick bed and sleep for days.

Instead, he slapped the hatch's control panel, and it slid open to let him leave.

Glancing down the corridor to his right, he couldn't see the rogue MIMAS, not that he'd expected to. He did see the motionless leg of someone in a marine uniform. *Unconscious or dead.* Probably dead, given the marine had gone up against a MIMAS.

He turned left, making his torturous way toward the hangar bay where his mech was housed. Every step was agony, sending fresh pulses of pain through his skull. It felt like someone, somewhere had a knob controlling the force with which the Ocharium nanites in his body attracted the Majorana fermion matrix in the ship's deck, and they were gradually turning it up.

After a few minutes, he came across a noncombat crewmember sprawled across the corridor, her body shredded by what had to be autocannon fire. Jake scowled darkly. *Whoever did this, I'm going to kill them.*

At last, he made it to the hatch that led into Hangar Bay Zeta, where another marine lay dead on the deck, eyes staring lifelessly across the cavernous space.

As Jake shuffled past, he heard the rhythmic pounding again, in the distance but getting louder.

They're coming to this hangar bay. He didn't know how he knew that, but he did. Somewhere deep inside his foggy consciousness, a grim logic had gone to work, and it knew exactly what to expect.

The distance between him and the twin rows of mechs that stood on the opposite end of the hangar bay seemed to stretch for miles and miles. One of the rows had only three MIMAS, of course, and the other row—the closer row, thankfully—had two, along with Rug's quadruped mech and his own alien mech.

He struggled toward it as the pounding grew louder behind him. It didn't seem as rapid as before, and again, his subconscious provided an explanation: *Whoever's piloting that mech is escorting someone who's not in a mech.*

Everything clicked into place for him, then, and he actually gasped, there in the middle of the hangar bay. *Andy.* The bastard had managed to gain access to the hangar bay somehow, and then he'd gotten inside a mech to begin his killing spree. All with the intention of freeing Lisa and then fleeing the *Vesta* together.

The treachery of it filled Jake with a berserker's rage, and the anger's intensity was such that it startled him, a little. But it didn't matter. *I won't let them get away. Not after this.*

Gathering his will, he forced himself to move faster across the hangar bay. The alien mech opened for him as he neared. Behind him, the pounding sounded like it was coming from the corridor outside. Jake let go of the IV rack and stumbled for the last few steps, catching himself on the ridged ramp projecting from the mech's front torso.

He wasn't sure how he managed it, but he climbed, turning to deposit himself into the smooth, metallic cocoon that awaited.

Andy reached the hatch just as the ramp was closing. He hesitated only a second before raising an already-exposed autocannon, but that second saved Jake's life. He fished out a sedative from an internal compartment and slapped it into his mouth as bullets ricocheted off the sealing mech.

He's ready to turn on me that easily? Jake entered the mech dream full of rage, ready to use the alien mech's might to rip Andy apart.

But the mech wouldn't move.

It wouldn't do anything. Try as he might, Jake couldn't get it to budge.

Bond with me, the mech whispered to him. *If you wish to ever access my power again, bond with me now, or be barred from it forever.*

Andy opened fire again.

CHAPTER 11

Rogue MIMAS

With her implant routed through her com, Ash could follow Major Gamble's progress through the ship. Ten minutes ago, he'd broadcast his location to every marine on the *Vesta*, along with orders to converge on him.

"A MIMAS pilot has gone rogue," the message had said.

"This way," Ash called to Beth when she made to run straight through an intersection. "It's quicker if we hang a right."

They sprinted down their chosen corridor, getting closer and closer to Gamble, who appeared to be heading toward Hangar Bay Zeta. *That's where our mechs are.*

She and Beth had been enjoying some private time in an unused bunkroom, but when they'd received the alert, they'd pulled on their jumpsuits with record-breaking speed, grabbed their sidearms, and rushed into the corridor.

They found Gamble with his back to a bulkhead, combat shotgun at the ready. In the corridor with him were eight of his marines, looking twitchy, to Ash's eye.

From inside the hangar bay, heavy gunfire roared, pinging off something metallic.

"Major, what's going on?" Ash asked, not bothering to raise her voice over the tumult—Gamble's embedded ear piece would deliver her voice straight to his ear canal.

"There are two active MIMAS inside the hangar bay, both firing on the alien mech, which apparently contains Price. I got a message from Bancroft that he left sick bay, and with the other mechs firing on it, that's where he seems likely to be."

Ash's heartbeat ramped up till it throbbed inside her chest. "What's our plan?" she asked, fighting to keep her voice steady.

"Till now, it's been to wait for MIMAS pilots to get here, in the hopes of getting you across the hangar bay to your machines. But it might be risky to go with just you two. Maybe we should wait for Rug and Odell to get here, too."

"No way," Ash said. "Sorry, Major, but Jake's mech can only withstand that kind of punishment for so long. I don't know about you, but I'm going now."

Gamble nodded. "Then we all go." He turned to the rest of the gathered marines. "Spread out as soon as you're through the hatch, covering Sweeney and Arkanian as best you can. Getting them to their mechs is our number one priority. The *Vesta*'s in danger, people. We protect our ship."

"Oorah!" came the answering cry, and Gamble turned toward the hatch, raising a hand then flicking it forward once. He charged through, raising his shotgun to his eye, and the other marines followed.

Ash drew her sidearm, locked eyes with Beth, and nodded. Beth nodded back, and they swept into the hangar bay together, pistols raised and seeking targets.

The two MIMAS mechs had turned their focus on the marines, who were spreading out to the cover provided by consoles, booths, and crates distributed throughout the hangar bay. Ash and Beth split up too, racing across the deck before the opposing MIMAS pilots could figure out what their plan was.

Ash could hear bullets deflecting off the deck behind her just before she reached her mech. She dove behind it, arresting her momentum by gripping the ramp that had already lowered, thanks to the command she'd sent while sprinting across the hangar bay. Two mechs over, Beth was just reaching her machine, and Ash felt a wash of relief as she swallowed a sedative and climbed into her MIMAS.

Once inside the mech dream, she stepped backward, using the other stationary mechs as cover against the attackers. Gunfire flashed to her left, and she realized that one of the attackers had already circled around the formation to get a cleaner shot.

Panic seized her an instant before she turned and registered what had happened:

Beth lay slumped across her MIMAS' ramp, her body riddled with bullets.

The entire hangar bay turned blood-red with Ash's rancor. Heedless of the autocannon rounds glancing off her machine, boring closer to her body nestled inside, she charged at the MIMAS, extending both bayonets and introducing a weave into her path to throw off her attacker's aim.

The other MIMAS began dancing backward, away from her, and it adjusted its autocannons to the right, but Ash anticipated the move. She jerked left while retaining most of her speed. Her enemy swept the autocannons back toward her, and she fell into a roll, coming up mostly unharmed—meters away from the other mech, who'd reached a bulkhead.

Momentum and fury carried Ash forward, and both bayonets struck true, piercing the MIMAS clean through and pinning it to the wall. She withdrew the blades and struck again, right where its human occupant was nestled. The mech slumped to the floor.

Then came the sound of a rocket whistling through the air, and Ash rolled sideways, coming up into a full-on sprint. The bulkhead exploded behind her, sending a blazing shock wave to speed her on her way.

Ash reached behind her back, seizing the heavy gun that was stuck there with powerful magnets. She dropped to one knee, took aim, and fired at the remaining MIMAS' head. It jerked backward just as it fired a second rocket, which went wide, taking out two marines.

The remaining marines continued to put pressure on the rogue MIMAS. Ash stood, walking forward and supporting their fire with hers. Then she dropped the gun and extended her bayonets.

The MIMAS raised both hands, and Lisa Sato's voice came from it: "I surrender!"

Like hell you do. Ash continued forward, intent on cutting Sato up into little bits.

"Sweeney, hold," Gamble barked. "She surrenders."

For a moment, incredulous rage burned through Ash, and she considered attacking anyway. *They killed Beth. They killed Beth and they both deserve to die.*

Almost, she resumed the attack. It felt like she had nothing left to live for, and she didn't know where she found the strength to restrain herself.

But she did.

CHAPTER 12

Some Unknowable Monster

"I should go in there with you, sir," Gamble said as he peered through the one-way mirror from the darkened chamber where he and Husher stood.

On the other side of the mirror, Lisa Sato sat in a brightly lit interrogation room, her hands bound together with metal restraints and her feet cuffed to her chair, which was bolted to the floor.

Husher looked at the major, the side of his mouth quirked upward. "Seriously? That's a bit much, Major, even for you. Sato isn't moving from that chair. You're welcome to stay in here and watch, but there's absolutely no call for you to accompany me into that room for protection. I'm pretty sure I'll be fine."

Gamble actually reddened slightly. "Right. Sorry, sir. I'm still shook up after what happened."

"Fair enough. It's unsettling when danger appears inside the ship you're charged with protecting—at a time when you were sure she was secure. That's not a criticism, Major. I've been in the exact same position myself."

Gamble nodded, though his eyes were on the deck. Husher headed toward the hatch leading into the interrogation room.

Sato tracked him with her eyes as he walked toward the chair opposite hers, but she said nothing. *She's remarkably calm.* Husher had no doubt that she'd seen a lot back in the Steele System, and that it took a lot to faze her. As much as he hated to acknowledge it, part of him admired her brazenness.

"I'm not sure who to trust, anymore," he said as he took a seat. "A few months ago, the mayor of Cybele proved a traitor, and now so have you."

"That's the idea," Sato said. "We don't want you to feel comfortable trusting anyone."

"We?"

"The Progenitors."

"Right. Well, before we continue, I should let you know that your treatment going forward will depend on how forthcoming you are during this session. I don't have time to keep questioning you, so you have one chance to decide your fate, and that chance is now."

"Is that right?" Sato said. "In that case, my future's looking bright, and I'll be treated like a queen. I have no problem answering whatever questions you have the sense to ask."

That surprised him, and he wasn't sure how well he was doing with concealing it. "All right, then. Tell me this, Sato. When did you turn?"

Sato chuckled. "I never *turned,* Captain Husher. To say I turned would mean I was on your side at some point, and I never have been. Yes, there is a Lisa Sato who was on your 'side,' such as it is, but you've never met her. She was taken aboard a Progenitor warship in the Steele System, and she was never released. Instead, I was sent to take her place."

Husher narrowed his eyes. "Are you...you're a clone, then? Have the Progenitors been cloning humans?"

Another laugh from Sato, louder this time. "You truly don't get it, do you, Captain? Let me spell it out for you. I'm not just another creation of the Progenitors, like the Ixa. I *am* a Progenitor."

Husher fell silent, and Sato's face blurred as he unfocused his eyes, attempting to process what she'd just told him. "I don't understand."

"I can see that, and it's really no surprise to me. You were expecting the species that's inflicted such suffering on yours would be some unknowable monster, yes? Some contorted beast, unrecognizable to such an upstanding human as yourself. Wrong, Captain. Wrong. The Progenitors are human. The Progenitors are you."

Husher could hear his own breathing, now—could feel it as it rasped against his throat. Otherwise, total silence filled the spaces between Sato's words.

"Just as I'm Sato's double, and she's mine, you have a double too," the Progenitor continued. "And what a bastard he is, Captain. You've been wondering where your good friend Fesky is, I'm sure, so let me dispel that mystery for you. By now, she's no doubt been apprehended and is undergoing an interrogation the likes of which you don't have the balls to put me through, not to mention the imagination. Would you like to know who will be administering that interrogation? You will, Captain. Where I come from, you're every bit as renowned for your ability to inflict agony as you are for your battlespace prowess.

"Whether your friend has broken or not—my bet is that she has—her captors know by virtue of her very presence that the IU now has the ability to reach our home dimension. That will make them abandon their subtle efforts to engineer the collapse of your society, and their scalpel-like attacks will come to an end. Now, the invasion will truly begin, using the thousands of ships they've held in reserve. They've kept those ships back because they hoped to make you destroy yourself, so that they would have the resources needed to attack the next galactic cluster right away. But your bird's appearance represents an existential threat, and now they will throw everything they have at you."

At last, Husher found his voice. "Why are you telling me this?" he asked. "Why are you so willing to speak?"

"Because I believe in evolution, Captain Husher, and I believe it operates at the level of societies. I believe the Interstellar Union was always destined to be the weak thing it has become, cowering as it waits for a better society to arrive and devour it. What I tell you or don't tell you makes no difference at all. You're about to witness natural selection, at a universal scale."

CHAPTER 13

Bargaining Chips

Ash wasn't in the crew's mess, and when Jake checked the Oneiri bunkroom, she wasn't there, either. He searched for another forty-five minutes, pushing the walker Bancroft had begrudgingly given him around the *Vesta*.

At last, he found her sitting in a bunkroom that wasn't currently in use, on a bunk whose sheets were rumpled beneath her.

"Knock, knock," he said.

She looked up, and he suppressed a cringe at the levity he'd spoken with. Tears streaked Ash's face, and her eyes were bloodshot. "What?" she said.

He crossed the room from the hatch and sat beside her. Ash didn't react, except to pull away almost imperceptibly.

"Remember when we first met during training, back on Valhalla Station?"

A sniff. "Sure."

"Did you know that, back then, I thought we might end up together?" He chuckled. "I was pretty wrong about that one."

The anecdote had been intended to cheer Ash, but she continued to stonewall his efforts.

So he dropped the attempt, letting his head droop toward the ground. *I'm bad at this, anyway.*

"I'm really sorry about Beth. I know saying that makes no difference, and I'm not sure I have the right words to make a difference, if there are any words that would. Probably there aren't." He glanced at her. Her face was still sullen and drawn. "I feel like I can relate, though, on some level. When Lisa came back from the Progenitor ship acting so differently—when she went with *Andy*, of all people, and later tried to kill me—I felt like I lost—"

"This is *nothing* like that, Jake," Ash hissed, though she sounded like she might start crying again. "Never compare Beth to Sato. I should have killed that monster."

Jake sighed. "I'm sorry. I know this is a horrible day for you—I can't even imagine how horrible. This is going to sound harsh, but I need you to bounce back from it, Ash. I need you to continue being an active member of Oneiri. We're in the middle of a war for survival, and you need to find a way to pick up the pieces and move forward."

"Oneiri Team's dead," Ash spat, which felt like a vat of ice water thrown in Jake's face. "Marco's dead, Beth's dead, that *bastard* Andy is dead. Lisa's a traitor. All that's left is Odell, Rug, me, and you. And you can't even control your own mech."

Jake drew a ragged breath. He'd heard the words Ash hadn't spoken: that if he'd been able to pilot his mech properly, Beth would almost certainly still be alive.

He pressed on: "Oneiri's not dead. We still have Lisa's and Beth's mechs, and we can find—"

"Just *go,* Jake," Ash said. "I want you gone!"

"All right," he said softly. He rose to his feet, and with a last glance at Ash's scowling face, he left the bunkroom.

For the next ten minutes, he paced some of the *Vesta*'s most underused corridors, walker scraping along the deck as he tried to calm down. His com buzzed, and when he told his implant to display the message, he found an order from Husher to come to his office.

I need to relax. If he carried this temper into the captain's office, there'd be trouble, and he didn't need to make today any worse.

Husher opened the hatch remotely as soon as Jake knocked. He shuffled in, then managed to come to attention and snap off a salute without the help of his walker.

"At ease, Seaman," Husher said as the hatch closed automatically. "Take a seat."

Jake lowered himself to the chair with one hand gripping the walker. He still felt raw from his conversation with Ash, but he struggled to keep himself in check.

The captain didn't seem to notice. "How's your recovery going?"

"As quickly as I can push it. I plan to be rid of this thing as soon as possible." He nodded at the walker.

"Glad to hear it." Husher cleared his throat. "I just finished interrogating Sato."

"Did you learn anything?"

"You could say that. She didn't seem at all concerned with holding anything back."

"Why did she try to kill me? What made her betray us?"

"That's the thing," Husher said, folding his hands atop his desk. "Technically, Sato *didn't* betray us, because she was never on our side to begin with."

Jake frowned, narrowing his eyes. "I've been friends with her since we were kids, sir. I don't think it gets any more treacherous than this."

"Your childhood friend isn't the one who betrayed you. There are two people named Lisa Sato, and it turns out there are two Vin Hushers, for that matter."

"I don't understand."

"Neither did I. Probably I still don't. Not completely. But the Sato I interrogated told me the truth about the Progenitors—who they actually are. She said they aren't an alien species at all, but a parallel version of humanity. When the Sato you knew was taken, they replaced her with the Progenitor Sato."

It took a few moments for that to sink in, and the implications took longer. At last, Jake said, "Does that mean the real Lisa might still be alive?"

"It's possible. The Sato I interrogated doesn't know for sure, but when I try to think from the Progenitors' perspective, it makes sense. We know they like to maximize the number of levers they can use against us, and they've likely kept alive whatever prisoners they've taken, in case they're ever needed as bargaining chips."

Jake noticed his own breathing getting heavier. Ever since fleeing the Steele System, he'd been trying to come to terms with Lisa choosing Andy over him—and since waking in the *Vesta*'s sick bay and remembering her attempt to kill him, he'd been filled with hatred for her.

This threw everything out of whack. It left him with the last several months to rethink, and once he did that, he needed to sort out his own conflicted feelings about Lisa.

"I debated with myself about whether I should tell you," Husher said. "Part of me thought it might prove distracting to you. But in the end, I decided you deserved to know, given your feelings for Sato."

Jake almost winced. He'd forgotten about telling the captain that.

It doesn't matter how I feel about Lisa. I know what I have to do. "I'm going to get her back," he said. "I don't know how, but I'm not going to stop until I do."

Husher nodded. "I intend to help you."

CHAPTER 14

At Least One Version of Me

Ever since the entire universe had collapsed down to just the Sol System, Husher had had access to less and less intel. The fact that he'd never even met Teth before was a testament to that.

With what he was learning from interrogating the winged rat, that made more sense, now. His double and Teth had been bitter enemies for twenty years. Letting him and Teth intermingle definitely posed a risk to them both, not to mention to the overall military picture.

The fact he was finally being allowed to meet the Ixan proved Darkstream was feeling the pressure. They were taking the bird's appearance in this universe very seriously. *Good.*

Husher waited in a luxurious leather recliner, and when the hatch opened, he rose to his feet, crossing to greet Teth and holding out a hand in friendship.

"Command Leader," he said as he approached. "I'm a great admirer of your work, and I think we have a lot to learn from each other."

The hulking Ixan came to an abrupt halt, staring at Husher's hand as though it was also a predatory reptile. Then, his cat-like eyes lifted to meet Husher's, and he hissed, his forked tongue protruding between his teeth.

Husher stood his ground, staring up to meet the genetically enhanced alien's eyes. "All right, then," he said, and returned to his seat.

"You should kill that," Teth said, gesturing toward the window that dominated the bulkhead opposite the hatch. It overlooked the Cavern from the rear, and Husher had turned the Winger's chair around so she could watch their meeting unfold. He'd stapled her eyelids open to ensure that she did. What was said would be lost to her, but he expected seeing Teth in repose would unsettle her greatly. She clearly thought of him as a brutal foe.

Except, Teth wasn't in repose. He refused to join Husher in sitting, instead standing stiffly in the chamber's center, as though barely able to restrain an impulse to go for the kill.

"Why do you say I should kill the Winger?" Husher asked mildly.

"Mercy. That creature is inferior, pitiful. Euthanize it."

"I believe she's much more valuable alive." *And I'm close to breaking her. I have to be.* That should be true, especially if she was as pitiful as Teth claimed. *She should have broken long ago.*

"Your double is also pitiful," Teth said. "They tell me you, however, are competent. If that's true, then you'll have figured out already that I despise you."

"It isn't me you despise, Teth. Surely you're capable of making the distinction."

"When I look at you, I see the human who killed my father. If I had my way, your face would be pulped and then erased from the multiverse. I would hunt down every version of you, no matter how innumerable, and exterminate them."

"This is quite a first impression."

The Ixan shifted toward him, so fast it was difficult to track his movements. He stopped himself just a foot away from Husher.

"Get out of my face," Husher snapped. "You're boring me, a lot. We both know you wouldn't dare attack me, and you're not going to get anywhere with trying to intimidate me, so why don't you drop the act and sit down to discuss how we can exterminate at least one version of me. Hmm?"

Husher maintained steady eye contact while he spoke, and he saw how Teth's body trembled with rage.

At last, the Ixan stepped back and lowered himself into the other chair.

"That's good," Husher said. "If you can believe it, I think we've already made a lot of progress. We've established that you hate me as much as it's possible for one being to hate another, for all intents and purposes. We can use that. We can channel it in order to win."

"You're saying my desire to rip out your throat with my fangs is productive," Teth said softly.

"That's exactly what I'm saying," Husher said, maintaining eye contact with the reptilian.

"My desire to revel in the lovely sound of cracking bones and ripping flesh. To tear off your jaw and break both your arms in half."

"I already mentioned you can't intimidate me."

"I'm not trying to intimidate you," Teth said, smiling. "I'm telling you the truth about what's inside. I want to do those things, not just to you, but to everyone."

"But you mostly want to do it to me."

"Don't underestimate my desire to harm *everyone*. I see it as mercy. Truly. When I'm finally finished my work, I'll grant myself the same mercy."

"Well, again, I call it good." He'd also call it insane. *I had no idea Teth was deteriorating like this.* He sniffed. *No matter.* "It means you'll do what needs doing with perfect enthusiasm. You'll hit Husher where he's weakest, with maximum vigor."

"Yes."

"I can help you. I *am* Husher, and I know him well. Better than anyone else. You need to exploit the tension inside him, the tension between saving the galaxy and saving those dear to him."

"Tell me how."

"Happily. But first, I want intel from you. I want to determine what Steele still isn't telling me, if anything. And I want to know things from your perspective—from the commander in the field."

Teth's grin widened. "Very well."

"I also want you to hear my advice, and heed it, in spite of your pride and hatred. Steele has counseled you to stop your measured, incisive attacks—to ramp up the invasion straight away. I think that, instead, you should triple down on those attacks. Hit them where they're weakest, again and again, with increasing tempo. Drive them like lambs to the slaughter. And once the entire galaxy is huddled together, as though for warmth...then, let the hammer fall."

CHAPTER 15

Just One Lifetime

Since the Progenitor was being so forthcoming, Husher saw no need for any theatrics designed to intimidate. He sat in the interrogation room as he waited for his marines to bring her, and when they did, he regarded her impassively while they bound her to the other chair.

"I have more questions," Husher said once they were alone.

"I'll give you answers," Sato said, and grew a sly smile. "Though I still haven't seen the promised improvement in my treatment, Captain. Everyone tells me you're a man of your word, but there's been no three-course dinner, no mani pedi."

"I meant that perhaps you'll be sentenced to just one lifetime in prison instead of two."

Sato laughed. "Ask me anything, Captain."

Husher frowned as he realized he wasn't particularly eager to proceed, despite the success of the interrogations so far. What she'd told him hadn't done much to inspire optimism in him over the fate of the galaxy.

"Why don't the Progenitors just conquer their own universe?" Husher said. "Why do they want ours? Surely one universe is enough."

"Ours isn't enough," Sato said, shaking her head. "Not anymore."

"Anymore?"

"In this dimension, you destroyed Darkstream. A long, clumsy process, but you managed it in the end. In our dimension, Darkstream seized power and kept it. The corporation absorbed the government into itself, and no one had the means to stop it from continuing to abuse dark tech."

"They destabilized the universe."

"Yes. So much that it began to collapse. We had enough time to throw all our resources at engineering forcefield tech, which you saw Teth use in the Concord System. That was enough to save the Sol System. The rest of the universe tore itself apart."

"Something's not adding up," Husher said, searching Sato's face for signs of deceit. "You created the Ixa, and the Ixa gave us dark tech. How did you get it, if there were never any Ixa in your universe to begin with?"

She shrugged. "We invented it ourselves, just as you would have, given enough time."

"All right," Husher said slowly. "So you lost your entire universe, thanks to Darkstream. Are they still in power?"

"Very much so."

"Does that bother you?"

"Not at all. The only thing that matters to me is that we survived. That's the measure of a truly strong society. For a universe to collapse and not kill us sort of proves that, doesn't it? Besides, only Darkstream would have had the wherewithal to invent interdimensional travel and inject self-improving AIs into your universe."

"Why did Darkstream hold onto power in your universe and not in ours?" Husher thought he might know why: without the Ixa, the Progenitors never had to contend with another species that exhibited their own worst qualities, and so they'd never had the same reasons for self-examination.

But Sato had a different answer. "I think we have you to thank for that, Captain."

"Explain."

"Where I come from, you're known as Darkstream's faithful hound, always eager to lap up the scraps of glory they let fall from the table of power. You've never opposed them—not once. You even killed your beloved Captain Keyes for them, though the Husher I knew never loved Keyes."

Husher felt his eyes widen, and he tried to clamp down on the reaction he knew was showing on his face. It was the same way he'd reacted to the first interrogation: utter disbelief.

I killed Keyes? The words didn't seem to belong together—the idea was completely alien, and he wanted to reject it outright. But the idea of serving Darkstream felt just as wrong. Somehow, he believed Sato's claim about Darkstream. *So why not the one about Keyes?*

"You should be grateful there's a version of you who isn't a coward," Sato said, clearly enjoying this. "*Our* Captain Husher helped create the society that will dominate the multiverse. The most perfect society evolution is capable of producing. You should be proud of that, but you're not, because you're weak."

He had nothing to say. To any of it.

"You're weak in specific ways," Sato continued. "And we know them all. If I were a betting woman, and I am, I'd say that the next attack will be custom-designed to exploit those very weaknesses. I'd warn you to prepare yourself, but it wouldn't make any difference. You're already going to act exactly as we've predicted, no matter what I say to you."

At that moment, his com vibrated in its holster, beeping stridently. He removed it, read the message it displayed, then froze. Slowly, his eyes drifted from the device to Sato.

She raised her eyebrows. "It's the attack I just predicted, isn't it? Don't worry, you don't have to tell me I'm good. I already know it."

CHAPTER 16

Something to Think About

Husher took the command seat from Ek and studied the tactical display, wishing for the thousandth time that they had the *Spire* back. The Progenitors were hitting Abdera from four locations dispersed around the globe, and the former lifeboat's flanking ability would have proved invaluable.

"Coms, order Captain Norberg and her battle group to engage the enemy ships just north of the equator. Tell the Quatro to target the battle group hitting the defense platform near the planet's south pole. Until we take out one of the other groups, Abdera's fighter group will have to take on the ships halfway up the northern hemisphere while we confront the ones at the north pole." Each of the Progenitor attack forces numbered ten, and given their ships' advanced capabilities, taking out forty of them dispersed around the planet was going to be a difficult fight.

"Aye, sir," Ensign Fry said, bending closer to her console as she queued up the transmissions.

With Fry occupied, Husher got in touch with Commander Ayam himself.

"Yes, Captain?" the Winger said.

"I want the Air Group to scramble as we approach, adopting formations designed for maximum versatility."

"What about my subspace squadron?"

"I was just about to get to that. Deploy with the rest of the Pythons headed for the north pole, and enter subspace right away. But the moment you transition, I want you to whip around and head toward the Progenitor ships further down the northern hemisphere. Help the Abdera defense pilots take them out as fast as you can, then come help us at the north pole."

"Can do," Ayam said, though his brevity didn't conceal his evident enthusiasm for Husher's plan. "Ayam out."

"The orders have been sent, sir," Fry said. "Captain Norberg's battle group is already underway toward the targets you designated."

"Very good. I've ordered Ayam to have his pilots use formations optimized to attack, so that's what the Progenitors will expect. We're doing the opposite. Coms, just as we're about to close, order the Air Group to go on missile defense, and tell our battle group captains to do the same." He intentionally hadn't told Ayam about his intended deception, since it would be much easier for the Python pilots to conceal something they didn't even know they were concealing. Husher's gaze settled on Tremaine. "Tactical, prep Banshees for loading into forward tubes, but mix in equal helpings of Hydras and Gorgons—they should account for half of the total missiles loaded. Everything we do in the next ten minutes will be aimed at getting Gorgons through as fast as possible."

"Yes, Captain," Tremaine said with a brisk nod before turning to his work.

As expected, Ravagers streamed forth from the Progenitor ships, and Fry sent the Pythons the order to engage them. Particle beams lanced out as well, but the battle group captains already knew to introduce lateral movement into their courses. Other than some superficial damage, they escaped unscathed.

The Ravager barrage met with a wave of Banshees, and then a wall of Pythons. Hundreds of them exploded within seconds, and Husher watched as the icons representing the Hydras and Gorgons crept across the tactical display.

"The first Hydras are splitting," Winterton said. "Enemy ships are turning their attention to dealing with the new threat, and they're getting some of our Gorgons too, but I think the sheer number of them is going to prevail."

The tactical display soon proved the sensor operator right: three of the enemy ships exploded, bringing a grim smile to Husher's face. *Now the real work begins.* "Tactical—"

"Sir, we've received a priority alert from a com drone that just entered from the Feverfew System," Fry said.

"What's the message?" Husher asked, though he dreaded the answer.

"Feverfew system is under attack from eight Progenitor destroyers and five of their carriers. There are Quatro ships stationed around Zakros, but with most local forces concentrated in the Caprice System, they don't think they can hold."

Sera is on Zakros. Despite their differences where their daughter was concerned—despite that Sera had let him believe their daughter was dead for nearly twenty years—he couldn't bear the thought of remaining in Caprice while her life was in danger.

"Noni, set a course that skirts the enemy formation and takes us to the Caprice-Feverfew darkgate. Coms, order the other battle group ships to follow suit. Recall the Air Group once we're clear of the enemy, and then broadcast a repeating transmission encoded to Commander Ayam's fighter: I want him to follow us in subspace until he catches up."

"Yes, sir," both officers answered, though he heard the notes of uncertainty in their voices. That they were unquestioningly following his orders to leave the battle around Abdera was a testament to how much they trusted him, and part of Husher couldn't help but feel like he was abusing that trust.

He sensed Ek studying him from the XO's seat, but she didn't speak, and he didn't invite her to. *How am I making this decision so easily?* It wasn't easy, truthfully—he felt on the brink of nausea. Still, he'd given the orders with barely a moment's hesitation. *How?*

He knew the answer, though it killed him to admit it, even to himself. Husher was losing hope in the galaxy's chances of survival. Abdera was almost certainly doomed, just as the rest of the galaxy was doomed. Faced with that, he would at least try to save those dear to him.

"Tactical, prep a starboard Hydra broadside and fire it as we pass the Progenitor formation."

"Aye, sir."

That will give them something to think about, at least.

The Hydras didn't take out any more of the enemy ships, but it did force them to expend more Ravagers in defense, and it let the *Vesta* and her battle group pass unharmed, with the help of the Air Group.

Husher instructed the Helm to adopt an acceleration profile equal to the slowest ship's maximum output, so that his supercarrier would remain in formation with her battle group. After that, the journey across the Caprice System passed in tense silence—except when Fry informed him of the panicked messages being sent by officials on Abdera's surface. He told her to ignore them.

After that, the silence inside the CIC grew tenser.

At last, they transitioned through the darkgate, and Winterton began to report on what he saw. "The Progenitor ships aren't attacking the colony, sir."

Husher stared at the sensor operator. "Then what are they doing?"

"They're hitting the shipyards."

Just as Winterton said it, the icons representing the Feverfew Shipyards winked out, signaling their destruction. At once, the Progenitor formation winked out of this dimension.

"Make for the colony with all possible speed," Husher said. "They'll strike there next."

CHAPTER 17

Missile Damage

The Quatro warships defending Zakros were mostly concentrated along the southern hemisphere, and so of course the Progenitors appeared over the north, above and below one of the orbital defense platforms there. They began bombarding it with Ravagers.

"Tell the Quatro ships to stay where they are," Husher ordered Ensign Fry. "We'll take on the thirteen attacking vessels—if the Quatro move to join us, the Progenitors will only reappear in a less defended location."

"Aye, sir."

With twenty minutes left before the *Vesta* closed with the attackers, the Progenitors succeeded in destroying the defense platform they'd been targeting. That done, they started dropping Amblers and Ravagers on the planet's surface.

A coldness washed through Husher as he watched that, but even so, he didn't give the order for Helm to accelerate beyond what the older UHF ships were capable of. They were already outnumbered and outgunned. If the *Vesta* arrived alone, the odds would be even worse.

Winterton looked up from his console at Husher. "Sir, analysis of one of the destroyer's hulls puts it at a high probability that it belongs to Teth. Repairs have been made to areas where his destroyer took missile damage in Hellebore."

"Then that's our target. Coms, order Ayam to scramble the Air Group, using the same formations we used in Caprice. We can reuse those same tactics here, since there's no way the two attack forces have had time to communicate with each other. Tell Ayam to use subspace to pressure Teth's destroyer as best we can. Tactical, prep a barrage identical to the one that took out three ships over Abdera, and center it on that destroyer."

His officers carried out his orders with the same efficiency they'd shown in Abdera; maybe more, since they were the same orders, which they'd executed just a few hours before.

But the attackers in Feverfew didn't behave likes the ones in Caprice. They failed to launch Ravagers at the *Vesta* and her battle group, and when Tremaine loosed his missile barrage, the Progenitor ships vanished before it could reach them.

Damn it. What's their angle? "Coms, tell Major Gamble to take ten battalions to help Zakros' ground forces clean up the mess on the planet's surface."

"Aye, sir."

"The enemy ships have appeared away from the colony, sir," Winterton said. "Just out of firing range."

"We're getting a transmission request from the destroyer likely to be Teth's," Fry said.

"Accept," Husher said, steeling himself. "Put it on the main display and give everyone access."

Teth's broad, leering face appeared, and his forked tongue flickered between his teeth as his eyes fell on Husher. "Hello, Captain. Your bird friend sends her regards. Or at least, I'm sure she would, if she wasn't otherwise occupied."

"What have you done to her?"

"I did nothing. You're the one who sent her to us so woefully unprepared. And now she suffers the consequences of your folly. Just like your galactic capital."

Husher fell silent, though his breathing had quickened.

Nodding, Teth said, "I see that you fear to ask the question whose answer you already know. Abdera has fallen, Captain. Overrun with our machines, who will take no mercy on the populace. Your precious capital is finished, and it will be far from the first colony to fall. You've failed to save your home. But don't worry. *I* will be their savior, by granting them the release of annihilation."

"How is that saving them?" Husher said.

"I'm saving them from life itself. This existence is a parade of devils that attack you relentlessly until you die. Surely you can see that. What better mercy can I show than to kill all who live, sparing them from endless suffering?"

"Will you show the same mercy to your masters?"

"I think I may. But you first."

With that, the Progenitor force vanished again and didn't return, leaving Husher and his crew in a galaxy changed forever.

CHAPTER 18

You Won't Be the Last

"Have you gone insane?" Iris stood over his desk, hands planted on her hips, glaring at him.

Suppressing a sigh, Husher met her gaze from where he sat behind the desk. "Iris, if you've come to berate me, get it over with. You won't be the first one to do that, and you won't be the last—not even the last one today. I'd bet my life on it."

"I'm sure you're right. You'll be lucky if the admiralty doesn't strip you of command for this."

"They won't take the *Vesta* from me," he said. "They've tried, many times, and I won't let them. I'll stay in command till the war is over, at least. If they haven't made their peace with that yet, they're going to."

His daughter shook her head, disbelief etched across her face. "How can you be self-righteous at a time like this? You abandoned the galactic capital, Vin. You let it fall."

"I'm Vin, now? Not dad anymore?"

Iris's shoulder fell a little. "You're dad, I guess," she muttered. "For better or worse."

"Indeed," Husher said, nodding. "And I came to Feverfew for your mother."

"You realize that makes you a colossal hypocrite, right?"

He squinted. "How?"

"This is exactly what I told you not to do. I told you that if you want to lead people, then you need to do it by example. By *living* by your principles."

"What principle are you talking about?"

"Dad, whenever you see mom, you're constantly preaching at her about how overprotective she is. About how she needs to learn to let me face the dangers of the world on my own. But when danger comes to her, you drop everything and run to protect her. You *abandoned the defense of the galactic capital*, and you came here, just to protect her."

Husher's eyes fell to the desktop, and he took a deep breath. "You're right," he said at last. "I know that. But there are certain things you aren't considering."

"Like what?"

"The Progenitors have too many capabilities we don't. Particle beams, and the ability to appear in any system without warning. We can't defend against that. We're too spread out."

"Then maybe we need to start consolidating our people, and our forces."

Husher paused. "That could work, if our society would concentrate on something other than tearing itself apart. But it's not going to. Not for any length of time. We're working to destroy ourselves almost as fast as the Progenitors are, and it's difficult to say who'll win that race."

Iris's eyes were wide, and she looked genuinely shocked. "You've given up on the galaxy. Haven't you?"

He didn't answer, but his eyes returned to the desk.

"It doesn't matter," she said, her voice strengthening again. "It doesn't make you any less of a hypocrite for what you did. You don't get a free pass just because you've lost faith."

He stayed quiet.

"As for mom, she would have survived the Progenitor attack either way. She can handle herself, and you know it. She used to command the *Providence* marine battalion, for God's sake!"

Husher still had nothing to say, and after a few more seconds of silence, Iris cursed, then turned toward the hatch.

"Where are you going?" he asked.

"Down to Zakros," she shot back. "I'm going to find mom."

CHAPTER 19

Long Shots

Husher trudged through the *Vesta* toward the supercarrier's conference room, wishing Fesky was by his side. Dealing with President Chiba still wouldn't have been easy with his friend there, but maybe it would have been bearable.

She made everything more bearable. He'd taken that for granted, and now she was gone. One of his many mistakes.

To top it all off, he'd gotten wind that Sera had agreed to return to the *Vesta* with Iris. Eventually he'd have to face her again, too.

He found the president of the Union sitting at the far end of the conference table, flanked by two marines. "Captain Husher," the Kaithian said. "You weren't on the flight deck to greet me."

"That's because you didn't alert me to your presence until your shuttle was at our hull, Mr. President," Husher ground out, taking a seat at the opposite end of the long table, so that they would have to keep their voices raised to converse. *Probably not the most diplomatic move, but I won't be pushed around on my own ship, either.* Chiba had already taken his usual seat, so Husher would take the other end of the table. "For hours, all we saw were eight Quatro warships who refused to answer our transmission requests as they approached from the Feverfew-Caprice darkgate. We were preparing to defend ourselves."

"Military preparedness can't be a bad thing, in the middle of a war. Surely you of all people agree with that, Captain."

"I do," he said slowly.

"Then why did you abandon Abdera while she was under full-scale attack?" Chiba demanded.

"That wasn't full-scale."

"The capital is *gone,* Husher," the president retorted, his voice like iron, which seemed strange coming from the childlike Kaithian. "It was full-scale enough, don't you think? If you'd stayed, we might have held."

"I had a decision to make."

"Between what?"

"Between saving Abdera and protecting the Feverfew Shipyards. It was a harsh calculation to have to make, but the shipyards were much more important from a military perspective."

The Kaithian's head twitched, causing his head-tail to swing to the right. "That's rather debatable, especially when you consider the damage losing the galaxy's capital will do to public morale. There's also the inconvenient fact that you *failed* to protect the shipyards."

"Nevertheless, the reasoning was sound."

"Was it? I think you're skirting the truth, Captain. You weren't choosing between Abdera and the shipyards at all. You were choosing between Abdera and your ex-wife."

Husher blinked. He hadn't expected that. *I guess you don't become galactic president without being perceptive.* His cheeks began to heat up, and he wondered whether they were close enough for Chiba to spot his shame. "Listen, Kaithian," he said, partly to mask it, and partly from genuine anger. Chiba's guards shifted their weight at his change in tone. "Let's get one thing straight. If you're here to try to remove me from command, then you'd better have your men shoot me, because that's the only way that's going to happen. Otherwise, I stay in the command seat. Understood?"

A brittle silence took hold in the conference room, and for a moment, Husher wondered whether Chiba would give the order to kill him. If he did, Husher had enough faith in his crew that he doubted they would react positively to that.

"I haven't come to remove you from command," the Kaithian said at last. "Attempting to do so has already proven a burdensome, aggravating experience. For the duration of this war, at least, we're stuck with you."

"Then what have you come to do?"

"After the Quatro evacuated myself along with thousands of other government officials and civilians, we owe them an even greater debt. I'm here to require you to turn over the Quatro aboard your ship, and to standby without interfering while we apprehend those aboard the Quatro warship in your battle group."

"I can't believe it," Husher snapped. "Are we really doing this again? You *know* what I'm prepared to do to prevent the Quatro with me from becoming political prisoners. I wouldn't recommend pushing me on it."

"Captain Husher, I don't think you fully comprehend the delicate balance I'm trying to strike here," Chiba said, and to Husher, the Kaithian almost sounded like he was pleading.

"The Quatro need us just as much as we need them," Husher said. "We offered them safe refuge in a galaxy we control, and without us, they'd fall to the Progenitors even faster. They don't get to pretend they can push us around and make demands."

"Clearly, you don't understand the Quatro," Chiba said. "Or at least, you don't understand their Assembly of Elders. They're willing to gamble with everything to get what they want."

"Then they're psychopaths. I don't strike compromises with psychopaths. It isn't possible. Sorry, Mr. President, but Rug stays on this ship, and I'll blast from space any ship that makes a move against my Quatro vessel."

Chiba's face hardened. "Then you've left me with only one option. I'll have to take other measures to placate the Elders, because without them, we're finished."

"What other measures?"

"I'm afraid you don't get to know yet, Captain."

Husher's jaw tensed. "I'd suggest you carefully consider whatever it is you're about to do, President Chiba. You and your friends have already done enough damage to the galaxy. It can't take much more."

"There's a lot you don't understand, Captain. You command a starship, and I hope you realize that comes nowhere close to the complex demands of governing a galaxy." Chiba paused, slim shoulders rising and falling more rapidly. "The loss of Thessaly and Abdera has made one thing clear: we need to begin evacuating systems."

Husher's eyebrows twitched at the near-echo of what his daughter had said to him inside his office. "Evacuate them to where?"

"That's yet to be determined."

"How about the Kaithian home system?"

That brought another prolonged pause from Chiba. Clearly, he was uncomfortable with the idea. Or at least, he thought it would be difficult to get the Kaithian Consensus to agree.

"You know it makes the most sense," Husher went on. "In fact, it would be criminally negligent to evacuate civilians to anywhere else. The superweapon you call a moon may be our last hope of survival."

"The Preserver was not meant for use in war."

Husher laughed. "What was it meant for, then? Decoration? Don't try to fool me about this, Chiba. It's shameful for you to try. I was with Captain Keyes when your superweapon gunned down the Ixa chasing us, and he told me how your brethren characterized the Preserver. They said it was programmed only for *defensive* war. And that's exactly what this is."

The galactic president met Husher's gaze for several long seconds. At last, he said, "You're right, and I believe the Consensus will agree. We'll begin the evacuation to Home immediately. Many supplies will be needed, and temporary structures. Our planet's land will be covered with beings."

Husher raised his eyebrows, a little surprised at how quickly Chiba had jumped on board with the proposal. "Yes, it will," he said.

"As for you, Captain, I want you to carry out a mission given to you at the very start of this conflict. One you still haven't completed."

"What might that be?"

"Go to the Gok, and find a way to forge an alliance with them."

Husher's eyes widened. "You can't be serious. They helped Teth fight us in Concord."

"Their government has been distancing itself from the Gok who did that. They say those were rogue ships."

"And you believe them?"

"Not necessarily. But I do believe that any chance of victory now depends on taking long shots. And this is one of them."

Husher was about to continue arguing, but the president was right, he realized.

"Very well," he said. "I'll approach the Gok."

He'd hoped to remain in this area of the galaxy for a little longer, in case Fesky returned. But she wasn't coming back. And as his conversation with the president had just attested, it no longer paid to remain in any part of the galaxy for very long.

CHAPTER 20

Lucid

As the *Vesta*'s crew made final preparations for her to depart Feverfew for the journey to the Gok home system, a shuttle entered the system from Hellebore.

Shortly after, a message arrived from a woman named Eve Quinn, who said she represented Invigor Technologies.

"I'd like to meet with Captain Husher," the message read. "I have a proposition that could change the war."

Husher read that with extreme skepticism, but like Chiba had said, it was time to start taking long shots. And they weren't slated to leave Feverfew for another three hours. So he could fit in a meeting.

Based on the name of the company Quinn represented, Husher figured that having Ochrim present would be a good idea. And so, after receiving Quinn on Flight Deck Delta, he led her toward Cybele.

"This place is actually less of a ghost town than I expected," Quinn said, peering around as they walked through the city streets toward Ochrim's residence.

Husher nodded, trying not to notice the smell of sanitizer, or to think about what it might be covering up. With the recent riots and general neglect that had come with a smaller population living in the same amount of space, the street-cleaning robots had increased the amount of sanitizer they used. Oculens overlays had also gotten more elaborate, to cover up the damage done to several of the buildings.

"A lot of the people who move to one of these starship cities do so for a reason," he said. "An agenda. That type of person isn't going to be turned off by unrest, or by flying into the middle of a war."

"Zealots," Quinn said.

"Basically. IGF Command welcomes them, since they're a major source of funding. Either way, Command's still dissatisfied with our population numbers."

They found Ochrim waiting for them on his front step, arms crossed. "I hope you don't have any more technologies for me to develop, Captain. I'm kept rather busy trying to find a way to move bigger ships through dimensions."

"You're in luck," Quinn said. "This one's already developed, and extremely straightforward to integrate with the *Vesta*'s existing systems."

To Husher, Quinn's words sounded exactly like the sales pitch he'd been expecting. "I only want your input, Ochrim," he said. "On whether whatever Quinn has come to propose is a good idea. We'll meet in the lab."

Ochrim uncrossed his arms to open his front door. "By all means," he said. "Not that I'm under the illusion that I have a choice in the matter."

"Good," Husher said. "We have enough illusions in this city as it is."

The Ixan led them to the back room where the lab's entrance, hidden in the floor, was now kept open. Without ceremony, he began descending the ladder, and Husher motioned for Quinn to follow.

As his foot left the bottom rung, Husher noticed two of Ek's six offspring swimming in the enormous tank that took up one wall of the lab. The Fins' exoskeletons allowed them to walk the ship freely, but to completely avoid the negative effects zero G had on Fin bodies, they had to regularly perform calisthenic exercises inside the tank.

It has to be better than living in there twenty-four-seven. That had been their situation before Ochrim had developed the exoskeleton.

Husher turned to Quinn. "What do you have for us?"

She grinned. "Right to business, I see. I like it."

"War doesn't leave much room for formalities."

Quinn's smile broadened, and then Husher's Oculenses notified him of an invitation to a shared overlay. When he accepted, a MIMAS mech appeared in the center of the lab.

"We already have mechs," Husher said, walking around it. "Unless you're one of the companies contracted to build more of them?" Whenever he beheld one of these machines, he couldn't help but admire the engineering that went into it. The mech bristled with artillery, and it vaguely resembled a human who'd broken free of the bonds of evolution to merge with technology.

"It isn't the MIMAS itself I wanted to show you," Quinn said. "It's the technology that allows pilots to control the mechs."

"Lucid, isn't it?" Husher said, still circling the mech.

"Yes. The pilot dreams she *is* the mech. And we've expanded on the tech; modified it for use with almost any vehicle."

Husher's eyes snapped onto Quinn's face. "Lucid is Darkstream tech. How did your company come to acquire it? My understanding was that the entire Darkstream board was sentenced to life imprisonment."

"That's true. But we've partnered with a lower-level employee, who was exonerated."

"Who is it?"

Quinn's smile tightened. "Invigor considers that information proprietary."

"Fascinating. Well, I'm surprised you'd come here to waste my time with Darkstream tech. You are aware of my history with the company, aren't you? Not to mention the universe's history with almost getting destroyed by it?"

Quinn managed to keep her chipper demeanor intact. "I can assure you, this isn't a waste of time, Captain. And the only reason you're surprised I would propose this is because you haven't seen the tech in action yet. Lucid would give the *Vesta* and her Python pilots a big edge in combat. Watch."

Apparently Quinn had sent her Oculenses a command, since the MIMAS disappeared, replaced by a battlespace in miniature. Inside it, a digital scale model of the *Vesta* was surrounded by gnat-like Pythons, all engaging an enemy that struck with particle beams and Ravagers. But Husher could see that the rate at which enemy fire found its target had been dramatically reduced, with Pythons turning on a dime. The *Vesta* also seemed to respond faster than should have been possible, given the time required for a captain to give the Nav officer orders based on information relayed by the sensor operator.

"Using lucid, a properly trained Nav officer can see and process what the ship sees, and respond accordingly. They can *become* the ship, and you can limit your orders to cases where you want the ship to move in a way that's counterintuitive."

"It's impressive," Husher admitted. "But we also don't have an abundance of time. The way I see it, our time is much better spent figuring out a way to get a ship like the *Vesta* to the Progenitors' home system. Preferably before they wipe out every last system of ours."

"But that's the beauty of this technology," Quinn said. "As I said, it can be seamlessly integrated with existing systems, and it doesn't take long to do that. You'll likely be finished well before you arrive in Gok space." She cleared her throat. "For all you know, Captain, this upgrade could buy enough time to make the discovery you just mentioned. And if you ask me, lucid will prove even more important for the war effort than interdimensional warship travel."

Husher drew a deep breath. "I tend to doubt that. But I do see your point." He expelled the air in a rush. "All right. My primary Nav officer happens to have a minor in sensor system engineering, so provided she agrees to this, she can probably be brought up to speed fairly quickly. All of this is contingent on her consent, however."

"I understand, Captain," Quinn said. "I think you're making the right choice."

I wish I did, Husher thought, still very apprehensive over using tech that had originated with Darkstream.

He reminded himself of Chiba's words. Husher and the president didn't agree on much, but in this they were united: it *was* time to start taking long shots.

"What about your Python pilots?" Quinn said. "Should I start work on having them outfitted with the tech as well?"

Husher shook his head. "I doubt we have the time. Besides, I want to see how the first upgrade plays out before converting my entire Air Group. If all goes well, we'll see to that later."

"Hopefully the war will afford us the opportunity to do all that, Captain."

CHAPTER 21

Lavender

As the *Vesta* sped through a dying galaxy toward the Gok home world, Doctor Bancroft suggested that Jake use the time wisely. "Getting a little fresh air would be good for your recovery," she said.

He'd quipped that fresh air wasn't available aboard the *Vesta*.

Bancroft hadn't seemed amused by that, no matter how true it was. The closest he could get to fresh air was Santana Park, where the simulated sun shone from above but provided no heat. Not that it was cold—the heating units out in the fake desert kept Cybele at room temperature, and the ceiling lights *did* emit UVB rays that triggered vitamin D production.

It's still not quite the same, he reflected.

He was used to being away from a real sun. He'd grown up in a great artificial habitat called Hub, which had shared a heliocentric orbit with the asteroids of Kuiper Belt 2 in the Steele System.

Still, he cherished the few memories he had of walking on Eresos outside of his mech. Real sunlight on real skin, unmediated even by the mech dream.

Santana Park pulsated with life, today: couples strolling the cobbled paths, youth chasing each other between the trees, students studying. It was as though the galaxy's rapid deterioration had chased everyone from their residences, to snatch what pleasantness remained to be had. No one seemed to be pushing a political agenda, today. Everyone was just living.

This is what I'm fighting to protect. Exactly this.

Except, Jake wasn't confident he could fight anymore. He could join Gamble's marine battalion as regular infantry, but he'd accomplish far less than he would in his mech, especially with the dizziness that continued to plague him. He could walk unaided now, but he still had a long way to go.

According to Bancroft, his prefrontal cortex had taken a beating after Lisa's shot caused his meninges to swell. *Maybe that's what's interfering with controlling my mech.*

Odell had suggested switching to one of the empty MIMAS mechs, but Jake wouldn't hear of it. Something deep inside him railed against the notion of abandoning the alien mech, and he justified it by pointing out how much more powerful it was. The war effort required everyone to strive toward their maximum potential, and for Jake, that meant piloting the thing, even if he had to master it all over again.

His gaze fell on a young woman wearing the spaced-out expression of an Oculens user. Another student studying….and he recognized this student.

"Hey," he said as he neared, trying not to hobble too much.

Iris looked up, and as she did, he caught the scent of flowers. *Lavender?*

"What do you want?" she said.

"To thank you. For saving my life."

"I would have done it for anyone. The fact that I saved *you* is proof of that."

Jake furrowed his brow. "What does that mean?"

"I've heard how you pushed for my father to meet with the Brotherhood. How you thought he should try to form an alliance with them."

Jake shrugged. "I thought they could lend us some muscle, in case the IU tried to put us in a position we didn't want to be in. And we *could* have used the muscle, it turned out."

Iris shook her head. "So, allying with the Brotherhood, that's a situation you'd prefer?"

"At the time, I thought it might help. Maybe I was wrong."

"Yeah, I'd say there's a good chance, considering they attacked a Union colony soon after that!"

"What's your problem with me, anyway?" he asked. "You were the first person I saw when I woke up. You were waiting by my bedside, for God knows who long. So I can't be all bad."

Iris rose to her feet, bringing her scowl close to him. *It's definitely lavender.*

"I felt responsible for you," she said. "Apparently that happens after you save someone's life. Hopefully you'll actually do something good with it, this time around. Because from what I've seen, you act first without thinking. You don't consider what the effects might be on other beings. Excuse me."

She brushed past him and headed deeper into the park, leaving Jake staring after her, feeling thoroughly baffled.

CHAPTER 22

Willing to Share the Galaxy

"The Gok ships seem to have registered our presence, Captain," Winterton said. "They're distributing themselves along a wide arc between us and their homeworld."

"The formation looks defensive," Tremaine put in. "No sign of their usual aggression as of yet."

Sounds like progress to me. Even so... "Stay on alert, everyone. Nav, take us close enough to their formation for real-time communication, but no closer." The Gok had stationed almost three dozen of their warships in this, their home system. While Husher was confident he would win an engagement if it arose, that wouldn't happen without heavy losses, and it wouldn't serve anything. He wanted the option to back out if things soured.

"Sir, a transmission request is coming in from a destroyer near the center of their formation," Ensign Fry said.

"Put it on the main display, and let everyone have Oculens access."

"Aye."

A Gok appeared on the screen, all forest-green muscle. Its rounded, bald head featured a forehead ridge that overshadowed small, onyx eyes, which were studying Husher intently.

"Have no business here," the alien said, its voice like gravel being ground together.

"On the contrary," Husher said. "Can I ask who I'm speaking with?"

"Am Fulm, Admiral of Gok Star Navy. State reason for coming here."

Well, I'm talking to the right person. He'd heard of Fulm—he was one of the Gok's few surviving officers from the Gok Wars. Husher knew next to nothing about the individuals that comprised the Gok navy, so he'd had no idea Fulm had risen so far.

He paused to gather his thoughts, in spite of how pointless this mission felt to him. He felt as optimistic about the chances of Gok joining the fight against the Progenitors as he was about the IU coming to its senses any time soon.

But I have to try. "I'm Captain Vin Husher. I've come on behalf of President Chiba of the Interstellar Union. I'm here to propose an alliance."

"Alliance," Admiral Fulm said, as though tasting the word and finding it foul.

"Yes. We understand your government has distanced itself from the ships that fought us in the Concord System, and we're prepared to let bygones be bygones. We're also well aware of your long history of working with the Progenitors—or at least with their creations, the Ixa. But we've come to you all the same. To be honest, we're desperate, and we think you should be too."

"Why Gok desperate?" Fulm asked, his expression broadening with what Husher guessed was an analog for disbelief.

"Your species and mine have a lot of animosity between us. You think humans are untrustworthy, manipulative. And in some cases, you're right. We captured a Progenitor agent who infiltrated my ship and tried to kill one of us. She's a human, Admiral Fulm. The Progenitors are just another version of humanity, from another universe. Humans have been manipulating your species for over forty years, using you as unwitting weapons of war. They were taken over by an alternate version of Darkstream."

Fulm's forehead ridge descended. "If humans treacherous, why should Gok trust you?"

"Because I'm not here to represent humanity. At least, not only humanity. The Progenitors are carrying out the agenda of a company that has exterminated all other beings in their universe. But the IU is a democratic coalition of species. We keep each other in check, and we balance out each other's weaknesses." *Somewhat,* Husher added, though only to himself. "The IU was designed to enable partnerships like the one I'm proposing. If we remain enemies, there's a near-certainty that the Progenitors will wipe us out. They don't want to share this universe with anyone. But if we unite, we could survive."

Fulm fell silent for a time, continuing to study Husher while his massive shoulders rose and fell. At last, he said, "Many Gok wish now to break cycle of war, which is starting again. New leader, Benth, has called for change, and many Gok agree, though even still, talk of the real problem is scarce."

"What's the real problem?"

"Virophage, which Ixa created to make Gok more violent."

Husher nodded. A cure for the virophage had been found during the Second Galactic War, and Keyes had attempted to distribute it to the Gok, but only a minority had accepted. They'd seemed to like the way they were, then.

"I believe what I'm proposing could serve as a solution, in the short-term, anyway," Husher said. "You just told me that the cycle of war is ramping up again. Does that mean the drive to make war is taking hold once more?"

"Yes," Fulm said.

"Join *us* in war, then. That way, you can satisfy your lust for combat and still be around afterward to figure yourselves out. The Progenitors want this universe for themselves, and if we fight each other, we'll effectively be handing it to them. But the IU will always be willing to share the galaxy with Gok."

Fulm raised a massive fist toward Husher. "Fulm does not speak for Gok. But will take your words to them. Time is needed for that."

"Time isn't something we have a lot of. You need to make your decision quickly. It shouldn't be hard. The right choice seems clear."

"Husher does not understand Gok," Fulm said. "Need time."

"We'll wait twenty hours," Husher said. "No more." Winterton inhaled sharply, and Husher looked at him. "What?"

"Twenty Progenitor ships have appeared behind our battle group," he said, his gaze lifting to meet Husher's. "The *Vesta*'s getting hit with three particle beams at once—severe superheating all along our stern!"

Husher winced. "Nav, evasive maneuvers now!"

CHAPTER 23

Close-In Alpha Strike

Even before Husher finished giving the order to begin evasive maneuvers, the *Vesta* had already begun shifting laterally.

It seems we'll get to field test lucid tech sooner rather than later.

So far, Husher was impressed. Plugged into the *Vesta*'s sensors, Noni's response time easily exceeded his expectations, even after Quinn's exuberant sales pitch.

"The superheating has subsided, Captain," Winterton said, his voice awash with relief. "We've escaped the beam."

"Very good. Excellent work, Chief Noni."

Thanks to the CIC crew's Oculenses, Noni appeared to be sitting at the Nav station. But in reality, the Tumbran was asleep in her bunk, under the influence of a sedative and wearing headgear that lent structure to her dreams, shaping them into a completely immersive simulation in which she *was* the *Vesta*, just as MIMAS pilots became their mechs inside lucid. But she could also communicate with the CIC crew, using her Oculens avatar.

"Ravagers streaming across the battlespace, sir," Winterton said.

"Acknowledged. Coms, tell Ayam to scramble Pythons and put them on missile defense for now." He returned his gaze to the sensor operator. "What's the posture of the Gok fleet?"

"They're showing no sign of joining the battle."

"Well, at least they haven't turned on us," Husher muttered.

"I'm picking up on encrypted coms traffic," Fry said. "It's likely the Progenitors are trying to get the Gok to do exactly that."

Husher found himself gripping the command seat's armrests as he tried to work out how to prevent that from happening. "What the Gok understand best is strength. We need to find a way to start knocking down Progenitor ships, fast, so that we look like the dominant side. Any ideas, Tremaine?"

The Tactical officer exhaled, and to Husher it sounded like a frustrated sigh. "It's difficult to commit to any offensive maneuver when their ships can just pop out of existence, forcing us to waste any missiles we fire at them. I'd recommend assigning our subspace squadron to offense, but other than that, I'm stumped."

"You're right," Husher said, turning over the Tactical officer's words in his mind. "Coms, let's implement Tremaine's suggestion to redirect Ayam's subspace fighters. And Tremaine, I want you to prep six missile barrages, twenty missiles each, with every barrage consisting of ten Banshees, five Hydras, and Five Gorgons. Have them loaded in tubes distributed all around the *Vesta*, so that we're ready to respond to any Progenitor ships who vanish and then reappear in our immediate vicinity."

"Aye, sir."

"Relay the following to our Quatro warship, Coms: I want them to leave missile defense to the other ships and start sending everything they have at the enemy. We'll have our Pythons do what they can to escort the missiles in, taking down any Ravagers that threaten them."

"Brilliant," Tremaine said. "The Quatro's missile salvage function should mean their rockets won't be wasted if the enemy ships decide to disappear."

Husher nodded. "We have a lot of work to do when it comes to efficiently coordinating our efforts with our new allies." Husher was just as responsible for that neglect as anyone else, he realized. He'd let his distrust of the Quatro draw his focus away from where it needed to be: on how best to work together to defeat a relentless foe.

"Sir, five of the Progenitor ships have vanished from the battlespace: two destroyers and three carriers."

"Here's our chance," Husher said. "Tremaine, are the missile barrages ready?"

"Aye, Captain."

"Excellent. Standby to fire on my mark."

He watched the tactical display as the enemy ships reappeared all around them, just as expected.

Switching to an overlay that showed him the distribution of missiles in the *Vesta*'s launch tubes, Husher saw the two destroyers were lined up perfectly, and close enough that they likely wouldn't be able to react in time.

"Fire five of the six barrages at once, Tremaine."

"Firing missiles."

Banshees, Hydras, and Gorgons streamed from the *Vesta* in all directions. The carriers were already deploying Ravagers, and since they weren't lined up like the destroyers, they seemed likely to back away and neutralize the missiles targeting them in time.

The destroyers weren't so lucky. They barely had time to activate their particle beams before the *Vesta*'s rockets flashed across the battlespace and into their hulls, obliterating both ships within seconds.

As usual during battles with the Progenitors, no one inside the CIC cheered. Every minor victory happened in the face of a broader, looming threat. Right now, there were still eighteen Progenitor ships to deal with.

As though to underscore that point, Winterton said, "The three carriers have recovered, sir. They're directing Ravagers at us again."

Husher nodded. "Put tertiary laser projectors in point defense mode, Tactical. Coms, tell Major Gamble to expect company." The marine commander would already be patrolling the *Vesta*'s outer corridors, but a little extra heads-up wouldn't hurt. "Send out a call for six Python squadrons to tighten up around us while we figure out a way to neutralize the carriers."

"Yes, sir."

"The Ravager cloud is denser than we've seen, Captain," Winterton said. "Some may get through our defenses before the Pythons get here."

"Acknowledged. Send the locations of any breaches to Coms for forwarding to Major Gamble."

The tide of robot-missiles washed across space, its front inching closer and closer to the supercarrier. At last, a robot made it through the point defense systems, even supplemented as they were by lasers. It latched onto the hull and burrowed inside.

A terrible shrieking arose at the Nav station. When Husher looked, Noni's avatar was flickering in and out of the overlay, spasming where it sat.

She slumped from her chair to the ground, her small body rocking in the throes of a violent seizure.

A single second of shock—that was all Husher allowed himself. Then, he turned to Fry. "Get the secondary Nav officer into the CIC at once. Contact Doctor Bancroft and tell her to check on Noni in her quarters."

"Aye, sir," Fry said.

Damn it. I never should have agreed to allow Darkstream tech on my ship.

Never again. He'd have lucid purged from his systems, never to return to the *Vesta*. He didn't care if the entire IGF adopted it and made it work. He would never leave himself or his officers this vulnerable again.

"More Ravagers are getting in," Winterton said. "Five breaches so far. Six," he added, consulting his console.

But the Python squadrons were arriving now, and they weaved between the cloud of Ravagers, shooting them down along the way. The six squadrons came together to form a protective blanket around their base ship.

A seventh squadron of fighters appeared behind one of the Progenitor carriers, executing a close-in alpha strike that tore up the ship's backside. In desperation, the carrier ceased its attack on the *Vesta* to direct Ravagers toward the subspace fighters, but they vanished.

"Hit that carrier with our primary, Tremaine," Husher said.

"Aye, sir. Firing laser." As always, Tremaine had followed Husher's standing orders to never be without multiple firing solutions at the ready.

The Progenitor hull began to warp, and the subspace fighters appeared off her stern, having sharply altered their trajectory. They added their fire to the *Vesta*'s, and the carrier exploded.

Husher's com beeped, and he answered it.

"Sorry, Captain," Ayam said. "I know I wasn't specifically ordered to do that, but you did tell us to go on the offense."

"No apology necessary," Husher said, chuckling. "Good work, Commander."

He noticed movement on the other side of the tactical display. The Gok ships were approaching, and they passed into missile range just as he noticed them. A flood of tiny icons crossed the battlespace.

"Is that for us or the Progenitors?" Husher asked, eyeing Winterton.

"It's hard to say, sir. With the two remaining carriers this close to us, it's difficult to tell who they're for. And the Gok seem to have chosen a firing solution that deliberately makes their targeting ambiguous."

"I picked up on more encrypted traffic less than a minute ago, sir," Fry said. "That may have been the Progenitors ordering the Gok to fire on us."

Husher's jaw tensed. "Tremaine, prepare a defensive Banshee barrage. Call two more squadrons back to us, Fry, for increased missile defense. How's our capacitor charge?"

"Twenty percent, Captain."

"Very good. Continue to supplement point defense with tertiaries."

The entire CIC seemed to hold its breath as the missiles surged across the battlespace. The fact that the Progenitors didn't seem concerned didn't do much to ease the tension.

But at the last possible moment, the missile barrage split, altering its course to target both carriers.

Rockets slammed into hulls, and the Progenitor vessels went up in flames promptly swallowed by the void.

That did bring cheering to Husher's CIC, and it did him good to hear it.

The Gok fleet continued to move forward, Slags pouring out of their carriers to scream toward enemy ships.

But the Progenitors had had enough. Their remaining fifteen warships vanished from the Gok home system.

CHAPTER 24

You Killed Him

"**H**ow close is the Interstellar Union to achieving interdimensional travel for capital starships?" Husher asked Fesky as he positioned a pair of slip-joint pliers around her left index talon. The pliers were large enough that he had to hold a handle in each hand.

Fesky's stomach roared with the insatiable hunger given her by the methamphetamine withdrawal—hunger which the meager rations Husher force fed her came nowhere close to satisfying.

She tried to answer, but her speech came out garbled, incomprehensible. Ever since Husher had ceased the massive doses of meth he'd injected her with, the Cavern had taken on a dreamlike quality, punctuated by spikes in pain that were all too real.

"What's that?" Husher said, leaning closer, though not so close she could bite him with her beak, which she'd tried to do before. His scar drew her eye, even though she could tell it bothered him when she stared at it. "Are you ready to start talking?" he asked.

"Burn in hell," Fesky managed to rasp.

"Ah." Husher slammed the plier handles together with her talon jammed deep in their jaws. Her index talon fell to the floor, and Fesky shrieked and shrieked.

"I need to know Ochrim's ideas for expanding the quantum engine," Husher said calmly. "I need his theories on how the multiverse works. I need everything."

Through the pain and the fatigue and the hunger, Fesky's head flopped to one side, and she saw Husher standing several meters to her right—not her torturer, but Husher, her captain of seventeen years, and her friend of even longer.

"Vin," she whispered.

"I'm right here," he said, backhanding her across the face. "Pay no attention to your hallucinations. Pay attention to me."

Still holding the pliers, he circled the table to where Fesky's other arm was strapped down. He positioned the jaws around her other index talon. "Care to tell me anything about your captain's progress toward interdimensional travel?"

Fesky clenched her beak and remained silent. For the past several days, she'd been attempting to use mindfulness meditation to contend with the torture, which she'd picked up from Ochrim but never really used.

She used it now.

"Any pain can be withstood," Ochrim said from the side of the chair opposite her torturer. "Any pain can be endured. Focus on it. Contemplate it. Catalog its quality."

The plier jaws closed, and fresh agony exploded, somehow worse than before. Fesky raged against her restraints, though they held her fast, and she shrieked again.

"As promised," Husher said, "you're slowly disintegrating. All of it you've brought on yourself. Talk, and you can halt the process. Where on the *Vesta* does Ochrim perform his research?"

Fesky said nothing, and Husher laughed. "You are quite a Winger, you know that? Not that it's saying much. The Wingers were exterminated from this universe, and for good reason. We thoroughly dominated them, and then they died out, as they deserved to. Weak, pitiful creatures with transparent motives. Insanely obedient to their superiors, well past the point it makes any sense to be. Irrationally attached to the Fins…though I suppose there are only seven of those left in the multiverse, as far as I know. All of them aboard the *Vesta*. They'll be killed too, soon enough."

"Where are my crew?" Fesky asked, as she had many times before.

Today, Husher's answer surprised her. "Funny you should ask that, actually." He walked away from the chair, and the darkness of the Cavern enveloped him, till she could only hear his echoing footsteps receding.

Soon, the footsteps began to return, and Fesky began trembling.

He reentered the light gripping a young man by the upper arm. Fesky recognized him as Petty Officer Milton, who'd worked in the *Spire*'s missile loading bay. His arms were bound behind him.

Husher shoved Milton forward, so that he stumbled and fell over Fesky. He didn't get up. He just lay on top of her, shaking, meeting her gaze with eyes full of fear.

Husher drew his pistol and placed it against the back of Milton's head.

"Tell me how close the IU is to true interdimensional travel."

Fesky said nothing, her beak clacking rapidly.

The gun fired, the report deafening at this range. The bullet exited through Milton's face, ruining it and barely missing Fesky. Brain and blood and flesh spattered her face.

"He died because of you," Husher said mildly. "You killed him, just as you'll kill the next crewmember. One every day, bird, until you start telling me all about the *Vesta*, her capabilities, and your captain's intentions."

Husher was back—her *captain* was back, standing at her feet, leveling a stern gaze at her. Captain Keyes stood beside him, wearing an expression that mirrored his protégé's.

"Burn in hell," Fesky gasped.

CHAPTER 25

A Form of Robbery

Wanda Carlisle stood when the receptionist called her name, and she smiled at the man as she passed toward the heavy oak doors of the governor's office. The receptionist returned her gaze with a blank one of his own.

Everyone's under a lot of stress, she reflected. And no wonder. With the galaxy falling down around their ears, who could blame them?

Wanda tended to keep her cool in trying times—that came with the territory of running a fast-growing interstellar shipping company. Even so, over the last few days, a lot of people had remarked on how baffled they were to see how upbeat she remained, despite the accelerating Progenitor invasion.

She couldn't help it. She'd always believed that the galaxy benefited from times like these: times when goodwill was allowed to shine through the drudgery of everyday life. The galaxy had been troubled even before this war began, and in her opinion, they *needed* this, if only to rediscover what was truly important.

Pausing before the closed door of the Office of the Governor of Pandosia, she smoothed her chic midnight blazer then reached for the door.

"Close it behind you," Governor Kessler said, without looking up from his desktop.

She was going to do that anyway, but she tamped down the flash of annoyance his words caused her and pushed the door closed.

At last, his gaze rose to meet hers. "Sorry for the wait," he said, his tone bland. "Have a seat."

"I understand completely," Wanda said as she approached the chair in front of his desk. "With the evacuation of the colony to coordinate, I'm surprised you were able to see me so soon."

Of course, Wanda wasn't *too* surprised. She was, after all, a prominent member of Pandosia's business community.

"What can I do for you?" he said.

"Actually, I was wondering what I could do for Pandosia."

Kessler titled his head to one side. "Hmm?"

"The galaxy's been through so much, Governor. Interspecies tensions have been getting out of hand, and it doesn't help when certain prominent fleet captains cling to old-fashioned ways of doing things. And now, with the Brotherhood on the rise...I want you to know that I've been fully on board with what the IU has been doing about all this. Our close alliance with the Quatro is going to be so good for society, I think, and I also stand by the arrests the IU has made of suspected Brotherhood supporters. I know a lot of people don't, but at a time like this, you have to do what you can to keep society from falling apart."

A brisk nod from the governor. "Yes, good. Sorry to cut you short, Ms. Carlisle, but there are countless matters for me to attend to. What is it you came here to discuss?"

Wanda's smile widened. "I came to offer to help with the evacuation. Every freighter I own is already being prepped to house and feed hundreds of civilians each. I want to use the wealth I've been lucky enough to build to help the less fortunate."

To her surprise, the governor didn't react—at least, not positively. Instead, he frowned, while nodding gravely. "Yes. Well, that's very gracious of you to offer, Ms. Carlisle, very gracious indeed. Unfortunately, many of your wealthy peers have failed to make similar offers of help."

"I...I'm sorry to hear that," Wanda said, unsure where this was going.

"So am I. As I'm sure you can appreciate, a migration on the scale we're looking at will require massive resources—resources the government simply doesn't have. Not without resorting to measures that some may call drastic."

"What measures?"

"It was decided just a couple hours ago by Galactic Congress that every private ship owner in the galaxy is to have their ships commandeered by local authorities, for use in the evacuation. So you see, your offer, while very generous, isn't quite relevant. Your freighters are likely being boarded as we speak."

For a long moment, Wanda found she had nothing to say. Then, at last, she found some words: "Will I be left a ship for my own use? And what about my employees—how will they escape?"

"You will all be entered into a lottery in order to determine who will receive the first spots on the departing ships. Everyone will be treated equally."

"But they're my ships." Part of her felt ashamed to point that out—but it was true!

"Not anymore," Governor Kessler said. "Not until after the war, at least. There's something else: everyone in your tax bracket will have fifty percent of their wealth appropriated by the end of the day, to help fund the evacuation."

Wanda's mouth was hanging open, she realized, and she snapped it shut. "This is not fair. I offered to *help* you. This is robbery!"

"Ms. Carlisle, please. You are human, and you come from a wealthy family. Many would say that the wealth you've extracted from the economy is a form of robbery."

Wanda squeezed her eyes shut, as though doing so might end the nightmare she'd walked into. "That's absurd."

"You should feel grateful you're being left with fifty percent," Kessler said. "If you ask me, fifty percent is probably a very conservative estimate of how much of your wealth you've accumulated inequitably. The government is finally taking steps to even out society, but they've actually been quite generous toward your class so far."

A wave of vertigo washed over Wanda, so that she feared to stand. It was hard for her to process how rapidly the ground below her feet had shifted, and how quickly her mind had been changed about the Interstellar Union.

"I'll have to ask you to leave, Ms. Carlisle," the governor said. "As I mentioned, I'm very busy. You will be contacted by those administrating the lottery once your name is drawn."

CHAPTER 26

You'll Pursue It Now

Ochrim was standing on his front step again as Husher approached, his scaled hands in his pockets.

"Captain," he said in greeting, nodding his ridged head, whose scales had faded to white in several places.

"Hello, Ochrim," Husher said. He'd given the Ixan advance notice of his visit, but he wondered whether that was why he stood out here. *Maybe he would have been standing there anyway.*

Husher climbed the step and turned to join the alien in gazing out at the illusion that was Cybele. From here, he had a pretty good view of the neighborhood, and of Cybele's taller structures. There was Cybele University, its ivory structures much higher in the Oculens overlay than in reality. The tip of the Epicenter poked over the city as well.

"The hydroponics facilities enable the *Vesta* to embark on longer voyages, when it's expedient," Ochrim said.

"So they do." Husher glanced at the Ixan, wondering where he was going with this.

"Having Cybele cuts down on your crew's need for planetside leave, as well. It gives them an environment with less structure, where they can blow off steam, even pretend they're truly outside as they walk through the elaborate overlay."

"What's your point, Ochrim? Are you making an argument for starship cities?"

"I'm making observations. Without Cybele, I wouldn't have been able to come and live aboard this ship. I wouldn't have been here to develop subspace tech, or the exoskeletons for Ek and her young. Where do you think you'd be without those two things?"

"Dead, probably." Husher sniffed. "Thank you for the extra perspective, Ochrim."

"According to narrownet talk, you've secured an alliance with the Gok."

"We have their word, yes. Now we get to find out how good it is. We're on our way back to IU space."

"And you've come to me about developing another technology."

"Well, expanding on one you've already developed. Shall we?" Husher said, gesturing toward the front door.

Ochrim nodded, turning to admit them.

"The living room will do," Husher said.

"Very well. Would you like a beverage?"

"Just water. The time for alcohol is long past, I think. At least until we've won."

Ochrim brought him a sweating glass of water, which Husher took a long sip from and then continued: "We can't win this war with the technology we have. Fesky still hasn't returned with the *Spire*, so clearly it isn't enough to send a ship that size to the

Progenitors' home. We need to send a capital starship. We need to take the *Vesta*."

For a while, Ochrim was silent, sitting across the room from Husher with no drink of his own. "I don't think it's possible," he said at last. "Not to develop the necessary tech in time to defeat the Progenitors before they wipe us out."

"How can you say that without at least trying, Ochrim?"

"Oh, I'll try. If that's what you want me to do, I'll do it. But I don't think it's what we should focus on. The galaxy is in grave peril, Captain Husher. The probability that the Progenitors will allow us to evacuate everyone to the Kaithian home system without a fight is extremely low. I believe we're better off helping with that effort. Then, under the protection of the Kaithian Preserver, perhaps we will have enough time."

Husher shook his head. "There's something you're not telling me. Something that would speed up the development of the tech but take us away from helping with the evacuation. But you think the greater good will be best served by the evacuation, so you don't want the *Vesta* haring off somewhere else, all for a mere chance of gaining this tech."

Ochrim looked at him with wide eyes, then his features relaxed. "I suppose by now I shouldn't be surprised at your ability to read me."

"I've certainly exercised it enough. Now that we've sorted that out, as captain of this ship, I order you to tell me what you've been holding back."

Ochrim sighed. "There is one way to achieve what you want, though the probability of it succeeding is quite low, I think."

"Tell me."

"If we could succeed in somehow disabling and capturing a Progenitor ship, I could probably reverse engineer their quantum engine, or whatever it is that allows them to shift ships that size through the dimensions."

"How do we disable one of their ships?"

"I don't know yet, because I haven't pursued this line of thought very far."

"You'll pursue it now. I want a report on the matter as soon as you have some ideas."

"Very well."

Husher's com buzzed with an incoming call. He checked it and saw that it was Ensign Fry, contacting him from the CIC. He answered. "Go ahead."

"Captain, we've just transitioned back into the Larkspur System. There's a Brotherhood force attacking a convoy of civilian ships headed toward Pirate's Path—presumably, they're evacuating to the Kaithe's home system."

Bounding to his feet, Husher said, "How many Brotherhood ships?"

"Twenty-three, sir. Over double what they had before."

"I'll be right there."

CHAPTER 27

Breaking Point

"Winterton, what defenses do the civilian vessels have?" Husher said, wasting no time as he crossed the CIC to the command seat.

"Very few, sir," the sensor operator said. "Some have hull-mounted turrets, most have nothing. Two ships went down while you made your way from Cybele, leaving thirty-nine still intact."

"The Brotherhood will pay for that. Are any other IGF ships responding?"

"A battle group has emerged from the Larkspur-Roundleaf darkgate. They have the *Artemis* with them. But we'll arrive first, by a wide margin."

The *Artemis* was one of the IGF's six remaining capital starships. *Why wasn't the civilian convoy under military escort in the first place?* He didn't bother giving voice to the question, since he already knew the answer. Between continuing to defend the Union's populated colonies and securing Pirate's Path so that civilians could flee down it, there simply weren't enough warships to go around.

A brief study of the tactical display told him that the Brotherhood's position put them between the civilian ships they were attacking and the *Vesta*. Meanwhile, the approaching warships out of Roundleaf were on a vector parallel to the battlefront.

"Nav, set a course that takes us around the Brotherhood formation, so that we're on their ships' starboard sides as we approach. Once you have it, forward the course to our battle group ships."

"Aye, Captain," Chief Ortega said, who'd replaced Noni as primary Nav officer for now. The Tumbran was still recovering from the seizure she'd suffered during the lucid field test.

"Coms, send Commander Ayam the order to standby to scramble Pythons on my mark. When I send the command, I want his Air Group to cut between the Brotherhood and civilian ships, running missile defense and taking shots when they can. Tactical," Husher said, turning toward Tremaine.

"Captain?"

"This will be our first opportunity to engage the Brotherhood directly, so let's make it memorable for them. Prepare a broadside that's predominantly Banshees, with enough Hydras mixed in to make it look like that's our main ploy. It won't be—I want even more Gorgons in the mix. Unlike the Progenitors, the Brotherhood probably won't be expecting such a move."

"A port-side barrage, then? It won't be as big as it could be with the damage we took in the battle for Thessaly."

"I'm aware of that, but this is what the positioning demands right now."

"Acknowledged. I'm on it, sir," Tremaine said, backing up his words by bending over his console.

"Be very careful with your firing solutions, Tremaine, and double check them in the moments before firing to adjust for any changes in our targets' position. A narrow miss might endanger our fighters as they fly between the two groups of ships, and a wide miss could hit civilian ships."

"Aye."

Husher hadn't had the opportunity to work with Ortega very much, and he wasn't sure how well the man handled multitasking. So as not to distract him, Husher performed some rudimentary calculations himself, to find that the Roundleaf ships would reach the engagement approximately a half hour after the *Vesta* did.

That confirmed for him that he'd made the right move in ordering Ortega to take them around to the Brotherhood's starboard side.

With any luck, we'll sandwich the bastards and rid the galaxy of them.

Eleven more civilian ships went down in the time it took the *Vesta* to cross the intervening distance, leaving just twenty-eight. Husher knew those ships had to be packed to the brim, meaning the Brotherhood had just murdered tens of thousands of defenseless beings.

If he were to check this convoy's passenger manifests, Husher felt certain he would discover they were from colonies with mostly nonhuman populations. The Brotherhood had gone from calling for the ouster of aliens from human colonies to simply exterminating them outright.

"Missiles prepped and firing solutions double checked, sir," Tremaine said. "Ready to fire on your mark."

"Mark," Husher said at once. He had complete faith in Tremaine's diligence.

The barrage burst from the supercarrier's port-side tubes, crossing the intervening space at speed. In response, the nearest Brotherhood ships diverted their attention from the civilian ships to the incoming rockets.

They failed to take out even half of the Banshees, and when the Hydras split into eight warheads each, the enemy ships seemed to panic. They turned, as though to flee toward the protection of their fellows, but the first missiles overtook them, converting four ships into short-lived explosions.

Tremaine had lined up his shot so that any misses would have a chance of taking out more Brotherhood ships down the line. The next ships also began to focus on defense, and they had better success than their downed comrades. Still, the size of the *Vesta*'s barrage was such that two more warships exploded.

Till this moment, Husher's battle group had trailed behind their capital ship, but now they swooped in behind her missiles, targeting Brotherhood ships with primary lasers. Three more enemy vessels went down in quick succession.

By the time the Pythons launched from their tubes, the enemy ships were already turning to flee.

"Tell Ayam to give chase until they're outside firing range of the civilians, Coms," Husher said.

"Yes, sir."

Husher frowned as he stared at the tactical display. Their strong showing had been enjoyable to watch play out, but the speedy retreat it had prompted meant the ships out of Roundleaf wouldn't arrive in time to tighten the noose.

The Brotherhood lived on, to help the Progenitors rain destruction down on the galaxy's inhabitants.

"We're getting a transmission request from the *Artemis*, sir," Fry said. "A lot of messages of gratitude from the civilian ships, too, but I assumed you'd want to hear what *Artemis* has to say first."

Husher nodded. "Tell the civilian captains we're deeply sorry for the ships their convoy lost, and that helping them on their way to Home was the least we could do."

"I will, Captain. And, sir—the transmission request from *Artemis* is apparently from President Chiba."

Chiba's aboard the Artemis? *Coming from Roundleaf?* "I'll take it in my office."

As soon as he'd lowered himself into the chair behind his desk, he instructed his Oculenses to connect him with Chiba. The Kaithian appeared in a throne-like chair upholstered in burgundy velvet, with ornately carved legs and armrests.

A second identical chair appeared beside the alien. It held Eve Quinn, of Invigor Technologies.

"Mr. President," Husher said, ignoring Quinn for now. "I'm surprised to find you're aboard the *Artemis*, and coming out of Roundleaf."

"Good," Chiba said. "The idea is to randomize my location and keep the enemy guessing. As for being aboard a capital starship, where else would you suggest the President of the Union should go? Abdera is gone, thanks to you. I'm likely not safe on any colony. Isn't it best for me to remain on the move, aboard one of our strongest ships?"

"I think the Progenitors had more to do with Abdera's destruction than I did," Husher snapped.

Chiba shrugged, and both he and Quinn regarded him in silence.

Husher itched to ask why Quinn was with the president, but he knew there was a more pressing question at hand: "Why does the Brotherhood have more ships, now?"

A look of studied innocence took shape on Chiba's face, though Quinn's knowing smirk remained intact. "I'm sure I don't know," the Kaithian said.

"I'm sure you do. For them to have a spike like that in recruitment, you must have done something. Those captains wouldn't have simply joined up with the Brotherhood on a whim."

"I'm afraid I can't help you with that, Captain," the Kaithian said. "And while we appreciate you saving what civilian ships you did, we haven't approached you to discuss the Brotherhood."

"What, then?"

"The field test. How did lucid perform in space combat?"

"Horribly. It sent my Nav officer into a seizure the moment the *Vesta* took some damage, and we were dead in the water until I could get my secondary to the CIC."

Chiba grimaced. "How unfortunate."

"A minor hiccup," Quinn cut in. "I stand by my statement that this tech will change the war. We'll work out the bugs that caused your mishap, Captain, and we'll have the next version rolled out to you soon. I actually think we're on the verge of fleetwide implementation."

Chiba nodded solemnly, but Husher stared at them like they'd both sprouted extra limbs from their foreheads. "I'm not letting lucid anywhere near my ship or crew again."

Eyebrows shooting up, Quinn said, "I thought you wanted to win this war, Captain."

"I do. That's why I'll have nothing to do with your product. Mr. President, why are you rushing Invigor's technology like this? It's beginning to remind me of the Darkstream days."

The president smirked. "Trust me, Invigor has no political clout. They're merely helping us bring our fleets to a level at which we can compete." The Kaithian shook his head. "I see a contradiction in your behavior, Captain. The capital starships have all had their lifeboats converted to warships capable of interdimensional travel, just like the *Vesta*'s. You must have received that report, yet you've raised no objections about that. Why object to one upgrade but not the other?"

"Because adopting lucid will weaken the Fleet. I sense an ulterior motive behind this. I don't know what it is yet, but there's a reason you're so keen to shove this down our throats, isn't there?"

"I have to wonder about your motives as well, Captain Husher," Chiba said, tiny teeth suddenly bared. "Why won't you take the sort of calculated risks we've already agreed are necessary to victory?"

"I don't consider this a well-calculated risk. Not after what happened to us while we were in Gok space."

"That's where we differ. You've never shown much faith in your government, and so your irrational opposition to this tech makes a certain sort of sense, I suppose. If you won't adopt lucid, I won't try to force you, Captain. I certainly have better ways to spend my time than that. But we *will* be integrating it with other ships, starting with the remaining capital starships."

The backbone of the fleet, weakened to breaking point. "Will that be all?" Husher ground out.

"No," Chiba said. "The Interstellar Union has adopted wartime policies, which will need to be implemented in Cybele as well. In order to fund the defense and evacuation of the galactic civilian populace, we are appropriating fifty percent of the wealth of its richest citizens. We're also commandeering every privately owned ship."

Husher nodded slowly as comprehension dawned on him. "So that's why the Brotherhood's recruitment has skyrocketed. You've decided to use the galaxy's death throes as an opportunity to make good on your goal of radical wealth redistribution."

"We are doing only what's expedient," the president said, regarding Husher imperiously.

"No, you're doing a lot more than that. You're leveling society, and it's going to finish the job of tearing us apart. I've said it before, or at least I've tried to: there are ways to reduce inequality that don't doom us. But you'd rather take a sledgehammer to the bedrock of society."

"Your opinion is irrelevant," Chiba said.

"Actually, it isn't. Not on my ship, anyway. This policy won't be enacted aboard the *Vesta*. I don't need even more unrest in the middle of my ship."

"You don't have a choice. The banks are granting us access to the funds stored in accounts on Cybele."

Husher whipped his com out of its holster and sent a priority transmission request to Ensign Amy Fry.

She answered immediately. "Captain?"

"Deny all outside requests to *Vesta*'s narrownet," he said.

"Aye, sir."

"Husher out." He ended the call and replaced the com back in its holster. "Now what?" he said, locking eyes with the Kaithian. "Are we going to go to battle with each other again?"

"Not at this time," Chiba said after a brief pause. "But you should know that for you, victory in this war isn't possible, Captain Husher. Whether we beat the Progenitors or not, I will see to it that you are ruined."

CHAPTER 28

Half-Baked

The alien mech accepted Jake inside of it readily enough, its front peeling away to form a ramp for him to climb.

But once he was inside, it bombarded him with whispers.

Do you want to win this? Or burn?

What good is dying along with your friends? They will die regardless. Merge with me, and we'll survive.

Embrace your destiny. Embrace the void.

He fought to withstand the whispers, like a boulder withstands the ocean's onslaught. That proved a useful way of conceptualizing his relationship to the whispers. They were nothing but waves of the sea: relentless, but devoid of content. They required nothing of him, and he would give nothing.

At last, after a half hour of meditating inside the mech dream, he was able to move the machine's foot, taking a single step toward Hangar Bay Epsilon's opposite bulkhead. The whispers raged at that, turning up the volume and mixing in obscenities. He continued to ignore them.

One step. It's more than I managed the day Beth died. It had taken him thirty minutes to accomplish, but he berated himself that he hadn't managed it then.

Ash still wasn't talking to him, spending a lot of time with Rug instead. Even though she'd known Jake a lot longer than she'd known the Quatro, he supposed it made sense. They'd both lost someone.

Though at least there's a chance Rug could get Lisa back.

The next step took him only twenty minutes to accomplish, and the third, twelve minutes. *So slow.* After everything he'd accomplished using the alien mech in the past, this pace felt excruciating.

But he was doing it. Gradually, he was learning a new way to control the mech. Hopefully, they'd come out of this even stronger than before.

Only if you integrate with me, the mech whispered.

Never, Jake answered.

Hangar Bay Epsilon wasn't currently in use, making it the best option for training with the unpredictable machine. In truth, there weren't any good options. Not anywhere on the *Vesta*.

The fact that they were willing to use Progenitor tech at all showed how desperate this war had made them. After what it had done to Gabriel Roach, along with most of the Quatro who'd climbed inside Progenitor-made mechs… *We're crazy to have this thing aboard at all.* Of all those who'd used the alien mechs, only Jake and Rug had managed to avoid losing themselves.

But this mech was also the reason he'd been able to evacuate anyone at all from the Steele System. It was the reason he was still alive.

I have to stick with it, at this point. I have to stay the course.

The truth was, he was addicted to the thing. He was self-aware enough to know that. *I just have to manage the addiction until the end of the war.*

"Hey," someone said from the hatch.

Jake didn't have to turn his head to see who it was—the mech had sensors all over its body, and he could see out of any of them from inside the mech dream.

"Iris," he said. His heart rate spiked, mainly from fear. "You shouldn't be here."

"Why not?"

The mech turned, then, of its own accord. That was more movement than Jake had gotten from it in an hour.

Then, it tried to raise its arms and convert them into heavy guns.

It also shut down Jake's ability to communicate with Iris—it would no longer let him speak through its exterior speakers. He couldn't tell her that she needed to flee.

The mech's arms raised halfway, and Jake brought his will down like a hammer, keeping the appendages at bay. His prior meditative approach wouldn't work, here. He had to attend to the whispers directly.

The mech stood in quavering tableau as Iris looked on in confusion and Jake did battle with it.

At last, he wrested control of the external speakers from the whispers. "Please," he grunted. "Wait for me in the corridor."

"All right," Iris said, and backed away, disappearing from the open hatch.

With its would-be target out of sight, the mech became slightly easier to manage, and Jake forced its arms down by its sides.

That done, he opened the front ramp and stepped out onto the deck.

He looked up at the hulking machine. "If you're going to kill me, go ahead. There's nothing I can do about it, and I'm not going to try to fight it."

But the mech remained motionless. *It doesn't want to kill me,* he realized. In a strange way, they truly had bonded, and there was nothing the mech wanted more than to merge with him entirely. Was the machine simply a tool of the Progenitors, or had it developed agency of its own at some point? If it was only the former, Jake should have died a long time ago.

"What happened in there?" Iris asked when he joined her in the corridor.

"You don't want to know," he said. "Why are you here?"

Her mouth quirked at the corner. "Sort of an abrupt question, but I deserve it. I know I was harsh, back in Santana Park. I came to apologize."

"Does the captain just give you free reign of the crew section, now?"

"I get in on family visitation passes. But I abuse them. I admit it."

That made him chuckle. "Well, apology accepted." He began walking along the corridor, with no particular destination in mind, and she fell in beside him.

"Did you hear about the wartime measures the IU's taking?" she asked.

Jake grimaced. "No, but I'm not sure I want to."

"Every privately-owned ship is being commandeered for the evacuation, and their owners are being entered in the same lottery as everyone else for spots on them. Plus, they're taking fifty percent of the richest people's wealth."

Suppressing a groan, Jake said, "Let me guess. You love these policies."

"I'm kind of torn about them, actually," she said, surprising him. "On the one hand, I can see the logic—the government needs a lot of money to get everyone to Home, and a lot of the wealth they're taking *was* gained dishonestly. On the other hand, this seems kind of extreme."

"I would say it does. Couldn't they *ask* the wealthy for their help first, before they swooped in and stole half their money and all their ships?"

Iris shrugged. "They're using what happened on Thessaly as justification—the fact that some shipowners didn't take any other civilians with them when they fled."

"So, because some of the well-off people are bad, it's time to punish all of them?" Jake shook his head. "This is what's been pissing me off so much since I came to the Milky Way. Politicians jumping at whatever criticism is lying around, just to justify screwing over everyone who's done well."

"But there *has* been oppression in the past, Jake, and plenty today. Plus, there's still plenty of bias between the species."

"I get that. But these half-baked, short-term solutions are only going to hurt everyone. There just isn't any way to fix this stuff overnight. Not unless you're okay with breaking society in the process."

"You sound like my dad."

Jake blinked. "Well, I never would have expected to say this, but...I think I'm on the same page as the captain, on this one. He's a lot better than me at explaining it, but you know, he might actually know what he's talking about."

Iris grinned. "I've been realizing that too. It's a painful process."

Cocking his head back a little, Jake said, "Why did you really come here today?"

Iris's grin took on a strange quality that Jake would have called a mix of playfulness and...well, shyness. "Because my mother didn't want me to." She winked at him and turned to walk in the opposite direction, leaving him to stare after her, speechless.

CHAPTER 29

Making a Play

Something about Price's demeanor seemed off as he entered Husher's office.

As well it might be. He'd heard the rumors about the young man spending time with his daughter.

But that wasn't what he'd called Price here to discuss—not right away, anyway.

"At ease, Seaman," he said, and Price separated one foot from the other, folding his hands behind his back. "Have a seat."

Price did, meeting Husher's eyes for a fraction less than he normally would.

Ah, yes. "I met recently with the president."

"Oh? How was that?"

"About as enjoyable as you might expect. There was a reward waiting for me at the end of the meeting, however, and it almost made it worth it." *Who am I kidding? Nothing could make a meeting with Chiba worth it.* But this did come close. "The IU has actually done something with the MIMAS you donated to them. At least, their scientists have done something with it. There are now a total of forty newly manufactured mechs, along with forty pilots who've trained on them, mostly using lucid simulations." Husher felt his mouth twist involuntarily at that, but his ban of lucid tech didn't extend to mechs. He couldn't afford to kick Oneiri off his ship because of what had happened in Gok space, not least of all because lucid seemed to work well when it came to controlling the mechs.

"The president decided it would make the most sense to assign the new mechs to the *Vesta*," Husher continued, "since you and your team are here to guide them. To lead them."

"There's not much of my team left, sir," Jake said.

"Well, there's about to be a lot more of it. The mechs are on Zakros, in Feverfew, and we're headed there now. You'll be responsible for all of them. How is progress going on regaining control of your alien mech?"

"Slow," Price said after a brief pause.

"Have you considered switching over to a MIMAS?"

A shrug. "Not truly, sir."

"What if I ordered it?"

Price raised his eyes. "I don't think you should order that."

"Okay. I'll continue to trust your judgment. In fact, I've decided to grant you a field promotion, to Petty Officer Third Class. It's still too low a rank to command a platoon, technically, but there's no one else with the experience you have. I wouldn't want to trust anyone else with the job."

"Thank you, sir." Price sounded both surprised and pleased.

"Do you think you can have your mech back under control by the time we reach Zakros? I'd like you in it when you go to meet your new pilots."

"I'll do everything I can to make that happen, sir."

Husher nodded. "Good. Oh, I almost forgot to mention—I hear you've been spending time with my daughter."

At that, Price's satisfied expression melted away, and his face lightened a little. "I mean, I've run into her a few times..."

But Husher could read the young men with relative ease, and it would take more than this to distract him from what was going on. "We have a war to fight, son."

"I know that, sir."

"You have feelings for Lisa Sato, correct? That's what you told me."

"Yes."

"We'll be making a play for the Progenitors' home system as soon as we can. Focus on that. Focus on getting Sato back. It isn't the time to let anything...*else* distract us. That's an order."

Price seemed to have no trouble meeting his eyes now, and Husher could sense the anger seething underneath. "Yes, sir," he grunted.

"Dismissed. We'll arrive back in Feverfew in seven hours to pick up the mechs and their pilots." *I guess it's a good thing I saved the colony after all,* Husher reflected.

Price left the office without another word, and Husher smiled to himself. *That couldn't have gone better.*

CHAPTER 30

Fly Again Someday

"Tell me how close he is to bringing the *Vesta* here," Husher said, his sidearm planted against the back of Chief Devar's head.

"Please," Fesky rasped. Devar was probably the best of her CIC officers—attentive, quick, and decisive. Fesky liked her as an individual, too.

"Please *what?*" Husher said. "Are you really going to insult your Nav officer like that, by pretending to beg for her life? You know there's only one way she leaves here alive. Tell me what I want to know."

Fesky remained silent, and the crack of the gunshot echoed through the Cavern. Devar slumped forward, her lifeless form flopping onto the metal deck.

Fesky wept, hard enough to shake her body as much as the restraints would allow. It sent jabs of pain emanating from her beak, which was now chipped and cracked.

Husher didn't react. Instead, he reached behind him and plucked from a metal table what appeared to be heavy duty industrial shears.

"How much will you allow your soul to deteriorate?" Husher said. "How much will you let me take away from you? Every minute you hold out will only make it taste more bitter when you finally break. You'll curse yourself for allowing your crew to die—for allowing me to rip out the core of your being. That day will come, bird, and soon. I've never had a subject hold out forever."

Without warning, Husher plunged the shears into her wing, clean through feather, skin, and membrane.

Fesky shrieked, louder than she'd shrieked before. Liquid fire crept through her nerves, her veins. The shears tightened in Husher's hands, and it seemed like the world was made of pain.

"These shears are nestled around your wing's main ligament. If I sever it, you'll never fly again. The IU's level of nanotechnology is too limited to rebuild something like this."

Fesky trembled.

"How close is he?" Husher hissed. "Just tell me that one thing, and perhaps you'll fly again someday."

She said nothing. Husher slammed the shears together.

Some time later, Fesky wasn't sure how long, she regained consciousness enough to see that Husher now stood at the foot of her chair, with three more crewmembers from the *Spire*.

"I'm losing my patience," he said, then shot all three of them in quick succession. They toppled face-first onto the deck.

That done, he picked up the shears again and began circling the chair they'd strapped her to. Every so often he would snap the shears shut, causing her to jump.

"You're running out of crewmembers," he said. "You've let so many of them die. I've decided that, once they're all dead, I'll kill you, whether you've decided to talk or not. I've been thinking...I'm actually not that concerned about killing you. If your misguided sense of duty is truly such that you'll die for it, so be it."

"What about the progress on *Vesta*'s interdimensional capabilities?" She found it darkly comic that she would bargain for her life like this, just so she could endure more agony. Husher was right. She barely knew why she bothered to continue fighting. She only knew that she had to. Nothing felt real, anymore, nothing except the memory of her friend, and her obligation to him. *I must not break.*

Husher chuckled. "It would definitely be better if you talked. But if you don't, I'm not sure it will make a difference. Clearly, my double wasn't very close to gaining the ability to come here, else he would have done so already. Meaning the AIs should have plenty of time to wipe out the IU before he ever has the chance. I *do* have a lot of faith in our AIs. They produced the plans, built the clones, gathered the necessary resources. And they're just cutting their teeth on your galactic cluster. They're only getting started on conquering your universe."

"But your ships are all captained by Ixa," Fesky said. "If the AIs are so capable, why not put them in direct control of your ships?"

"We did, during the Second Galactic War, though clearly that AI was inferior to its more evolved siblings, since it lost. If we gave them control of our ships now, it would be suicide."

"How?"

"The AIs have been programmed never to interface with tech that allows interdimensional travel, just as they're programmed to self-destruct the moment they've completed the task we've assigned to them, of clearing out your universe for our habitation. We know better than to ever occupy the same universe as a superintelligent AI. They're far too dangerous, and we've taken multiple precautions to prevent that from ever happening." Husher smiled. "Once the AIs are finished with you and with everyone else in your universe, they will turn themselves off."

"Something doesn't add up," Fesky said. "To create superintelligences, you must have been in the same universe with them at some point."

Husher smiled, continuing to circle, continuing to brandish the shears. "Your ignorance is the only reason it makes no sense to you. We didn't create superintelligences—instead, we created low-level AIs, just sophisticated enough to do two things: to adhere to our safeguards and imperatives during every iteration of their evolution, and to improve themselves. They accomplished the latter via a machine learning protocol that involved interacting with their environments, testing multiple strategies for efficient resource-gathering and domination, and optimizing for the ones that worked best."

"Still makes no sense," Fesky said, her voice a low rasp. "The Ixa have been around thousands of years, and your AI created them. How is that possible, when thousands of years ago you were still confined to your planet, just as the version of humanity I know was?"

"It's possible because the form of interdimensional travel that you have mimicked was not the first type we invented. First, we discovered how to send a modest amount of matter and information—not just to another dimension, but to a prior point along that dimension's timeline. It was a very imprecise process, and your future was inaccessible to us, but after plenty of trial and error we were able to prepare the ground for our conquest by sending AIs thousands of years into your past; AIs that would eventually turn themselves into superintelligences while using the fewest possible resources. The AI that appeared in the Milky Way, for example, spawned the Ixa and then used their brains as the bulk of its processing power."

Husher pulled out his com and pressed a button on it. When he did, a rectangle of light appeared in the distance—the hatch into the corridor, opening to admit five more of her crewmembers, escorted by a single marine.

Once they reached the foot of Fesky's chair, the marine shoved them into line. They were all from the *Spire*'s missile loading bay, though it took her a moment to discern that, as they'd been beaten until their faces were swollen and multi-hued. Their IGF uniforms were covered in their own blood.

Husher took out his pistol and shot them all, one after another.

Fesky wept, feeling completely hollow. *To tell him what he wants would be to betray those he's already killed.* But to continue to hold out meant more would die.

Eight bodies surrounded the chair Fesky had been strapped to for days. *If he plans to keep killing crewmembers at this rate, I don't have much longer.*

Without warning, Husher leapt toward her, seizing her uniform by the chest and shaking her as much as the restraints would allow her to be shaken.

"Why do this?" he hissed. "Why hold out? Tell me Husher's secrets. Tell me what he knows. Why do this to yourself?"

"You, Husher," Fesky said through her sobbing. "I'm doing it for you."

CHAPTER 31

Concerto

A MIMAS orbital insertion was a thing of incredibly precise engineering; a concerto of gravity, friction, and aerospike thrusters.

Next to it, the alien mech's insertion amounted to a show of brute strength.

Jake crashed to Zakros' rocky surface at an angle, already having transformed into a spiked wheel meant to grip the ground and slow him. Once he'd created a long furrow, he sprang to his feet, a biped again, to skid the rest of the way.

He'd spent every waking moment of the journey to Zakros working at regaining control of his mech, and he'd surprised himself with his progress. It scared him a little, too. *Did the mech submit too easily? Is it planning something?*

Rug stood nearby, having pulled off a landing sequence similar to his, and beyond her Ash Sweeney and Maura Odell descended the rest of the way on aerospike thrusters, their landing sending tremors through the ground.

"It's good to see you back in action," he said to Ash over a two-way channel. The connection made her human form appear next to him in the mech dream, just as his would be standing next to Ash, from her perspective.

She answered his remark with a cold glare. "Not here for you. Not here for the galaxy. I'm here for revenge."

It probably wouldn't have been wise to point out that she wasn't likely to find any revenge here on Zakros. They were just here to meet the new mech pilots and make sure they were clear on the procedure for rocketing up to orbit and rendezvousing with the *Vesta*.

But that's not what she means. He also decided not to point out that it had been Andy who'd killed Beth, not the Progenitors. *Same difference.* Andy had been trying to save a Progenitor—he'd been corrupted by one. *He lost his way, and he paid the price.*

Either way, for Jake to call out Ash for confused motives would have been obscenely hypocritical. He couldn't even tell whether he wanted to defeat the Progenitors to rescue Lisa or to have a life with Iris—if that was even an option for him. All he knew that, after the captain had told him to stay away from his daughter, Jake had realized how badly he wanted her.

A shuttle touched down to his left. The airlock opened immediately, and Gamble emerged with half the platoon he'd brought. *They must have been already waiting in the airlock.*

The marine commander had wanted to be there for the first look at the new mech pilots. *Can't say I blame him.* Jake would be in charge of them, but Gamble was in charge of Jake, and the major would decide how the new MIMAS force would be deployed.

"Let's move," Gamble said, nodding toward the broad hangar sitting at the other end of the LZ. The marines began jogging toward it, but for the mechs to match their pace meant adopting a leisurely stroll.

When Jake entered the hangar behind the platoon of marines, he found his forty new pilots arrayed in crisp ranks, all standing at attention outside their mechs. They were already saluting, from Gamble's entrance into the hangar.

Jake looked them over from the vantage point of his mech. Towering over them, he could see them all, and he began looking for weak points. Impressively, he couldn't find many—a man slouching here, a woman barely suppressing a yawn there. Anyone caught shirking would need to shape up or ship out, and given replacement pilots would likely be in short supply, it was Jake's job to make sure they shaped up.

Gamble turned, nodding at Jake, who began to speak: "You've been assigned to the IGS *Vesta*," he said, his voice booming out of the mech to fill the hangar. "I hope you know what that means. We're the IU's secret weapon, whether they know it or not. We're the IGF's flaming sword. We go where others do not, we show up where we aren't expected. Captain Husher plans to take us into the belly of the beast to rip its guts out. If you don't think you're up for that, say so now. I don't want anyone on my team who isn't willing to sacrifice everything for the galaxy."

No one moved. No one spoke.

"Good. Till now, the mechs serving aboard the *Vesta* have been called Oneiri Team, a name we brought with us all the way from another galaxy. Starting today, we'll be known as Oneiri *Force*. Now, I know you've read up on launch procedure—at least, you were ordered to read up on it—but reading about it is nothing like executing. Technically, we should have you run multiple drills on this, but we're time-limited, and I'm lucky you have even half a clue about operating your machines. Listen carefully, because—"

A priority com transmission cut him off, and Husher's likeness appeared on the hangar floor, halfway between Jake and Gamble.

"We're under attack," the captain said. "Progenitor ships have appeared around the *Vesta* and her battle group in overwhelming numbers. We can't win this. We need to retreat, but we're not leaving without you. The Progenitors have already started deploying ground forces to the surface. Avoid them if you can, and get back to orbit immediately. Husher out."

"Inside your machines," Gamble barked at the new mech pilots, and they fell out in a confused mass, popping sedatives as they ran toward their waiting mechs.

Jake walked toward the wide hangar bay entrance, then ducked inside again in time to avoid heavy gunfire from an Ambler that was overhead, plummeting toward the ground. The Ambler crashed to the planet's surface, followed by a second, and then a third. Soon, Amblers and Ravagers covered the LZ, which the mechs needed clear in order to launch into orbit.

Then the enemy surrounded Gamble's shuttle, cutting it off from the *Vesta* marines, and things got real interesting.

CHAPTER 32

Playing the Martyr

Thirty Progenitor vessels surrounded the *Vesta* and her battle group ships, which were clustered around her as tightly as their captains dared. The supercarrier's Air Group formed a rough sphere around them all, doing their best to keep the endless waves of Ravagers at bay, and through the gaps the *Vesta* and her battle group fired hundreds of defensive Banshees.

"Missile stores are running low, sir," Tremaine said. "We can't keep this up for much longer."

Husher's grip tightened on the command seat's armrests. "Have tertiary lasers target Ravagers as well, but only after they break through the Pythons." To do otherwise would have risked hitting their own fighters. A missile could broadcast its position to nearby friendly forces, but a laser could not, and the coordination that avoiding friendly fire would have required was simply too intensive.

If it wasn't for Zakros' nearby orbital defense platform, both the *Vesta* and the old UHF ships likely would have been vaporized during the first few minutes of the engagement. But because the

Progenitors had decided to focus everything on Husher's forces while in range of the platform, it had been left to pound away at the enemy ships with impunity.

He watched it destroy a fourth enemy ship, a carrier, and with that, some of the enemy forces began to divert their attention to the defense platform. Two destroyers disappeared from the opposite side of the Progenitor formation, and Husher knew they would soon appear underneath the defensive structure. The planetary fighter group would rally to defend it, but how long could they hold?

"We need to press the attack now," he said. "Tremaine, calculate a firing solution for the nearest carrier, and prepare a volley of Hydras and a volley of Gorgons for two more carriers, which I'll designate."

"Aye, sir."

The Progenitor carriers were causing them the most grief, and Husher wanted their numbers cut. The enemy destroyers were mostly focused on pressuring Pythons, to make sure they couldn't get a decent attack angle. To use their particle beams would take out too many Ravagers to make it worth it, Husher suspected.

"Coms, alert Commander Ayam of our intentions, and Tremaine, forward your firing solutions to him as soon as you have them."

"Commander Ayam is currently in subspace, Captain," Fry said.

"Then send it out in a repeating, encrypted broadcast, coded for both his fighter and that of each squadron leader. We don't have time to wait for Ayam to come back. We need to act now."

Even managing multiple encryption keys, Fry moved fast, and Husher watched on the main display as Pythons cleared the space where Tremaine would strike.

One of the carriers started to react the moment the nearby space cleared, but it was too late. The *Vesta*'s primary laser lanced out, striking the hull near her prow and cutting a melted furrow down her port side as she tried to flee.

Seconds later, she exploded.

The second carrier took several Hydras on her hull, but survived. The carrier they'd targeted with Gorgons wasn't so lucky, which Husher attributed to how cluttered the battlespace was, making it harder to pick out the stealth missiles from everything else. *I should have gone with Gorgons for both.*

Ayam's subspace squadron popped into existence, directly behind the carrier who'd managed to survive the Hydras.

But she didn't survive Ayam. A single alpha strike finished the job.

Husher squeezed his fist to celebrate the victory, and he noticed grim smiles sprouting on some of the other CIC officers' faces.

That was the extent of the celebrations. Though they'd relieved some of the pressure, everyone could clearly see that victory today simply wasn't going to happen.

A successful retreat was the best they could hope for, and that depended on Gamble and Price returning with the new mechs in time.

Husher's com beeped with an urgent transmission, and Husher answered right away.

It was Major Gamble. "Sir, we've run into a problem."

"What is it, Major?" Husher asked, trying to inject his voice with calm, despite the fact he wasn't sure they could handle any more problems.

"The Progenitors just destroyed our only shuttle. My marines and I are fine with staying on Zakros and covering the mechs' escape, but I figured I should let that be your call instead of playing the heroic martyr."

Thank God. Men like Peter Gamble were way to rare to lose. "I'm sending two gunship shuttles and a squadron of Pythons as escort. No way I'm leaving my marine commander behind, Major."

"Yes, sir."

"Husher out."

He resisted the urge to curse, or to slam his hand against the command seat's armrest. Instead, he turned toward Ensign Fry and gave the necessary orders in as level a voice as he could manage.

CHAPTER 33

Gunship Mode

Once Jake's new pilots got their mechs up and running, they were able to start delivering some serious punishment to the robots outside.

But that wouldn't last. More Amblers and Ravagers were raining down with every second, and when he saw the shuttle taken out by a few well-placed rockets, Jake realized that getting out of here would require some drastic action.

For starters, they needed to control the terrain better. There wasn't much in the way of cover, inside the hangar bay—the walls were reinforced steel, but the front was completely open. Yes, they might have closed the doors, but that would have cut off every firing lane and trapped them inside.

We need outside access if we're going to get out of here.

Gamble had split his platoon in two, with each half taking cover on opposite sides of the open doors. That left the rest of the hangar bay's floor to the mechs, who Jake had arrayed in a staggered line to fire on the enemy encroaching from outside. The mechs' staggering allowed easy dodging to the left or right without colliding with a fellow mech pilot.

Even so, it left fifteen mechs with little to do, other than leap over the heads of their fellows to take occasional potshots. That might have been fine, if the new pilots were more proficient with their mechs. But they weren't.

We have a lot of work to do, and no time to do it.

Jake established contact with one of the mech pilots forced to stay back behind the staggered ranks of MIMAS. The mech's pilot appeared before him in the dream, a lithe brunette who couldn't be more than nineteen.

"I'm guessing there's no rooftop access to this place," he said. "I didn't see any as we approached."

The pilot shook her head. "None that I've seen, PO."

Jake nodded, a little impressed that she'd used his new rank. He shouldn't have been, but it felt nice to hear it. "If there's no access, then we'll make some."

His arms merged into a single energy cannon, which he directed at the ceiling near the wall. A single blast of blue-white energy left a melted, smoking hole almost three meters wide.

The young pilot's simulacrum widened her eyes.

Jake leapt into the air, his mech's lower legs converting to thrusters in a heartbeat, which carried him to the roof. There, he transformed his arms into long, diamond-sharp blades, which he plunged into the corrugated steel at the edge of the hole he'd created.

He tore across the rooftop, his blades dragging behind him in a shower of sparks, cutting twin furrows in the corrugated steel. When he reached the roof's halfway point, the blades shortened and widened into arms. Both his forefingers became superheated blast torches, which he used to carefully warp the metal. Behind him, the three-meter-wide path he'd cut creaked as it parted from the rest of the roof and groaned to the floor below.

Inspecting his work, he saw that it had come out as he'd intended—a fairly stable path with a gentle incline thanks to its length.

He raised Gamble on a two-wide channel. "Major, I've created a way to get to the hangar roof. From what I'm seeing, controlling it is the only way anyone's getting out of here—you in your shuttle, and us in our mechs. We need a stable launching surface too, and it doesn't look like we're retaking the LZ."

"Good thinking, Price."

"I'd suggest getting your marines up here, and taking the inactive mechs with you. Getting you back to the *Vesta* is our main priority. Once that's done, my pilots and I can use the roof to leave."

While he waited for Gamble and the other mechs to join him on the roof, Jake sprinted to the edge, turning his arms into long-barreled energy cannons and peppering the forces below. A full-powered energy blast took an Ambler square in its rounded torso, knocking it backward onto the ground, and another suffered the same fate as it turned to respond to Jake's presence.

A group of ten Ravagers leapt from the ground in a wide arc that would end with them on the rooftop. Jake sent rapid-fire energy bolts to meet them in midair, neutralizing six of them. The remaining four landed all around him and charged.

He seized one and used it to smash another, both their spindly metal bodies disintegrating in a shower of shrapnel. The other two made it to his legs, scrambling up them to reach his torso and tearing at the metal as they went. He grabbed one and threw it to the ground below, but the second robot refused to stay still, so he impaled it on a spike that protruded suddenly from his abdomen.

More Ravagers were on the way, thirty at least, hurtling through the air. Jake blasted more of them, backing up across the roof, worried that they were about to lose control of it.

Gunfire sounded behind him, picking off half of the Ravagers before they landed on the corrugated surface. Glancing through one of his rear sensors, Jake saw MIMAS mechs pounding across the rooftop to back him up, metal fingers retracted against wrists to let rotary autocannons fire at full bore.

The rooftop was soon cleared of the metal devils, but more and more were coming, some of them from the sky. The Progenitor robots seemed to know that if they could take the corrugated steel surface, they could deny the *Vesta* forces their evac.

An Ambler clanged to the roof, followed by two more. Jake charged toward the nearest one, arms becoming broadswords. He leapt, transforming his calves into powerful thrusters, and the added momentum caused the blades to punch through his enemy, sending them both hurtling toward the roof's edge.

Jake formed feet again, adding claws to grip the metal for added purchase. His movement arrested, he spun in place, hurling the Ambler he'd skewered at another one threatening the rooftop. The hulking robot didn't see it coming, and it was knocked to the ground below. Jake turned just as his new pilots were finishing off the third.

Not bad. The mech dream made a patch of sky flash green, and Jake looked up, engaging his visual sensors' zoom.

Sixteen Pythons escorted two combat shuttles, closing with their location fast. He wanted to cheer. Instead, he raised his arms toward them, both broadswords becoming energy cannons.

"Price," Gamble said over a two-way. "What are you doing?"

But Jake couldn't answer. It took every ounce of concentration to prevent his mech from firing on the approaching craft.

Do it, the mech whispered. *You don't need them. We don't need anyone. We have the power to stay here and slaughter them all. You know what you have to do.*

More robots were crashing to the rooftop—four more Amblers, and a host of at least fifty Ravagers. The MIMAS pilots and marines reacted instantly, and the roof's sloped metal surface turned into a confused battlefield, with bullets firing in every direction. Grunts of pain came from Jake's right, where a marine was pumped full of bullets before he collapsed to the deck.

The Ambler that had killed the marine turned toward Jake and opened fire.

Destroy the starfighters. Destroy the shuttles. Only then will we allow you to defend yourself...and defend yourself you will, with might unseen in this universe.

The Ambler stalked forward, its heavy fire quickly burrowing through Jake's mech, to where his body was nestled at its center. He could deal with Amblers, but it involved remaining in motion, and putting them down as quickly as possible. Allowing them to attack unchallenged was not a healthy move.

Do it, the mech said, no longer whispering, but shrieking directly into Jake's consciousness. *Do it!*

With a roar of animal rage, Jake wrenched himself away from the bead he'd drawn on the incoming fighters, spinning sideways to protect the part of him the Ambler had made vulnerable. Then he fired massive energy bolts at his attacker, blasting it off the roof.

He became a spinning dervish of death. Pairing a broadsword with an energy cannon, he let the mech dream sing to him, and when harmonies aligned, he struck.

Sensing the danger, Ravagers threw themselves at him, but discordant chords alerted him to their proximity and location in space. Without having to look, his blade always followed the right arc, and his shots always found the weakest point.

Ravagers shattered and Amblers staggered back. It took him less than two minutes to clear the rooftop.

Gamble approached, R-57 held at the ready. "Price? Did you...did you give in to it? Are you merged with that thing?"

Am I? For a moment, Jake wasn't sure, and he performed a scan of the entire mech.

"No," he said. "It almost got me, but I'm still here."

Gamble nodded, though he still studied Jake uncertainly. All of the marines did, and the MIMAS pilots, too.

Then, another group of Ravagers landed on the roof, giving them other things to worry about.

When the Pythons arrived, they began executing strafing runs on the robots occupying the LZ, which greatly reduced the pressure on both the roof and the mechs still inside the hangar below.

One of the shuttles went gunship-mode, joining the fighters in blasting the enemy, but the other touched down, its outer airlock hatch already opening to admit the marines. They poured inside without another word.

Once one shuttle was full, Jake waved it into the sky, then got on a wide channel.

"All right, Oneiri Force. Get to the rooftop and initiate launch. I don't have time to run through it with you, and I don't have time to take questions. Just do it right. Go!"

The mechs on the rooftop began to take off, launch thrusters streaming fire and smoke.

A group of Ravagers collided with one MIMAS as it left the rooftop, and five of them managed to stay on it as its rockets carried it upward. Seconds later, the mech exploded, hundreds of meters into the air.

"Ignore that!" Price yelled. "Go, go, go!"

He turned to continue defending the rooftop, which he intended to do until the last MIMAS launched.

CHAPTER 34

The Power to Stop It

When Eve and Bronson disembarked from the shuttle onto the *Eos*, Captain Norberg was waiting.

The captain glanced at Bronson, then looked at Eve again. "Is that Bob Bronson?" Norberg said, voice sharp.

"Hello, Katrina," Bronson said. "How long has it been?"

"Not long enough. What is he doing with you?"

Eve cleared her throat. "Captain Bronson has been helping Invigor Technologies implement lucid tech in ways Darkstream hadn't yet started on. His knowledge of lucid has proven invaluable to us." Almost, Eve let her plastered-on smile waver. She was growing tired of this charade, necessary as it was. There really was an Invigor Technologies, and they were fine with her acting as their ambassador, but she wasn't actually on their payroll. She was an agent with the Galactic Intelligence Bureau, and the president had given her a direct mandate to accelerate the widespread adoption of lucid tech by any means necessary.

"Does Husher know you're working with Bronson?" Norberg said, eyes narrowed. "I can't see him agreeing to field test any new tech that he's had his fingers all over."

Quinn forced herself to smile wider. "That fact was concealed from Husher, given his temperament. But I'm told you have *much* stronger loyalty to the IU." Eve really meant that Norberg was more pliable, but she doubted saying so would help accomplish her objective. She glanced around. "Where will we be meeting, Captain Norberg?"

Norberg sniffed. "There's a ready room closeby that should suit our purposes. It's equipped with a large display, in case you have any overlays you'd care to show me."

"Excellent. Lead on, Captain."

They trailed Norberg across the flight deck and out into the corridor. Both Norberg's capital starship and her battle group was stationed in the Dooryard System, the first system along Pirate's Path. Here, she could protect the evacuation route while remaining in position to answer any threats to the Interstellar Union's core systems.

While they made their way to the ready room, Norberg remained silent. Eve didn't bother to attempt any small talk, sensing that it would only irritate the old curmudgeon, and Bronson also seemed perfectly at ease with the awkward silence. Of course, Bronson didn't seem capable of social discomfort, so that didn't come as much of a surprise.

Once they entered the ready room, Norberg didn't wait for them to find seats before beginning the meeting. "It's going to take some doing to convince me to implement an entirely new technology in the middle of a war," she said, her voice steely. She reached the front of the room and turned to face them, spreading her feet apart and clasping her hands behind her back, in typical military style. "I'm not Vin Husher, who seems willing to try out anything with half a chance of having some effect. And even he won't use your tech, according to rumors I've heard from other captains."

At Norberg's self-importance, Eve's smile almost returned, but she checked it. The woman captained a supercarrier—thousands of crewmembers, marines, and Python pilots. On top of that, she was responsible for keeping safe the civilian city at the center of her starship. By custom, this woman was owed a lot of respect, even if Eve didn't personally think she deserved all of it.

"Captain Husher did in fact implement lucid," Eve said, "and it took him just a few hours to incorporate it with his existing systems. Since then we've smoothed out the process even more, and it should go even quicker for the *Eos*."

"Husher's Nav officer also experienced what amounted to a grand mal seizure because of your tech. The *Vesta* was immobilized until they could bring their secondary Nav officer into the CIC and have him operate in the traditional way. I hope you weren't planning to withhold that information from me, Ms. Quinn."

"Of course not," Eve said, though she would have withheld it if she thought she could get away with it. "We're here to fully inform you about the risks and all of the benefits that come with implementing our product. But before we continue, I should tell you two things that will preempt a lot of unnecessary discussion. First, we've ironed out the bug that led to the unfortunate incident with Captain Husher's Nav officer. And second, the admiralty has issued a fleetwide order to implement lucid tech, starting with the capital starships."

Norberg frowned. "And yet, Husher still won't do it. Will he?"

Bronson stirred beside Eve. "Husher is following in the footsteps of his old mentor, Leonard Keyes. He's bucking Command for now, but he'll pay for it, just like Keyes did."

Resisting the urge to glare at Bronson, Eve said, "We've been assured that Captain Husher will be allowed to think he's waging a successful rebellion until the war's end, at which point the IU intends to bring the full force of the law down on him. His rebellion is meaningless, and it will not serve him well in the long run."

Nodding slowly, Norberg fell silent for a time. At last, she said, "It seems I don't have much of a choice when it comes to this technology." She cleared her throat. "Among the rumors I've heard about your company is that you have a close relationship with the Interstellar Union. Are you close enough to know whether they consider these sweeping new policies a success?"

"Which policies are you referring to?" Eve said, cocking her head to the side.

"You know which policies," Norberg shot back, scowling. "The drastic redistribution of wealth. Seizing all private ships. It's causing no end of unrest in Attis." Attis was the city at the heart of *Eos*.

"Well, I'm not a politician," Eve said. "But if I were in your position, I would remind the people of Attis that the galaxy is in crisis. No one is happy, least of all the IU, but they're only doing what is necessary."

"There are many who would disagree about what's necessary," Norberg said.

"Do they have the power to stop it?"

"Likely not."

"Then I wouldn't worry too much about it, Captain Norberg."

Back on the shuttle, strapped into her crash seat and waiting for the pilot to take them out, Eve noticed Bronson studying her. "You look pleased with yourself," he said.

"Why wouldn't I be? I'm signing up capital starship captains faster than anyone expected." Tomorrow, Invigor's technicians would arrive on the *Eos*, and within hours the supercarrier would be fully outfitted with lucid. "Once the power of lucid becomes accepted across the fleet, it will spill over into the public at large. When it does, people won't want to wear those clunky headsets for very long. They'll want implants, just as the public in Steele did. And we'll be ready to sell them."

"Complete with backdoors for the IU to spy on users."

"Of course." Eve tilted her head to the side. "You're not sour because we're stealing your idea, are you? Come on, Bronson. It isn't like Darkstream is using it anymore. Darkstream is dead."

His face remained impassive, but Eve had learned to tell when Bronson was smoldering internally.

That lifted her mood even more.

CHAPTER 35

Unmatched

"Certainty is gone," Husher told the officers he'd gathered together in the *Vesta*'s main conference room. "We don't even have a coherent battle plan. And safety was never truly ours in the first place. But for seventeen years, we did have peace. The galaxy hasn't been thrown into chaos like this since the Second Galactic War. Everyone is panicking. Flailing. This is what dying looks like."

A heavy silence hung over the chamber. His officers had been quiet before, but now they were as statues, not moving, barely breathing.

"As we speak, the beings left on Zakros are in the process of being slaughtered, and there's absolutely nothing we can do about it. From here on out, our options are extremely limited. Unless we decide to flee to the Kaithian home system and huddle in Home's orbit with as much of the Fleet as has made it there…unless we do that, we'll have to stay on the run from now on. The Milky Way belongs to the Progenitors. They're just finishing the process of scouring it—killing off those unlucky or foolish enough to have not evacuated yet."

He drew a deep breath and let it out in a slow hiss. "From now on, even when we move through IU core systems, we're maneuvering through enemy territory. The Progenitors could strike at any time, surrounding us, and when they do, we must be ready to punch through and continue on toward our destination."

"What is our destination?" Chief Benno Tremaine asked.

"That's what we're here to discuss," Husher said. "The decision is ultimately mine, but a lot rides on it, which is why I've called you all here: to get your input before I make the final call. We need to decide what our priorities are. Do we think simply defending Home is a viable long-term goal? Personally, I don't think it is. The Progenitors' resources are virtually unlimited."

"What do you consider a viable long-term goal, Captain?" Ek asked, from the other end of the long, oaken table.

"I don't think we have any," Husher said. "I think we have a *single* viable goal, and it's a short-term one. We need to make it to the Progenitors' home universe. And we need to kill those we find there."

Scot Winterton spoke up. "Apologies, Captain, but—"

"Don't apologize for disagreeing," Husher said. "I called you here to speak your mind, and everyone here has my full permission to do so."

"Yes, sir," Winterton said. "I was going to say that the way you've framed things seems to suggest that making it to the Progenitor home dimension is a single objective, when in fact it's a set of multiple objectives. We don't know how to transport a ship as big as the *Vesta* through the multiverse, so that has to be priority number one. Assuming we're able to obtain that knowledge, in order to implement it, we'd need shipbuilding facilities as large as those the Progenitors destroyed in Feverfew. We're not sure any such facilities exist any longer. But let's entertain for a moment the possibility there is still such a facility and that we're able to reach it—we'd still need to defend it while making the modifications. The *Vesta* will be inactive while any upgrades are made, so I'm not able to guess how we might do that. Even supposing we did...that would still leave transitioning through the multiverse on a voyage without historical precedent, to face an enemy we know very little about, and to either defeat them or force them to call off the attack."

Winterton fell silent, expressionless, and Husher raised his eyebrows. Then, he chuckled—he couldn't help it. He was pretty sure no one but the stoic sensor operator could have mustered such a dry account of all the problems confronting them, right to the captain's face.

"That was an extremely comprehensive analysis, Ensign," Husher said, still smiling. "And I'm glad you gave it. It's good to have every possible objection on the table from the outset." He met the gaze of the other officers, one by one. "Winterton's right. What I'm about to propose fails every objective analysis. Every analysis except one, that is: we have no other option. When you have only one shot at victory, you must take that shot, no matter how improbable it is. The other option is to lay down and die, and everything about how I was raised and how I was trained rebels against the thought of that. I know you all feel the same. I've lived and worked with you on this ship for many months—most of you,

I've done so for years. I know you. And I know you refuse to say die."

"What's your plan, sir?" Ensign Amy Fry asked.

"The last conflict the galaxy faced, the Gok Wars, ended with the defense of the Arrowwood System." He didn't mention that he'd been the one to lead that defense. His officers knew that already, and bringing it up would only amount to boasting. "I'm hoping Arrowwood can play a vital role in ending this war as well."

As he paused to gather his thoughts, he noted the heavy silence inside the conference room. Despite Winterton's skepticism, which probably mirrored that of several others, his officers were clearly desperate for a way forward. Some action they could take that might give the galaxy hope.

"Like Winterton pointed out," Husher went on, "for all we know, the Progenitors have taken out every shipbuilding facility in the galaxy. But if not, then Arrowwood's facilities are the most likely to have survived, thanks to the way that system is laid out. Their facilities occupy orbits below the orbital defense platforms protecting Summit, the system's only colony. The Gok Wars taught the IU the importance of Arrowwood, and their fighter defense group is unmatched throughout the Union, either in skill or in numbers.

"If Arrowwood stands, then that also addresses the problem of how we'll defend *Vesta* while she undergoes upgrades. We can rely on the system's existing defenses, bolstered by our own Air Group, as well as our battle group."

Winterton cleared his throat. "We still haven't gotten to the part where we figure out what those upgrades should be, exactly, Captain."

"Yes," Husher said, nodding. "And as you've already pointed out, Ensign, shipbuilding facilities will serve as prime targets for the Progenitors. If Arrowwood hasn't been attacked yet, it soon will be, especially when the enemy detects our interest in it. We're going to use that to accomplish our objectives. When they hit Arrowwood, we're going to disable one of their ships, and then we'll steal their interdimensional tech from it."

Husher looked around the conference room one last time, meeting each of his officers' eyes in turn. "I'm open to being dissuaded, but that will involve one of you proposing a plan that's more likely to work."

No one spoke. Not even Winterton.

Husher nodded again. "Okay, then. We're doing this."

CHAPTER 36

Shrapnel-Laced

"Transitioning into Arrowwood now, sir," Winterton said. "Waiting on sensor data to come in."

"Acknowledged, Ensign."

Several minutes later, Winterton spoke again, and when he did, he confirmed his own predictions, made in the conference room just two days before: "Summit is under attack by fifty Progenitor ships. Fifteen of thirty destroyers are positioned underneath the colony's defense platforms, and the fighter defense group is spread thin trying to deal with them all. The remaining destroyers and twenty carriers are focusing on three separate defense platforms from above, while being engaged by the system defense group."

"How many warships remain of that system defense group?"

"Twenty, sir."

Husher closed his eyes. In one sense, the attack represented incredibly good fortune. After all, it gave them plenty of targets to try and disable in their effort to steal the Progenitors' interdimensional tech.

But fifty ships...

It was the largest Progenitor force he'd seen in the field, and it was clearly meant to break Arrowwood. Without the *Vesta*'s intervention, it would almost certainly succeed. Even with their help, the colony's survival was far from certain.

"Nav, set a course that takes us around the colony and terminates at an uncontested defense platform, well away from Progenitor missile range."

"Aye, sir," Chief Ortega said. Noni was still recovering from her episode caused by lucid, though Doctor Bancroft said she would soon be cleared for duty again.

"Coms, order our battle group captains to set courses to join the system defense group in engaging enemy ships positioned above the orbital platforms."

"Yes, Captain."

The journey through the beleaguered star systems between Feverfew and Arrowwood had been an extreme test of Husher's resolve to see this mission through. Almost every system they'd entered had been under attack, and to watch orbital defense systems compromised by a merciless attacker while doing nothing to step in and help…it had required Husher to harden himself, more than he ever would have wanted to.

It made him wonder how much of the galaxy's population was actually going to make it to Home. A long rebuilding phase had followed the Second Galactic War, but Husher wasn't sure it would be possible for the galaxy to ever recover from this one. *Providing we survive it at all.*

At last, they reached the end of Ortega's course. Throughout it, Husher had kept every missile tube loaded, with a mix of

Banshees and their last remaining Hydras. He'd also ordered Commander Ayam to standby to scramble the Air Group at a moment's notice.

But to his surprise, the Progenitor ships hadn't used their interdimensional capabilities to surround the *Vesta* at any point.

Maybe they have an inkling of what we intend. If the enemy thought there was even a chance of Husher using the Arrowwood shipyards to gain the ability to travel through the dimensions, they would want to destroy them as quickly as they could.

"Nav, make for the nearest destroyer positioned underneath the defense platforms' orbit, while keeping the *Vesta* above them, of course." The supercarrier's mass was such that, if she strayed very far below the defense platforms, there would be no escaping Summit's gravity well. "Coms, get me Captain Syms."

Within seconds, he was talking to the captain—audio only, of course, since the captain of Summit's fighter defense group was currently engaged in furious combat.

"Syms here," the Winger said. "Go ahead."

"Captain Syms, this is Captain Husher of the IGS *Vesta*. I'm—"

"By the talon," Syms said. "Captain Husher, I can't believe you've come to our aid once again!"

"We'll do what we can. But I'll be honest with you, Captain: our main reason for coming is access to your shipyards. I'm keen to make an upgrade to the *Vesta* that I think will prove essential to winning the war."

"That's certainly something I can get behind," Syms grunted—he was probably coping with tremendous g-forces at the moment. "Either way, my pilots will get quite the morale boost once they learn you're here."

"I don't want to distract you, Captain. I'm getting in touch to ask that you disengage from the Progenitor destroyer we're approaching—I'll have my Coms officer send its designation to you now." He nodded at Fry, who nodded back, then did as he'd indicated. "That should help you pressure the enemy's other low-orbit positions a little more, and hopefully keep them from compromising any defense platforms in a way that can't be repaired quickly. In the meantime, we'll bring everything we have to bear on neutralizing our target. Then we'll switch to the next target, send you the designator, and have you disengage from it. As long as your defenses continue to hold, we should be able to increase the pressure on the enemy until it becomes overwhelming and they disengage."

"I'm fully on board, Captain Husher," Syms said. "I think I'd be crazy to say no to a plan from the savior of Arrowwood."

Husher suppressed the urge to wince. "Uh, thank you, then, Captain Syms. I look forward to wiping the Progenitors from this system with you."

"Thank *you,* Captain. Syms out."

Husher released a breath he hadn't realized he'd been holding, then turned to Tremaine. "We need to make every missile count. The Progenitors likely know we're running low. I want you to have all Hydras pulled from the forward missile tubes and replaced with Gorgons. Standby to fire the entire forward barrage at the target."

The Tactical officer frowned. "Sir, if the Progenitors know we're running out of missiles, aren't Gorgons exactly what they'd expect from us?"

"Yes. And that's why I'll be scrambling the Air Group at the same time, including Ayam's subspace squadron." He turned to Coms. "Fry, tell Ayam not to bother having his squadron enter the launch tubes. Instead, order them to transition to subspace directly from the hangar bay, and do their accelerating within subspace. They won't have the same energy, and it'll take them longer to reach the target, but when they do arrive it should be unexpected enough to let them strike the final blow."

"Yes, Captain."

Husher waited until the *Vesta* was halfway between two defense platforms, affording them the safest firing solution for their missiles—one that had the lowest chance of hitting either a platform or the planet itself.

Once they were in position, he gave the order: "Fire missiles, Tremaine. And launch Pythons."

"Aye."

Pythons streamed from the *Vesta*, shooting down Ravagers as they worked their way toward the destroyer, which had been abandoned by the planet's own fighters mere moments ago.

Now, the *Vesta*'s Air Group stepped up the pressure, keeping the destroyer occupied, so that it had no opening to use its particle beam. The missile barrage Husher had ordered helped with that.

Without the backup of its fellow warships, the assault proved too much for the destroyer, and missiles began to get through, even though they'd clearly anticipated the Gorgons. Even some Python squadrons managed to evade point defense turrets long enough to get in volleys of kinetic impactors, along with a few Sidewinders.

Then Ayam's subspace fighters appeared out of nowhere, connecting with a flawless alpha strike. The destroyer exploded, and the subspace fighters vanished before colliding with the shrapnel-laced conflagration.

"On to the next," Husher barked.

CHAPTER 37

Redouble

Two more destroyers fell in quick succession, to roughly the same approach.

The Progenitors are getting sloppy. Husher could see why: they were too focused on breaking the colony's defenses. Each ship was acting independently to do its part to accomplish that, which harmed their coordination overall.

In the meantime, both the *Vesta* and Summit's fighter defense group worked in tandem, whittling down the destroyers trying to take advantage of the defense platforms' unprotected underbellies.

When the *Vesta* succeeded in taking down the fourth destroyer, letting Captain Syms and his fighters put even more pressure on the remaining ones, Husher knew they'd stabilized. To back up that assessment, a group of squadrons commanded by Syms took down a destroyer of their own, allowing them to split up to attack the remaining ten targets occupying orbits below defense platforms.

But the Progenitor warships were finally changing their tactics, doing more to support each other. The carriers and destroyers above the defense platforms were inching toward their fellows below, trying to back them up.

Easier said than done with those platforms pounding away at them. After what had happened at the end of the Gok Wars, Summit's planetary government had lobbied the IU hard for beefier orbital defense platforms, and they'd received them. Judging by their performance today, they were just as deadly as advertised.

On the other hand, only fourteen system defense warships remained of the twenty that had been active when the *Vesta* entered the system. And the *Vesta*'s own battle group had been whittled down to seven ships. Slowly, Arrowwood's defenses were crumbling.

"It's time," Husher said, his eyes on the tactical display. "That carrier there, moving to support our next logical target." He sent the designator to each CIC officer's console. "That's the one we'll disable. Winterton, is Ayam still in realspace after taking down the last destroyer?"

"He is, sir."

"Get me him, Coms."

"Ayam here," the Winger said a few moments later, over a two-way channel.

"Commander, your squadron will be instrumental in disabling a carrier so we can steal its tech—here, I'll send which one to your computer now. I don't see how else we can execute the type of surgical attack we need to destroy her capacitors so that she can't transition out. We don't have the luxury of deciding which of our missiles gets through, and the same goes for non-subspace fighters. But if we send everything directly at a main capacitor, our intention of disabling her will become obvious."

"And that's where I come in."

"Indeed. We'll do everything we can to make it seem like we simply intend to target the destroyer, but at the last second, we'll switch to the designated carrier, hitting them with enough to keep them busy. That should give you the opening you need to flit into realspace and target their main capacitors, on the port and starboard side. With those gone, they won't have the energy to power their quantum engine." *Assuming that is how they travel between the dimensions.*

"A lot of variables here, Captain," Ayam said. "Luckily, it's the type of situation I thrive in."

"I know it. God speed, Commander."

"Thanks, sir. You too. Ayam out."

Ayam's squadron vanished from the tactical display seconds later, and Husher turned to Tremaine. "Time to use those last Hydras, Chief. I want a barrage loaded into the forward tubes consisting of only Hydras. Calculate two firing solutions; one that sends six at the destroyer, and another that sends the rest at that carrier."

"Yes, sir."

"Coms, tell the Air Group that if any of the Hydras make it through, they're not to fire on the enemy carrier. We're trying to capture her, not destroy her."

"Aye."

The *Vesta* reached a point equidistant between two defense platforms, and a slight tremor ran through her and up Husher's chair as the Hydras left the forward tubes.

"Missiles away," Tremaine said. "Pythons are closing in."

"The carrier's reaction seems disproportionate to our attack," Winterton said. "She's dumping Ravagers toward the incoming missiles and fighters. It appears they may have some suspicion about what we're trying to do."

Husher winced, turning to Coms. "Give our pilots the go-ahead to engage fully."

On the tactical display, most of the Hydras split into their separate warheads, many of which were intercepted right away. Pythons made war on Ravagers, unloading Sidewinders and kinetic impactors on the kamikaze robots. They succeeded in pushing back the tide—but not nearly enough. The carrier's point defense systems weren't engaged at all, which meant Ayam and his fighters would get torn to shreds once they reentered realspace.

"Helm, adjust attitude upward thirty degrees and bring engines to fifty percent, now."

"Aye, sir," Ensign Vy said.

"Nav, I need you to whip up a deceleration profile as fast as you can—one that brings us to a stop just above those Ravagers." Husher turned toward Tremaine. "Tactical, supplement point defense turrets with tertiary lasers. We need to help our Pythons punch through, and we don't have very much time to do it."

Husher's breath came in ragged bursts, and his stomach felt like stone. He'd been so confident his ruse would work out that he'd risked sending his CAG and the other subspace pilots to their deaths. If that happened, he wouldn't just lose his most talented pilots. He'd also lose his last subspace-capable craft, which had proven vital to the *Vesta*'s survival so many times.

The supercarrier arrived above the Ravagers, and her augmented point defense systems went to work. By now, all of the Hydra fragments had been cleared by the enemy, but seeing their base ship join the fray seemed to cause the Python pilots to redouble their efforts.

Partner-pair formations wove in and out of the barrage of robotic missiles, one partner taking the lead while the other pilot watched the leader's back. With the *Vesta* thinning the cloud of Ravagers substantially, her Air Group was able to cut through the remainder within ease.

In less than two minutes, the Pythons had pushed through to threaten the carrier's hull, forcing her to engage point defense turrets. Five Pythons went down as they ensnared the carrier, surrounding her. Another four went down. Two more.

Then Ayam and his subspace squadron reappeared, in perfect position to execute a strafing run all along the carrier's starboard-side main capacitor bank. Explosions ripped through the massive ship's hull in a neat line, and then Ayam's squadron vanished to perform the feat on the other side.

Husher opened a two-way channel with Price. "Is Oneiri Force ready to deploy, PO?"

"Ready as they'll ever be, Captain."

"Go take that ship."

"Yes, sir."

Dozens of new icons appeared on the tactical display, deploying from the *Vesta*'s flight decks: the new MIMAS mechs, commanded by Price and accompanied by Rug in her own alien mech. They sailed toward the disabled carrier.

"Sir..." Winterton said, with a note of uncertainty. "The entire Progenitor force attacking Arrowwood has vanished."

"Should I recall the Air Group?" Coms asked.

But Husher could feel his heart begin to pound in his chest as he realized what was about to happen.

"No," he said. "Tell them to continue surrounding the carrier and ready themselves to defend it. Contact Petty Officer Price to tell him that I need the carrier's point defense systems deactivated as soon as possible."

Winterton was looking at him with his head tilted sideways. "Sir?"

"The Progenitors aren't leaving," Husher said. "They realize what's happening. Coms, tell every ship and every fighter in the system to converge on our location, immediately."

"Aye, sir."

But it was too late. The remaining enemy ships began reemerging into the Arrowwood System in a tight sphere, with the *Vesta* at their center.

CHAPTER 38

Viper-Like

"Rug, let's break through the hull where it's already damaged," Jake said over a two-way. The airless void had already quenched the explosions that had taken out the carrier's starboard capacitor bank. "I don't want to risk hitting her anywhere else. I'm afraid of compromising the integrity of the structure any more than it has been."

"I am in accord with your plan, Jake Price."

"Awesome." He used his implant to paint two red dots on the damaged section, within fifty meters of each other. "How's this? I'll take the left, you take the right?"

"Yes. Let us."

"Get ready. We'll be in range in a few seconds."

The carrier's point defense turrets directed some fire at the incoming mechs, and one MIMAS had already gone down. But mostly the turrets were hitting Pythons, who in turn attempted to execute surgical strikes meant to take out individual turret banks.

That's a dangerous game. If this ship exploded with Jake and Oneiri Force inside, they'd all be wiped out. He doubted even he or Rug would survive that. Maybe if they were merged with their mechs, like Roach had been—that had seemed to make him nearly invincible. But Jake still refused to do that, no matter how hard it had become to resist it.

The red dots painted over the carrier's shredded hull grew larger, and Jake yelled, "Now!"

His arms became energy cannons at his mental command, and he sent twin blasts at the red spot painted by the mech dream. He'd calibrated the blasts with just enough power to make a hole big enough for his alien mech to get through, and when the explosion dissipated, it left exactly that.

Rug had done the same, using shoulder-mounted energy cannons she'd morphed for the purpose. Together, they crossed the remaining space and passed through the ship's jagged hull.

Jake's metal feet found the deck, and he ran forward to clear the area for the MIMAS mechs coming in behind him, spikes sprouting from his feet to cling to the deck and help him slow his momentum.

The rest of Oneiri Force came in with much less speed: they used thrusters to decelerate before entering the ship, to avoid damage to their mechs.

As his pilots streamed into the carrier, Jake took a moment to take in his surroundings. He stood in a long room filled with row upon row of the hulking metal boxes that held the capacitors, most of them charred and twisted from the explosions triggered by Ayam's strafing run. The chamber was open to space now, so anything not bolted down had already been sucked out. Emergency lighting provided a dim murk, enough to see that the carrier's interior was fairly similar to the *Vesta*'s crew section. The same gunmetal grays, the same function-driven aesthetic.

As the last of Oneiri Force boarded the Progenitor ship, Jake received a call directly from Captain Husher.

"Price here."

"PO, I want you to take the CIC as soon as you can," Husher said. "I'm sending Major Gamble aboard as well, along with two platoons of marines, and my tertiary CIC crew. The Tactical officer is a skilled hacker, so with any luck he should be able to take over the carrier's point defense systems and help us defend."

"How's it going out there, Captain?"

"Not great."

Jake cleared his throat, waiting for Husher to elaborate, but it quickly became clear he didn't plan to. "Should I hold here till Major Gamble arrives, then?"

"No. Make for the CIC and do what you can to disable those turrets. Just give Gamble encrypted access to your path through the ship. He and his marines will follow behind you."

"Roger that, sir."

"Good luck. Husher out."

Jake didn't waste any more time in mobilizing Oneiri Force. "Let's move, people." Leading by example, he walked toward the nearest interior hatch, which was sealed off, almost certainly in response to Ayam's attack.

Jake blasted it apart with his energy cannons, leaving a gaping hole large enough for a mech to push through.

He did so now, and as soon as he emerged into the corridor beyond, the roar of gunfire sounded from opposite directions.

Turning right, he peppered his attackers in that direction with balls of energy, while his sides slid open to reveal rocket launchers. The missiles sailed down the corridor, quickly filling it with flame and sound.

The shooting from that direction ceased, and behind him, Rug was already engaging the other group of attackers.

As Jake waited for the smoke and fire to clear so that he could observe his handiwork, a hulking form sprinted into view—an Ixan, made massive by the Progenitors' genetic enhancements.

It also moved with unnatural speed. Before Jake could react, the alien crashed into his mech, causing him to stagger backward while he reformed hands to attempt to deal with his assailant.

The Ixan battered him with ham-like fists, apparently oblivious to the way the mech's metal hide shredded its knuckles. Then the berserker drew twin shortswords and launched a flurry of viper-like attacks, slashing and thrusting.

The blades proved incredibly sharp, and the mech dream flashed blood-red as Jake realized they'd actually pierced his machine. He danced backward, but the Ixan followed, swords darting and stabbing.

Letting instinct take over, Jake sprouted swords of his own—broadswords, which he used to parry an overhead cut, then to knock aside a thrust. His blade found the Ixan's throat, and just like that, it was over. With a flick, Jake's blade burst from the alien's thick neck, half-severing its head from its body, which slumped to the deck.

He was ready for the pair of Ixa that charged at him next. One of his broadswords became a heavy gun to spray across the corridor at his foe—an avoidable volley, but one that slowed them. Then he was between them, parrying a blow with the gun's barrel while running his other attacker through, pinning him to the bulkhead.

The first Ixan hit him from behind, twin shortswords sinking deep into the mech, but Jake sprouted spikes from his back that were longer and thicker than the alien's weapons. They struck home, and when they withdrew, the alien crumpled to the deck.

By now, most of Oneiri Force had crowded into the corridor. "Don't underestimate the ship's defenders," he told them over a wide channel. "Their enhancements make them almost as strong as us. But unlike us, they aren't walking armories. Focus your fire and take them down before they get close."

He divided his force into four squads, each with orders to radio the others if they found the CIC. Then he ordered them to form ranks, and they did so with parade crispness. "Share your trajectories through the ship with Major Gamble," he said. "By the time he arrives, I'd like this vessel mostly cleared."

Jake took one squad, putting Ash, Rug, and Maura Odell in charge of the other three. Ash still wasn't thinking straight from losing Beth, but she needed to see that he still trusted her. He worried about Rug, too, given she piloted an alien mech like his. But she'd shown no sign of losing control like him, so if he was going to put faith in himself, he would count on the Quatro, too. As for Odell, he still considered her new, but she wasn't as new as the rest of Oneiri Force, and to put one of them above her would have been a needless insult.

"Look alive," he told his squad as he started down their chosen corridor. They moved together in tight formation, and whenever they encountered resistance, the forward rank dropped to one knee. The corridor was wide enough that this allowed all ten MIMAS to fire on anyone confronting them. If the defenders were entrenched behind cover, the mech squad simply continued approaching, keeping them pinned with overwhelming firepower, until they were upon them.

At that point, they'd either neutralize their targets at point-blank range or Jake would take them out with a little broadsword work.

I do believe I'm getting used to having this many mechs. Oneiri Team had never numbered more than eight, but this squad alone had ten. The MIMAS design was finally doing what it had been intended to do: revolutionizing warfare.

Twenty minutes later, Ash got in touch. "We found the CIC and locked it down, PO," she said. "Gamble's boarded the ship and he's already here."

"Good work," Jake said, and he meant it. He was glad Ash had been the one to do this. He could tell she needed a win. "Though I heard the Ixa call it the bridge, not CIC."

"Whatever."

"Do the officers there seem cooperative?"

"They're dead. They refused to surrender, so hopefully our crew can figure out how to make this thing work."

"Yeah," Jake said, and couldn't think of anything else to say. He had a sudden suspicion that the Ixa on the bridge hadn't refused to surrender at all—that instead, Ash had ordered them murdered in cold blood.

He shook his head to clear it. *Have a little more faith in your teammate than that.*

CHAPTER 39

Insanely Ambitious

For the first time since the war began, the Progenitors fought to the last ship.

"They know exactly what we're trying to accomplish," Husher told Ochrim as they walked through the captured carrier, toward the main engine room. "That means they'll be back soon, with more ships."

The Ixan remained silent. Tension drew his features taut, and the whitened scales around his eyes seemed even lighter than the last time they'd spoken.

He knows what's about to be asked of him.

Husher laid a hand on Ochrim's shoulder as they walked. "This may very well be the last time I call upon you in this war, friend. After this, you can rest."

"Yes. All I have to do is accomplish the impossible." The Ixan offered a wan smile to soften the sarcasm, but Husher got the message, and he couldn't say he disagreed, exactly.

After the Progenitor ships had appeared all around her, the *Vesta* had expended the rest of her missiles defending herself against the constricting sphere. She'd lost forty-nine Pythons to go with them, her Air Group's heaviest losses ever. The number of Pythons the supercarrier could field was dropping, and at this rate, they'd soon approach the *Providence*'s maximum capacity.

If Arrowwood's defenders hadn't rallied around the *Vesta* with admirable speed, they would have lost many more. But with the system and planetary defense groups, the supercarrier's own battle group, her Air Group, and the colony's advanced defense platforms, they took out every enemy ship, except for one. With hundreds of missiles headed its way, the final destroyer had vanished, no doubt to report what had happened in Arrowwood.

If only we could have taken out that ship, we might have had some reprieve.

But Husher knew their only reprieve would be the time it took the enemy to rally enough forces to deliver Arrowwood a crushing blow.

They reached the hatch leading into the engine room, which was flanked by a pair of MIMAS mechs guarding it. They both came to attention and saluted the moment they spotted Husher.

"At ease," he said as he passed them, impressed that even inside such hefty machines, they could pull off textbook salutes.

Inside, a massive metal construct hung suspended in the air, surrounded by four consoles situated near the bulkheads, though they all faced the floating construct in the center.

Ochrim immediately went to the console nearest the hatch and went to work, pausing only to occasionally glance up at the massive quantum engine.

Though he knew he shouldn't interrupt, Husher couldn't help himself: "How did they get it to float like that?"

"Ocharium nanites, would be my guess," Ochrim answered. "Evenly distributed throughout the shell containing the engine. It would also require a Majorana fermion matrix woven through not just the deck but also the bulkheads and ceiling."

"Why bother making it float in the first place?"

Ochrim stopped working altogether to peer at Husher, blinking. "The quantum engine aboard the *Spire* also floated, using powerful magnets. How else could a spherical wormhole be generated around it without separating it entirely from the ship?"

"Ah," Husher said, reddening slightly. He should have known that. He should have taken the time to familiarize himself with the workings of the ship he'd sent Fesky to another dimension in. But a war for survival had a way of stealing one's time for studying engineering schematics.

After that, he let Ochrim work uninterrupted, while he stared at the strange construct suspended in the chamber's center.

At last, the Ixan stepped away from the console. Husher raised his eyebrows.

"The good news is that I found exactly what I hoped to," Ochrim said. "While the design is different, the Progenitor quantum engine appears to function according to the same principles as the engine I designed for the *Spire*."

"And the bad news?"

"The limiting factor is energy. Since the *Vesta*'s bigger than this carrier, we'd need a bigger engine, or at least one with an upgraded power bank and alternators. It would take weeks to build one, working around the clock with no hitches."

"I need it to be hours, not weeks, Ochrim."

The Ixan stared at him blankly. "I'm afraid that simply isn't possible, Captain."

"What if we rip this engine out of the ship, put it in the *Vesta*, and make the necessary modifications to it there?"

"That..." Ochrim coughed. "If you're willing to open up your ship like that, I suppose it could speed things up. A timeframe of hours still seems insanely ambitious, but it would be faster."

"Then we'll do it. As for the timeline, I'm not the one setting it, Ochrim, trust me. It's being set by the Progenitors, who are coming very soon to kill us all."

CHAPTER 40

Permanently Compromised

"Ortega, adjust our attitude downward half a degree," Husher said as they inched toward dry dock, his eyes glued to the telemetry readings. "We're looking pretty close up top."

"Aye, sir."

While Ochrim and Husher had been investigating the Progenitors' quantum engine, the controllers of Summit's biggest ship construction platform strove to raise it to a higher orbit as quickly as possible. If the *Vesta* had attempted to enter dry dock at its previous orbit, the planet's gravity would have dragged the supercarrier down till it smashed against the rocky surface.

Luckily, the shipyard had two dry docks of this size, and the Progenitor carrier had already been guided into the other. Once they removed the quantum engine, it would be a simple matter of transporting it across the shipyard, as long as the *Vesta* was ready to receive it in time.

Husher felt thankful that the logistics of modifying his ship were working out as well as he could have hoped, since they would surely need every advantage they could get. He suspected that defending the *Vesta* during the mods would be nowhere near as straightforward.

However necessary, raising the shipyard to an orbit nearly as high as the nearby defense platforms probably wasn't going to help with defense. It would force those platforms to work twice as hard just to protect the shipyard from Progenitor missiles. And the platforms themselves remained just as vulnerable to any destroyer that appeared below them.

Worst of all, Husher would remain aboard the *Vesta* if and when the Progenitors attacked. He had to: in case any problems arose, he planned to stay in position to attend to them immediately. And if Ochrim succeeded in making the modifications on time, they'd likely need to join the fight right away.

Or flee. But he didn't like to think of that.

Husher drummed his fingers on the command seat's armrest and stared at the tactical display. Four hours passed without any sign of an attack. More time than he'd expected.

It proved long enough for them to cut through dozens of decks with a hole sized for the carrier's quantum engine to be lowered into a central cargo bay, which Ochrim had identified as the ideal location, given its proximity to the more traditional main engine room.

While laborers cut through the supercarrier, another crew cleared out the supplies stored in the cargo bay, which had been stocked full because of its central location. That done, engineers swooped in, working feverishly to install a Majorana fermion matrix into the bulkheads and ceiling, so that the quantum engine could be kept suspended in midair. Then they started laying down the necessary wiring.

Station workers were also working overtime to restock the *Vesta*'s arsenal with Banshees, Hydras, and Gorgons. They'd already exhausted this facility's missile stores, and more were being brought over from other orbital shipyards. Extra shipwrights had already been transported from the other shipyards, and they were hard at work repairing the supercarrier's port-side main capacitor, after which they'd patch up the hull there as best they could.

Moments after the quantum engine was lowered into place, Winterton twisted to face the command seat. But Husher's eyes hadn't left his own console, and he already knew what Winterton was going to say.

"The attack has begun, sir. One hundred Progenitor ships: the computer has tallied sixty destroyers and forty carriers. Half of the destroyers have appeared in positions beneath orbital platforms, all over the planet, and the rest of the enemy ships are bombarding them from above."

Husher nodded grimly. Both the *Vesta*'s battle group and the system's original defenders were dispersed evenly around the planet, though he suspected everyone already knew what he'd realized hours ago: there was no way they'd stop this attack from piercing Summit's defenses. Which meant that anyone remaining on the planet was doomed.

That meant the optimal configuration—for his battle group and for the system and fighter defense groups—would have been to cluster around the three defense platforms surrounding the shipyard where the *Vesta* was undergoing repairs. That was where the most vital thing in this system was happening…a cold calculus, but no less true for that.

Except, he hadn't had the heart to make that argument to Captain Syms, or to the planetary governor. Like him, Husher knew their consciences would require them to try their best to protect the civilian populace before being forced to draw the same harsh conclusion.

Winterton's face hardened. "Relayed visual feeds show that a defense platform just went down near the planet's southern pole, sir." Then, the sensor operator's expression grew even more austere. "Another has been destroyed, near the equator."

"We're getting a transmission request from Captain Syms, sir," Ensign Fry said.

"Put it on the main display," Husher said, feeling suddenly weary.

The Winger's face appeared, looking just as grim. "Captain Husher, as you've no doubt just seen, Summit's planetary defenses have been permanently compromised. This colony is lost. I'm giving the order for all craft to execute a tactical withdrawal to your location."

"Acknowledged, Captain Syms. And thank you."

"Syms out." The Winger disappeared.

The Winger officer had made exactly the right move, which didn't surprise Husher at all. Still, the situation made him want to curse. Had they been as cold and unfeeling as their enemies, they would have simply arrayed all their forces around the *Vesta* from the outset. But now, they would take extensive losses as every ship in the system attempted to make the maneuver.

Unnecessary losses. He squeezed his hands so hard that even his neatly trimmed nails bit into his palms. *Everything depends on Ochrim, now.*

The quantum engine was in place, and workers had already started resealing the *Vesta*'s hull. If Husher was right that the fate of the galaxy depended on the supercarrier leaving this universe for the Progenitor's, then that fate now rested in the Ixan's clawed hands.

CHAPTER 41

Blast Backward

After the first two defense platforms went down, the rest began to follow in rapid succession. So did the IGF vessels that attempted to effect an orderly retreat around the planet, toward the *Vesta*: the Progenitors destroyed them at an alarming rate.

Unlike with other attacks Husher had seen the Progenitors launch against colonies, this time they didn't seem interested in deploying Amblers and Ravagers to the planet's surface.

They'll have plenty of time to do that once they've destroyed the Vesta. Right now, the enemy seemed desperate to reach his supercarrier.

Arrowwood's remaining defenders closed in around the shipyard, joining the *Vesta*'s battle group in a desperate attempt to protect her. Husher had ordered the Air Group fully deployed as well, and they were giving a good showing, as always: enemy ship after enemy ship fell to their incisive strikes. But for every Progenitor ship that fell, two more broke through to replace it.

"We're getting a transmission request from the *Melvin*, sir," his Coms officer said.

"Put it on the display."

Vanessa Harding's gaunt face appeared. "It's been a pleasure serving with you, Captain Husher," she said.

He opened his mouth to respond, then closed it again. At last, he said, "What are you talking about?"

"This situation. Only one ship has a hope of leaving Arrowwood intact, and that's the *Vesta*. I hope your strategy incorporates that fact."

His shoulders rose and fell with a long breath. *My entire battle group, gone. Arrowwood, gone.* It was too much loss to process, let alone to accept. He forced the words out: "It's been an honor to serve with you, Captain. If we do escape this system, then it will be the second time you saved us. If there's anything you'd like to ask of me, ask it, and I'll see it done."

"Kill these bastards," she said, her voice admirably steady in the face of her own impending death. "Don't let them do what they're trying to do."

"I'll try my best," he said.

"That's not good enough, Captain Husher. I want your word."

He hesitated, for a drawn-out moment. Then: "I promise you, Captain Harding. I will win this war."

She nodded, said, "Harding out," and then disappeared from the main viewscreen.

"Coms, get me Summit's governor at once."

"Aye, sir."

Soon, the CIC's main display showed Governor Tyson's gray-feathered face. "Captain Husher, if the *Vesta* is able to depart, the time is now. I'm not sure how much longer the Progenitors can be kept from that shipyard."

"I haven't heard from Ochrim yet, Governor. He's going to contact me the moment his work is complete. In the meantime, I'd like you to use as many of your fighter squadrons as you need to start escorting shuttles full of civilians to the *Vesta*. If we're to escape today, I'd like to do it with as many beings on board as possible."

Slowly, Tyson nodded. "A noble sentiment. I'll give the order now."

"Very good. Farewell, Governor."

"Farewell, Honored Captain."

Husher blinked. He'd never been called that by a Winger before, and he'd never heard any other captain called it, either. It sounded a little like "Honored One," which was what the Wingers had once called each Fin. Whatever the case, the form of address was clearly a profound compliment, and he felt humbled by it, not to mention undeserving.

On the tactical display, the defense was crumbling. The system defense group was cut down to nearly half its numbers from the end of the previous engagement, and what fighters remained of the *Vesta*'s Air Group and the planetary fighter group struggled desperately to keep the flood of Ravagers at bay.

Twenty minutes after his conversation with the governor, a great fleet of shuttles launched from the planet. Clearly, the governor believed he would only get one shot to evacuate civilians, and he'd put everything he could muster into it.

He's probably right. Four squadrons of fighters escorted the shuttles, and the Progenitors paid them little mind, instead remaining focused on their ultimate target: the *Vesta*.

The shuttles had reached the halfway point when the system's defense gasped its last breath. Husher watched his battle group's sole Quatro ship go down, followed seconds later by Captain Harding's destroyer.

It was as though a chain reaction had been ignited, and defending ships began to explode in quick succession. There were twenty ships left guarding the *Vesta*, then seventeen, then twelve.

His com gave the shrill beep of a priority transmission, then, and Husher ripped it from its holster.

"Yes?" he said.

Ochrim's weary voice filled his ear: "I've done it. Provided I've performed the calibrations correctly, the *Vesta* is ready to transition out of this dimension."

"Thank you, Ochrim." Husher turned to his Nav officer, whose console had already been installed with a modified version of the software interface Ochrim had designed to allow the *Spire* to travel the multiverse.

But he couldn't bring himself to order the *Vesta* to leave. Doing so would mean abandoning over one hundred civilian shuttles that might otherwise have been saved.

Instead, he said, "Helm, full reverse thrust. We don't have time to ease the *Vesta* out of dry dock, and if we take some superficial damage, then so be it." *We certainly needn't concern ourselves about damaging the shipyard.* "As soon as we're out, bring us about as fast as possible. Nav, set an intercept course for those shuttles."

"Yes, sir," Ortega said, followed by Vy's "Aye, Captain."

"Coms, broadcast orders for every Python to make for a flight deck on the *Vesta*—Air Group and system fighters alike. We're not stopping, so combat landings will be necessary."

Before Fry could acknowledge his order, he'd already started on the next: "Tactical, put secondary lasers in point defense mode, and have Banshees loaded into every launch tube." Using secondaries like that normally wasn't done, since it drained capacitors so quickly. But Husher wasn't planning to stick around for long. *We should have enough charge left to transition out when we need it, with the main port-side capacitor restored. We should.*

The *Vesta* blasted backward out of dry dock, swung around as fast as it was possible for a ship her size to do so, and began accelerating toward the approaching shuttles.

As she did, the last defending IGF ships were destroyed, and the Progenitor forces constricted, like a pack of wolves incensed by the smell of blood.

Pythons converged on the supercarrier, taking heavy losses as they did, though that still left hundreds. The surviving pilots fought desperately to stay alive, using every guns-D maneuver in the book, even as they continued to protect the *Vesta*.

For her part, Husher's ship laid about all around her with the might capital starships had become known for. Banshees screamed from their launch tubes, slamming into Ravager and warship alike, and the supercarrier sailed through the void too fast for the enemy destroyers to affect her with particle beams.

At last, they reached the shuttles, which poured into the flight decks, every one of which was open. The Pythons followed behind them, under the covering fire of Banshees and secondary lasers.

"Capacitor charge is getting dangerously low, Captain," Ortega said. "A few more seconds and we won't have enough to use the quantum engine."

"Transition out," Husher barked. "Now!"

The Milky Way disappeared, and a starless void took its place.

CHAPTER 42

To Home

Refugees lined the streets of Cybele, some of them napping right on the asphalt as they waited for the city council to find them better accommodations.

"Captain Husher!" a young man called out as he passed. A pair of young boys clung to his legs. "Thank you!"

Husher raised a hand and smiled. A few called out to him like that, but not many. *They're downtrodden. Broken by war.* Displaced, like the rest of the galaxy, many of them separated from families who they could be certain were dead by now.

"A grim scene," Ochrim said from beside him.

Husher nodded. "I'm glad we were able to save some." *Not nearly enough.* The seven-thousand or so that had made it to *Vesta* from Summit were a mere sliver of the colony's population, but to the colonists who'd survived, it certainly made a big difference. At least, it would, once the shock wore off.

"It's all thanks to you, Ochrim," Husher said as they continued down the street. "Everyone on this ship owes you their life. You performed a miracle, today."

The Ixan avoided Husher's gaze, instead staring ahead, at the endless sea of refugees. "It doesn't feel like a miracle. It feels like the end."

"No matter what it is, I thank you. You deserve to be rewarded, and if your efforts lead to us winning this war, then I plan to see to it that you get what you deserve."

"I require nothing. I've never done anything for payment."

Payment of a different sort, perhaps. Husher was about to say as much, but decided against it. "Then you're a rare individual indeed, Ochrim."

A woman stepped forward from amidst the masses of new arrivals, and her composure provided a stark contrast with those around her. She stood with excellent posture, and her gaze never left Husher's.

"Hello, Sera," he said, coming to a halt.

"Hi, Vin. Can we talk?"

Husher glanced at Ochrim, who nodded, and continued down the concourse.

"Whatever it is you want to discuss, I doubt it's suitable for the street," he said. "Shall we go to my office?"

She gestured over her shoulder. "The Secured Zone is right there," she said. "We could rent an enclosure."

"All right."

But once they were inside the bar, they found it packed with more refugees, in and out of the enclosures. Apparently the owner had opened up their establishment to the newcomers, to offer them rest while cutting down on congestion in the streets. That impressed Husher.

"Let's just discuss it here," he said, turning and leaning back against one of the clamshells. "It's fine."

She nodded toward the exhausted people filling the bar. "You've done good work here, Vin. Taking on all these people, helping them escape—it's admirable."

"It isn't nearly enough."

"Of course, not," she said. "No one can ever do enough to reduce suffering, even in the normal course of life. In a war as drenched in pain as this one…" She shook her head. "It's not possible. But you did what you could, and that has to be enough. So in case no one's said it yet, thank you."

He raised his eyebrows, feeling somewhat off-balance after receiving the first compliment from his ex-wife in seventeen years. "What did you want to discuss with me?"

She sighed. "I wanted to…apologize." The last word came out sounding a little strangled. Sera had never had an easy time with apologies. "I've been treating things with us, and with Maeve, like we're on opposite sides of a war. I never gave a thought to the idea you might be right about some things. But watching the way the IU has used this crisis as an opportunity to shove through a political agenda, it gave me a lot to think about. And I realized I've been acting sort of similar when it comes to Maeve."

Husher hesitated for a few seconds, wanting to tread lightly, especially given the unexpected progress they were suddenly making. "Thank you for acknowledging that," he said at last.

Sera nodded. "I'm still not anywhere near comfortable with my daughter living on a warship during the worst war the galaxy's ever known. But I am starting to accept that I can't stop her. So I'll do the next best thing: I'll be here with her."

"She's tougher than you might think," Husher said. "She *is* the daughter of the *Providence*'s former marine commander, you know."

That got a smile. "I guess that's true." The smile faded. "Have you decided what you'll do next? You're not taking us straight to the Progenitors' home dimension, are you?"

Husher shook his head. Currently, they were sitting in the first dimension they'd entered, and the Nav officer on duty was ready to flit out of it at the first sign of danger.

The *Vesta*'s capacitors were recharging, and he'd wanted to take a moment to breathe, to give everyone a chance to collect their thoughts, and to decide what his next move would be. Somehow, his conversation with Sera had clarified that.

After Arrowwood, the Progenitors seemed more invincible than ever, or as close to invincible that drawing a distinction almost seemed pointless. But that didn't mean he was going to roll over and die.

It was exactly like Sera had said: he would do what he could, and he would keep doing that until he won or was killed.

"We're going to take these people to join the rest of the IU refugees," he said. "We're going to Home."

CHAPTER 43

Asking Price

Captain Anthony Flores cracked his knuckles, an action that usually brought a wince from his Nav officer. He monitored the officer's face, but no wince came this time. *Ah, well.*

All this waiting bored him, but he knew it was necessary—indeed, it had been the key to his success so far. Even though he'd managed to grow the Brotherhood to thirty warships, more than double their original number, that paled in comparison to the IGF. And so, any time the Brotherhood struck, they were first forced to wait for a civilian convoy to happen by with a particularly sparse escort.

We would have more ships if it wasn't for what Husher did to us in Larkspur. But it didn't pay to dwell on that. Flores would have his revenge. He just needed to figure out how.

Currently, they were several systems along Pirate's Path, stalking prey that fled through the stars. Whenever his intel told him that the civilians on board a given convoy were mostly human, he left them alone. He still expected to be recognized as a hero by his species someday, but that would become less likely if he blundered by slaughtering them in large numbers.

The galaxy belonged to humans, and it was the Brotherhood's goal to shape reality until it reflected that fact. To allow other, lesser species to inhabit viable colonies and suck up all the resources...that was a waste. The Progenitors recognized that. Flores could see it too, and so could his fellow Brotherhood loyalists.

But how to show the Progenitors that the Brotherhood should be given the Milky Way on humanity's behalf? *If we were allowed to stabilize here, and grow, then in time we could help with their conquest of the universe.*

Flores knew the answer, of course: they could prove their worth by making a meaningful contribution to the Progenitor victory over the IU. Except, that was basically impossible with just thirty warships. While the Progenitors might appreciate their efforts to disrupt the exodus to the Kaithian homeworld, it didn't actually move the needle very much.

"Sir, a shuttle has transitioned into the system," his sensor operator said.

"Just one?"

"Aye."

Flores studied the tactical display through narrowed eyes. His connections in the IU hadn't told him anything about this shuttle, meaning that either its occupants were nobodies, or the craft's flight was so classified that even Flores's moles knew nothing about it.

"Coms, coordinate with Tactical to figure out how long we should wait before contacting it. I don't want there to be any chance it might escape us."

The Coms officer glanced at Flores. "The shuttle's already broadcasting a transmission request throughout the system. It's as though it knows someone's here."

Flores sniffed. The *Marblehead* was currently positioned behind an outer gas giant's moon, just as the other Brotherhood ships were concealed throughout the system, forming a wide net that could constrict at a moment's notice. There was no way the shuttle's sensors detected them.

Whoever that is, they already know we're here. "Accept the request," he said. "Put the video on the main display, but I want exclusive access to the audio." He saw no reason to give his crew information they didn't need.

Captain Bob Bronson appeared on the large display, rendering Flores momentarily speechless. "Captain Anthony Flores," Bronson said. "Correct?"

"Yes, that's right," Flores said, surprised Bronson knew his name. He knew Bronson, of course. The man was a legend, and his long track record proved he valued human ascendancy just as much as Flores did.

"I thought I might find you here. Panicked reports are flying through government channels about marauders attacking convoys on their way through Pirate's Path, but of course the IU lacks the wherewithal to actually deal with it."

Grinning, Flores said, "That's what we've been counting on."

"It's a safe bet. But that doesn't mean what you're accomplishing here is having much of an effect on the war, other than tanking public morale."

"Tanking morale is something," Flores said, struggling to restrain his temper with such a great man.

"It's barely anything, Captain Flores. The public was already panicking. They are abandoning the galaxy, after all. Making them panic even more doesn't meaningfully reduce the likelihood of IU victory."

Say nothing, Flores told himself, afraid that speaking would reveal the fact that he was seething inside. But he couldn't help himself: "What would you do differently?" he asked through gritted teeth.

"I would target the IU's last source of strength. What they call the backbone of the Integrated Galactic Fleet."

"The remaining capital starships."

"That's right. Destroy those, and you'll serve the IU to the Progenitors on a silver platter."

"How?"

"I can show you. Other than the *Vesta*, every capital starship was recently fitted with a new technology called lucid. For now, all you need to know is that I have in my possession a backdoor for lucid, which can be used to take over those ships' navigational systems. Do that in the middle of battle, and they'll be rendered helpless."

Flores regarded Bronson for a long time. At last, he said, "What do you want in exchange?"

"Command of your best ship. My sources tell me that would be the *Marblehead*—your destroyer. I'm sure you can take over from the captain of your next-best ship. Once we have that out of the way, I'll share the backdoor with you, and we can begin getting into position. The Progenitors will strike Home soon, and if you want to make your mark, we need to move now."

Flores made a show of taking time to consider Bronson's proposition, but he already knew what his answer would be. Bob Bronson would be a valuable ally in his own right, especially since he appeared to have inside knowledge of both the IU's and the Progenitor's intentions. If he could provide what he claimed, then this could easily become a historic moment.

Giving up the *Marblehead* was annoying, but in the end, it was just a lump of metal with engines and weaponry attached. A means to an end. Truly, Bronson's asking price was quite low.

"Very well," Flores said. "You have a deal."

CHAPTER 44

Becoming Something Else

Despite how crowded the rest of Cybele was, Santana Park was almost deserted as Jake and Iris strolled through it, with artificial evening descending all around them.

Iris's fingers slipped through his, and he allowed it. He should have pulled away, given how conflicted he felt. But no part of him wanted to.

Where is everyone? Santana Park would have been the perfect place for the Summit refugees to gather and relax. Even at "night," the park was kept at a comfortable temperature, and the fake grass was always soft. Anyone who hadn't been given temporary accommodations could simply come here.

They're too restless, he realized. They all wanted to remain in the city center, where news would disseminate the quickest, and where they could have their say in case of unfair treatment. True, their Oculenses would have performed both those functions, but there was still something about being in person that carried more weight.

"Why haven't we arrived at Home yet?" Iris asked. Apparently, she was thinking along the same lines as him.

That's not overly surprising. Probably, everyone in Cybele is asking themselves the same question. "I heard they're having trouble with the new quantum engine. Something about the *Vesta*'s size throwing off the calculations."

"That poor Ixan," Iris said. "He probably thought he'd finally get a break."

"I would say Ochrim's smarter than that. Besides, if you ask me, that Ixan is far from repaying humanity for what he did to us. I don't think he'll ever be able to repay us."

Iris pulled her hand away from his. "You're always saying I shouldn't be so wrapped up in identity, and yet here you are doing it."

"This is different. He killed hundreds of thousands of people, Iris."

Part of him felt relieved that she'd pulled away. He'd been trying to get Oneiri Force ready for the mission he knew was coming: to travel to the Progenitor home system and save anyone held captive there, if they could. That included Lisa. The real Lisa; the one he'd grown up with.

In the weeks before evacuating the Steele System, he'd felt a strong connection forming between them. Something that went beyond just friendship. And now that he knew the Lisa who'd abandoned him for Andy was really a Progenitor, he felt even more certain that what he'd felt with the Lisa he'd always known was real.

But so were his growing feelings for Iris. He knew he shouldn't act on them till they could extract Lisa and he could figure himself out. But Iris was often by his side, now, her piercing, ice-blue eyes muddling his thoughts.

In his most honest moments, he knew he was spending time with Iris in part because Husher had told him not to. Jake had always had that rebellious streak. But in the end, Husher was right. *War is no time to let myself get distracted like this.*

They were coming up on a thick copse of trees, which looked just as abandoned as the rest of the park did.

"Millions of people have died in this war," Iris said. "And millions more may die."

"Yeah."

"You'll be getting back inside that thing soon, won't you? You'll climb back inside and you'll risk becoming something else." He'd told her about his increasing struggles with the alien mech. "As if going to war isn't bad enough…you're at risk of losing what makes you Jake."

He shrugged.

She took his hand again and tugged him gently toward the thicket of trees—toward a path that led to its center. He trailed behind her, silently cursing himself all the while.

They found a fountain at the center, quietly burbling to itself. Iris sat on the lip, pulling him down beside her.

Their lips met, and for a while, Jake forgot everything else.

CHAPTER 45

Nothing's More Destabilizing

Husher stared at Ochrim, who stood bent over the Nav station, working with Noni to figure out how the hell they were going to make it back to their native dimension. They were at least moving, now, but getting a warship of the *Vesta*'s size to their desired dimension was proving more complicated than expected.

The Tumbran was recovered at last from her traumatic episode in the Gok home system, which gave Husher a measure of relief. Ortega was good, but he came nowhere near Noni's precision and thoroughness. He knew the war would end soon, one way or another, and he wanted his best officers in the CIC for that.

"We're getting close, I think," Ochrim said, perhaps sensing Husher's impatience.

Normally, Husher would have required everyone in his CIC to be seated and strapped in while his ship was in transit, but interdimensional travel didn't require any movement. Not in the traditional sense, anyway. The ship remained basically stationary during the entire process, meaning Ochrim was fine to simply hover over Noni's station as they flitted from universe to universe.

"With every dimension we enter, I'm able to refine our trajectory to a smaller region of the path integral, often by an order of magnitude," Ochrim said. "Of course, with infinity possible directions, it still takes time."

"Less chatting, more getting us to Home," Husher barked.

Ochrim's scaled face tightened momentarily, and he returned his attention to Noni's console.

As they worked to find a path through the multiverse that led back to the Milky Way, Ochrim was also reprogramming the Nav station on the fly, to incorporate what he was learning about moving a ship the *Vesta*'s size through the dimensions.

At last, he looked up. "I believe we've done it."

Husher remained skeptical. "Winterton, can you confirm?"

The sensor operator eyed his console as he waited for it to populate with data. "Location confirmed, Captain," he said with a nod. "We're in the Kaithian home system. I've identified their superweapon, and visual analysis puts the number of spacecraft present at five thousand, eight hundred and ninety-four. Three thousand and eight of those are warships, including all five remaining capital starships, not counting the *Vesta*. Would you like to know the breakdown of how many of our warships there are versus how many Quatro and Gok warships?"

"Not at present, Winterton. Thank you." He turned to the Ixan. "Good work, Ochrim. Go get some rest, but keep your com close. I don't know when we'll be heading for the Progenitor home system, but I mean to make it as soon as possible."

"Of course, Captain," Ochrim said, doing an admirable job of keeping the fatigue out of his voice. With that, he left the CIC.

"Coms, give Major Gamble the order to begin evacuating every civilian aboard the *Vesta*."

"Aye, sir."

Husher stared at the tactical display—at the largest number of friendly ships he'd ever seen gathered in one place. *So this is where the galaxy makes its last stand.*

"We're getting a transmission request from Home's surface, sir," Ensign Fry said.

"Put it on the main display and grant everyone Oculens access."

President Chiba's narrow face appeared on the display, headtail swishing through the air behind him, as though it had a mind of its own. "Captain Husher. That's quite an entrance you made. It's causing something of a stir among the fleet."

Just another day at the office, then. But Husher didn't indulge himself by actually making the joke—especially not at a time like this.

"To be honest, I wasn't sure we'd see you again," the Kaithian continued.

"Sorry to disappoint," Husher said.

"On the contrary," the IU president said. "We continue to recognize your value to the galaxy's defense."

Heartwarming. "I have thousands of refugees on board, Mr. President, and I'm only here to drop them off. After that, we're bound for the Progenitor's home system."

Chiba's eyes widened. "But you can't abandon us, Captain Husher. Surely you wouldn't. Not at an hour of need as dire as this."

"That's precisely why I have to leave. We can't hold here indefinitely, Mr. President. If we don't hit the enemy in their home, we'll crumble here."

"We'll crumble even faster without the *Vesta*," Chiba said. "Too fast. You'll return to find that there's nothing left to protect."

Husher raised his eyebrows. "I'm not used to such flattery from you."

"This isn't flattery. I recognize what you mean to the other Fleet captains, and I recognize your skill. I want you to command our defense, Captain Husher. Without you, I truly don't know what we'll do."

Mouth quirking, Husher studied the Kaithian's face. This was a somewhat pathetic display, but he did believe it was authentic. The galactic president was getting desperate. He had to be, if Husher was the straw he'd chosen to grasp at.

"Sir," Winterton said, and trepidation filled the syllable. That got Husher's attention. If his stoic sensor operator sounded worried, then he should probably worry, too.

"What is it, Ensign?"

"New contacts appearing in a wide circle centered on Home, roughly twenty light-minutes in diameter."

"How many ships?"

The sensor operator swallowed, his Adam's apple bobbing. "They're still appearing, but…they appear to be slowing. Visual analysis puts the last count at over twenty-thousand warships."

Husher felt his eyes bulge. *Twenty-thousand?* His stomach became a chunk of ice.

"They're broadcasting a message," Fry said. "I'm not sure how we're getting it so quickly, at this distance—it's possible they've transitioned in a com drone closer to us, and it's getting lost in all the noise." She shot an inquisitive glance at Winterton, who shook his head, presumably to indicate he didn't detect such a drone. Fry's gaze returned to Husher's face. "Should I play the message, sir?"

Husher nodded.

Teth's face replaced President Chiba's on the main display. "Beings that remain of the Interstellar Union," the Ixan hissed, his eyes wide and filled with fervor. "You must be filled with envy for your fallen neighbors. I have slaughtered most of the family members, friends, acquaintances, and strangers who once shared this galaxy with you. And yet, you are unfortunate enough to still exist. But don't worry. Salvation has come.

"All your life, each of you has sensed how irredeemable you are. How vile. Deep down inside, you've wished for the release of death—the ultimate penance. Well, I am an agent of death, and I come to deliver you to it. Make your peace. Or don't. Either way, this is the end."

Teth vanished from the display, leaving Chiba's fearful face in his wake. Before the president could speak, Winterton did: "The Progenitor force is closing in, sir. Most of them are moving through space toward us, but hundreds of their ships have vanished."

"I'm sure we'll be seeing them shortly," Husher said, his jaw tight.

The president seemed in a state of shock. He'd ceased his pleading, and indeed, he seemed to have ceased most functions. He sat there, shaking.

"President Chiba," Husher snapped, and the Kaithian gave a start. "Can the Preserver hit the Progenitors from this range?"

Chiba seemed to shake himself. "Uh—yes. It has a range-extending function whose existence is little-known. It involves the use of what you would call dark tech, however. And so, potentially, it could destabilize—"

"Activate every function that thing has," Husher said. "Nothing's more 'destabilizing' than twenty-thousand enemy warships at your doorstep."

"Yes. Okay. Captain Husher, do you—"

"I'll take command of the defense," Husher cut in, unable to keep the frustration from his voice. Yet again, Teth was forcing his hand, and that made him very angry. He meant to make him pay. "Go," he yelled. "Activate the Preserver!"

"It's already activating," Chiba said.

"Get me a visual, Winterton."

The sensor operator complied right away, and Husher saw that the president's words were true. Massive clouds of dust were drifting up from the moon-sized superweapon as ravines appeared all along its length, which widened rapidly into canyons.

As soon as the four, behemoth-like segments were far enough apart, they turned their concave insides outward, rotating them to face the enemy fleet approaching from the outer system.

The system's sun glinted off the silver innards of the nearest segment as it turned, and Husher realized he was holding his breath.

Then, at last, the Preserver began to fire.

CHAPTER 46

Looking to End This

Great storms of energy coalesced inside every circular impression that dotted each Preserver segment. Seconds later, broad energy beams flashed across the system toward the oncoming fleet.

It would take several minutes for those beams to reach the constricting circle of Progenitor ships—more than enough time for them to maneuver out of the way. Husher's heart sank as he saw the enemy doing exactly that on the tactical display. Gaps opened in their ranks where the beams would strike.

But it appeared the Preserver knew what it was doing. Only a few of the energy storms had produced beams, and now wormholes opened above most of the others. The beams poured into those wormholes and then out of their exit points, which were situated directly behind the enemy ships.

It took only one direct hit from the Preserver's great energy lances to destroy even the largest Progenitor ships; the carriers. Energy surged into their pierced hulls, overwhelming them and exploding them in great flashes of light and flame.

This happened hundreds of times, to hundreds of enemy ships, within seconds. Husher had seen the great superweapon in action only once before, from aboard the *Providence*, when they'd been fleeing a large Ixan fleet.

Then, the Preserver had repelled the Ixa with ease. But Husher didn't remember anything like this orchestrated display of might. Clearly, the superweapon possessed enough intelligence to have kept some of its capabilities in reserve, like the ability to open wormholes to extend its range, or the ability to coordinate those wormholes and fire through them with a rapidity that was difficult to track.

By concealing those capacities till now, the Preserver took by surprise an enemy it hadn't faced for twenty years. Clearly, the Kaithe's ancient ancestors had engineered and programmed the moon-sized construct with the ability to play a very long game, which helped explain why the Kaithian homeworld had never been harmed.

As Husher monitored the tactical display, a surge of hope began to push through him. Clearly, even the Kaithe themselves hadn't known the exact nature of the gift their forebears had given them. Less than a minute ago, the Progenitors had outnumbered the allied fleet almost seven-to-one, and in that time the Preserver had destroyed over one thousand ships.

There's nowhere they can go to escape those wormholes. Unless they left the system entirely. Presumably, the superweapon had no ability to track the Progenitors across the universe, and certainly not through the multiverse.

But the enemy ships remained, continuing to close in. Then, destroyers and carriers began to appear all around Home, within and around IGF formations, above and below Home's orbital defense platforms.

Dispersed as these enemy ships were around the IGF, Gok, and Quatro forces, it was too dangerous for the Preserver to risk firing on them, lest it hit friendly forces. As that realization seemed to take hold inside the rest of the Progenitor ships, more of them began to disappear from among their ranks, no doubt to reappear closer in. Still, the Preserver continued to savage the enemy ships that remained at a distance, neutralizing dozens at a time.

"Coms, put me on a fleetwide channel—one that includes the Gok and the Quatro."

"Aye, sir. You're on."

"Species of the fleets defending Home," Husher said. "Gok, Quatro, Kaithe, Tumbra, Wingers, Fins, and humans. This is Captain Vin Husher, and I have been given the command by President Chiba. As you're seeing, the Kaithian Preserver has given us some breathing room, but it would be stupid to assume it's going to win this for us." On the tactical display, more and more of the great circle of Progenitor ships were vanishing from the universe. "The Progenitors will continue to appear amidst our ranks, and they'll try to rip us apart from the inside. This will be like no battle you've experienced, and a new kind of combat requires a new kind of thinking. One thing holds true, though: if our capital starships are beaten, then the fleet is beaten. Let's arrange ourselves so that neither happens—so that our formations allow our capital starships to protect the fleet, and vice versa.

"I want all our forces to cluster around the planet we're defending, in a distribution I will describe now. As I've alluded to, we protect the planet by protecting our capital starships. We salvage the galaxy by staying alive to fight. I want one hundred warships, mostly destroyers and missile cruisers, to cluster around every capital starship that isn't the *Vesta*. Each sphere of warships is to defend against attack from without, while the capital starships and their Air Groups defend against attacks from within."

Husher's abdomen tightened as he glanced at the tactical display and saw that most of the encircling Progenitor ships had now either disappeared or been destroyed. In a matter of seconds, the battle for Home would begin in earnest.

"Frigate and corvette captains, you are responsible for patrolling underneath Home's orbital defense platforms and supporting the fighter defense groups that have made it here from other systems. I want any ship I haven't mentioned to envelop the planet in a protective blockade, to support either the capital starships or the planetary defenders, as needed."

Husher cleared his throat, knowing that this would likely be the last thing he'd have time to say. "I've been informed that every capital starship lifeboat has now been converted to a warship capable of traversing the dimensions. To those captains, I say this: you are our Secret Service. Detach from your capital starship and flit through the dimensions, to return and strike wherever your damage can be maximized. Even with the Preserver's aid, the odds are stacked heavy against us, and we must use every capability at our disposal. We must also fight with more intelligence and determination than we ever have before. Keep your heads, and give them hell. Husher out."

He nodded at the Coms officer to terminate the transmission, and then he turned to Winterton. "How many Progenitor ships have been destroyed by the Preserver, Ensign?"

"Nearly eight thousand, Captain."

Incredible. If Husher had been taking losses like that, he would have backed off the attack. The fact that the Progenitors had remained was worrying. For one, it showed they held no regard for the lives of their crews. That pointed not only to their coldness, but also to the possibility that they'd kept even more ships in reserve.

Either way, they're clearly looking to end this today. The allied ships were still outnumbered four-to-one, and on average, the enemy vessels were much more advanced, much more powerful.

But if the Preserver can manage to continue picking them off—

"Sir, the Preserver is under attack," Winterton said.

"Can you give me a visual?"

The Ensign nodded, putting a zoomed-in view of the engagement on the main display.

A battle group of two hundred Progenitor carriers had appeared between the four superweapon segments, so that its weapons faced away from them. They'd already begun to pump thousands of Ravagers across the void toward the four megastructures.

Wormholes opened above and below the carriers, and energy beams began to explode the attackers. But the superweapon was limited by the danger of hitting itself with its own energy beams, and it had to select its angles carefully. There was also no way it could meaningfully target the smaller, robotic ordnance that moved through space in a dark wave.

Soon, Ravagers covered all four segments, tunneling into the barren, moon-like parts, with many of them racing around to attack the infrastructure supporting each energy weapon.

The carrier force positioned between the four segments now numbered half its original number, but that didn't seem to matter to them. Those that remained continued to belch Ravagers, and the Preserver's fate seemed sealed.

Without warning, the first segment burst apart in a titanic explosion of blue light, hurling great chunks of moon and metal in all directions. The second segment followed, then the third, and the fourth.

The Preserver was no more.

CHAPTER 47

Limbs

Wanda Carlisle was shaken awake from bizarre dreams filled with shadowy monsters that lurked in a jungle beneath trees made of human limbs.

She gasped as she was ripped from her slumber, and she fought to steady her breathing as her gaze fell on the face of Lopez, her head of security. He clutched a military-issue assault rifle in the hand not shaking her awake.

Normally, she hated having bodyguards, or anything else that marked her out from the general public. Despite her success, she considered herself a woman of the people. But since arriving on Home, she'd been forced to use what resources remained to her in order to hastily put together a security detail. Anti-rich sentiment was prevalent all over the Kaithian homeworld, and as the battle raged in space all around it, the temperature only seemed to be rising on the planet's surface.

"Ms. Carlisle," Lopez said. "We may have to move."

At that moment, the sound of angry shouting all around her penetrated her awareness. "What is it, Lopez?" she asked, unable to keep the fear from her voice. "What's going on?"

"The sky lit up with this huge explosion around thirty minutes ago. Everyone's pretty sure it was the Preserver."

"Oh, God, no," Wanda moaned.

"It's really setting people off. They're feeling helpless, I think, and they're looking for someone to blame for all this. They're...they want to hurt people like you, Ms. Carlisle. I think we should move."

"To where?" Wanda said. "The entire planet's surface is a sea of tents and temporary structures, and every camp is filled with beings thinking the same way. There's nowhere to go. Not on Home. And there's no leaving the planet, either."

"What are we going to do?"

Wanda drew a couple of steadying breaths. "I have to talk to them. Let me talk to them."

"I'm not sure that's a good idea."

"We're out of options," she said, pushing to her feet, glad that she'd slept in her robe.

On her way out of the tent, she glanced at a mirror propped up against the side of a bureau. She looked a mess, but there was no time to run a comb through her hair, and certainly no time to put on makeup. The people outside were yelling for blood, and she only had so many guards, whereas the mobs outside were limitless.

Lopez kept pace beside her, R-57 held at the ready.

"I don't want that used," Wanda said. "Under any circumstances. The guns are just for show. Understood?"

Lopez raised and lowered his eyebrows, but said nothing.

Once outside, she managed to make it to the bed of an open-backed truck before the crowd spotted her and closed around it, arms snaking over the sides, faces contorted with anger.

Seven of her guards had made it to the side of the truck before the mob closed in, and now they shoved beings back, keeping them from reaching Wanda.

Holding up a hand, she waited for silence so she could speak, though she wasn't sure she would ever get it. Instead, the crowd lobbed degrading curses at her. One man spat, and the glob of mucus and saliva barely missed her left foot. She suppressed a wince.

At last, somewhat miraculously, the crowd settled down enough for her to be heard.

"Oppressor!" a female Winger shouted into the relative silence.

"That's ridiculous," Wanda shot back, surprised at how upset the comment had made her. "I'm far from an *oppressor*. I've always gone above and beyond to provide jobs, and to make sure the beings filling those jobs are fairly compensated—also, that they feel appreciated. I've done a lot of charity work. I care about the galaxy, and I've given back to it."

"You're just trying to escape your guilt," yelled a Kaithian who Lopez was holding back with a hand on its shoulder. "Get off of me!" it yelled at him.

"Ease up, Lopez," Wanda said. "Guilt for what?" she asked the alien.

"For all the privilege you've benefited from. Your species openly oppressed the galaxy for decades, but now they've just gotten more subtle. If you weren't human, you never would have risen as far as you did. The government left you half your wealth, but you don't deserve any of it. You've kept nonhuman beings down. That's why we weren't prepared for this war!"

"That's quite a leap of logic," Wanda said, shaking her head. "You have to stop this," she added, looking around at the rest of the mob. "All of you. You want to know who's tearing this galaxy apart? *You* are. You all are. I understand you've suffered. I understand life is unfair, and right now you're afraid for your lives. I am too. But if you use your bitterness to attack beings who've had success, then what are you going to accomplish? Are you trying to abolish wealth altogether? Because that's foolish. All beings need an incentive to contribute to society. Our system isn't perfect, and it doesn't have all the answers, but if you remove every reward for working hard, where will that leave us?"

"Get down, Ms. Carlisle!"

It was Phillips, the first guard she'd hired since arriving on Home. She turned to find him grappling with a human male clutching a pistol, whose barrel was inching toward Wanda's head.

Instead of dropping to the truck bed like she should have, Wanda froze, totally paralyzed by the mortality suddenly confronting her.

The gun went off, and Wanda felt the air stir near her left temple. Phillips brought a fist against the man's head, once, twice, and the handgun fell to the ground, lost below the press of bodies.

The crowd roiled, surging against the truck until it rocked back and forth. The only reason it didn't tip right away was that the pressure was coming from all sides at once.

Wanda finally regained the ability to move, and she dropped to the truck bed, pulling the robe tight around her and curling into the fetal position. No more shots came—not yet. Her guards were following her orders not to use their guns, and the crowd hadn't yet produced any more would-be killers.

But she felt far from safe. Tears slid down her cheeks to pool on the corrugated metal beneath her, and she began to tremble.

CHAPTER 48

Enter the Brotherhood

All was chaos.

Progenitor destroyers and carriers began appearing around the planet in the thousands, wasting no time before lashing out at the nearest targets with particle beams or Ravagers. The last of the shuttles carrying civilians had left the *Vesta* minutes before, and now some of them were caught in the crossfire on their way toward the planet, forcing the pilots to engage in evasive maneuvers.

Allied destroyers and missile cruisers struggled to get into the formations Husher had prescribed, and he watched the *Eos* take heavy damage from a particle beam before her battle group of destroyers could pressure her attacker enough to take some heat off.

Most of the frigates and corvettes were out of position, and now they scrambled to reach the region between Home's defense platforms and the planet's surface. There, destroyers were already felling allied starfighters by the hundreds.

"Sir, we're getting hit by seven particles beams from three different directions," Winterton yelled.

"Nav, transition us out!" Husher barked.

Noni's hands flew over the console, and the *Vesta* left the universe for another.

"How soon can you get us back—preferably to a location on the edge of the battle, where we can start attacking the edge of the enemy fleet?"

"I estimate seven minutes, Captain."

Husher nodded. "Excellent." Reverse engineering the Progenitor quantum engine had helped Ochrim iron out a lot of inefficiencies inherent in his initial design—the design from which the *Spire*'s engine had been constructed. He'd managed to cut voyages through the multiverse from over an hour to a matter of minutes.

"Coms, tell Ayam to prepare to scramble the Air Group the moment we return, but only Pythons that were originally aboard the *Vesta*. I want to keep the Arrowwood Pythons in reserve."

"Aye, Captain."

He turned toward the XO's chair. "Ek, to capitalize on the element of surprise, I'll need your help to analyze the battlespace as quickly as possible."

"Yes, Captain Husher."

The seven minutes felt like two, and then they were back in the Kaithian home system, hard against the edge of the battle.

Using a shared Oculens overlay, Ek indicated a battle group of twenty Progenitor ships; half carriers, half destroyers.

"This formation will soon be hemmed in by allied forces, and they know it. Soon, they will target these ships," Ek said, indicating a group of five Gok ships. "That is their best point of egress, and they will struggle hard to avoid becoming surrounded."

"So we deploy our Pythons to weave through the battle and engage them at the same moment they engage the Gok ships," Husher said, nodding. "Tremaine, standby to fire Banshees and Gorgons if a decent firing solution opens to us."

"Yes, sir."

Most of the *Vesta*'s Air Group deployed from launch tubes, with orders to randomize their movements until the optimal moment.

Minutes later, when the Progenitor force attacked the Gok ships, just as Ek had predicted, the hundreds of Pythons converged like a fist clenching. The sudden movement helped mask Ayam's squadron, which had dropped into subspace only to pop back into reality to hit a carrier with an alpha strike, taking out its main engine.

Then, as the rest of the Air Group closed with the enemy, so did the dozens of Gorgons Tremaine had found the space to fire. Six ships went up in flames, and when the Gok ships realized what was happening and joined their power to the *Vesta*'s, more began to fall.

The Progenitors managed to strike back some, taking out two of the Gok ships and eleven Pythons. Husher was loathe to take any losses, but he had to admit it was an incredible trade. Clearly reluctant to continue the exchange, the remaining enemy ships transitioned out of the dimension, relinquishing their position.

"There," Ek said, indicating a point on the battlespace a few light seconds away. "If we can reach that space within three minutes, we will be in position to hit a battle group of six Progenitor ships who will believe themselves safe. For self-preservation, we will have to strike and then transition out immediately."

"Noni?" Husher said. "Can we make it there in three minutes?"

"I can try, Captain, with a reasonable expectation of success. Our mapping of the multiverse is limited, but based on Ochrim's calculations, I—"

"Just do it. If we take too long to reach it, we'll find something else to target once we get there."

"What about the Air Group, sir?" Tremaine said.

"We're leaving them here for now. Transition out, Chief Noni."

As it turned out, they reached the position Ek had designated in two minutes and forty-seven seconds. Husher had Tremaine unleash a massive missile barrage, complete with Banshees, Hydras, and Gorgons. The Progenitors launched Ravagers to help with missile defense, but Husher had calculated his barrage to be overwhelming. Two ships went down before the *Vesta* transitioned out, and when they returned to the universe less than five minutes later, sensors confirmed that he'd calculated correctly: there was no trace of the four remaining ships they'd targeted. Either they'd been destroyed or they'd transitioned out.

So it went, for a time: the *Vesta* flitting in and out of her native reality, exploiting vulnerabilities in the enemy's positioning. The Progenitor's numbers were great, but no ship in the battlespace rivaled the *Vesta*. Husher wedded his tactical knowhow to Ek's advanced perception, and in doing so they ensured the supercarrier did real work wherever it appeared.

The Secret Service of lifeboats-turned-warships were also making outsized contributions. It seemed the battle for Home had granted Winterton an opportunity to fulfill his vast potential, and managing several data streams produced by the *Vesta*'s sensor suite, he observed and analyzed the battlespace with a skill that rivaled Ek's. He reported on the Secret Service's activities whenever one of their ships reappeared. "Captain Okane just played a large role in disrupting a Progenitor assault on the *Eos*' formation, sir," Winterton said at one point, and moments later he reported that Captain Deeley, another Secret Service captain, had single-handedly taken out three destroyers.

Despite these successes, and despite that the Progenitors were losing ships at a faster rate then the allied fleet, they weren't losing them fast enough.

Especially not if they've kept ships in reserve. If that was the case, the allies seemed doomed.

Even so, they fought on.

Without warning, a destroyer appeared directly in front of the *Vesta*, followed by a cohort of eleven more warships of the same make.

All twelve hit the *Vesta* with particle beams.

"Transition out, Noni!" Husher barked.

The Nav officer did—just in time, as Winterton confirmed: "They almost had us, sir."

"That first ship to appear," Husher said. "That was Teth's, wasn't it?"

Winterton gave a grim nod. "Aye."

"Noni, take us directly behind that formation, and Tremaine, be ready to hit them with everything."

"It will take nearly eight minutes for us to return to that location, sir," the Nav officer said.

Husher cursed under his breath. "Can't we just transition back the way we came?"

"I'm afraid the multiverse doesn't work like that."

Eight minutes proved too long: when they reappeared, Teth and his destroyers were gone from their previous position.

"Watch out carefully for Teth's destroyer, Winterton," Husher growled. "I want to take every opportunity to kill him that presents itself."

"Aye, sir," the ensign said, though he was staring hard at his console. "Sir, it appears the Brotherhood has entered the system. Thirty ships with profiles matching those that turned to their side recently transitioned through the darkgate, and they've been joined by an escort of hundreds of Progenitor ships."

Husher frowned. He had no idea why the Progenitors would prioritize the Brotherhood ships like that, but it couldn't be good. Either way, with so many ships protecting them, he couldn't see a way to attack the former IGF ships without losing his own ship in the process.

CHAPTER 49

Snapped in Half

"Help me anticipate Teth's targets," Husher said to his Fin XO. "Neutralizing him could cut the enemy's morale in half."

Ek nodded. "I expect his skill is greatest among the enemy captains. As such, he will pursue important targets, but only ones not surrounded by too many defending ships. I have identified three targets that meet those criteria, given the battlespace's current configuration."

"What are they?"

"The sparsely defended underside of an orbital defense platform—though I doubt he will pressure it, since the situation over the planet is fluid enough that Teth may find himself under more threat than anticipated, which I am sure he will account for. The *Ceres*' Air Group has been thinned enough that she offers a likely target for Teth, provided he gets in and out before the destroyers and cruisers encircling her can act. Finally, a Gok battle group of thirteen assorted warships has isolated itself from allies, and Teth will know he and his destroyers can overwhelm them handily by taking them from behind."

Husher frowned at the overlay he shared with Ek, which highlighted the three targets she'd indicated. *The Gok have had a tendency to operate on their own throughout the battle, to their own detriment.* But would Teth bother to target them? "I think we should count on Teth wanting to take down the bigger target," he said at last. "He'll go for the *Ceres.* At least, I think he will. Let's roll the dice. Noni, take us inside the formation protecting the *Ceres.*"

"Aye, Captain," Noni said, and an instant later, the *Vesta* left the Milky Way once again.

When they returned four minutes and twenty-nine seconds later, just where he'd ordered Noni to put them, Teth wasn't there.

Winterton looked up from his console, not quite concealing his frustration. "Teth chose to target the Gok ships, Captain," he said. "He and his destroyers have almost neutralized the entire battle group." Winterton's gaze fell to the console, then flicked back toward Husher. A fearful expression had replaced the hints of frustration that tightened his features before. "Sir, the *Ceres* is speeding toward us—as though she means to ram us!"

Husher narrowed his eyes. "Helm, full reverse thrust, and Coms, contact Captain Riggs and ask what he's doing. Once you've done that, make sure the destroyer and cruiser captains behind us are aware of what's happening. They may have to get out of the way, too."

"She's gaining on us, Captain," Winterton said. "She has a full head of steam."

And we're starting up from a complete stop. "Noni, standby to transition out on my mark."

"Aye."

"Sir," Winterton said, his voice hitching with something that sounded very close to panic. "The other four capital starships are also behaving erratically. They're all traveling at full speed toward the edges of their protective formations. Some of the cruisers and destroyers are getting out of the way, but many of their captains are slow to react."

That's fair enough, given how bizarre this is. But it also wasn't acceptable. "Coms, get me on the fleetwide at once."

"You're on, sir."

"Captains of the *Eos, Artemis, Ceres, Ormenos,* and *Simon,* please provide an immediate explanation for why you're breaking formation." That done, Husher waited, monitoring the tactical display to anticipate the moment he'd be forced to transition out. He'd intended his transmission to warn the fleet as well as get answers.

"Incoming transmissions from all five capital starship captains, sir," Ensign Fry said.

"Accept them all, and put them on the main display."

All five captains appeared on the now-segmented display, in various states of panic. Unsurprisingly, Captain Katrina Norberg seemed the most composed. She spoke first.

"Captain Husher, my Nav officer is experiencing what seems tantamount to a grand mal seizure, just as the one your Chief Noni experienced while in Gok space," she said. "The Invigor Technologies rep assured me they'd ironed this out."

"Same here," Captain Riggs said, his voice tremulous. "Exact same thing happening to mine."

"You all need to get your secondary Nav officers to the CIC at once," Husher said, "as well as your chief engineers, to help you rip that tech out of your systems as fast as possible. Everyone on that planet is depending on you to make it happen inside of the next few minutes. Give the orders now, but don't disconnect from this transmission. We need to figure this out. Clearly this was triggered somehow, and we need to make sure it can't be again."

On the tactical display, the capital starships continued to move toward the edges of the spherical formations protecting them. Most of those formations had responded quickly, moving with the rogue capital starships to keep them in the center. But the *Artemis'* formation had failed to do that, and she now sailed past the destroyers and missile cruisers that comprised it.

At once, a host of hundreds of Progenitor destroyers and carriers converged, targeting the *Artemis* with Ravagers and particle beams. It was far too much firepower to bear. Explosions tore the *Artemis* apart, and Captain Updike disappeared from the main display.

Meanwhile, the *Ceres* was nearing the *Vesta*. In less than a minute, he'd be forced to give Noni the order to transition out.

"Back in Gok space, my primary Nav officer's seizure was triggered by the *Vesta* taking damage," Husher told the four captains that remained on the display. "But the Progenitors couldn't have damaged all of you at the same moment. In fact, unless I missed something, none of your ships took any damage during the last ten minutes. But something had to cause this. Think, Captains. What preceded your Nav officer's seizures?"

Norberg's eyes narrowed in thought, and then she spoke up: "One of the Brotherhood ships sent us a transmission request. I thought that odd, but I ordered my Coms officer not to accept."

"We got the same thing," Riggs said, and the other two captains echoed him.

Something clicked for Husher, then, and he knew what had happened. "The Brotherhood must have access to some sort of backdoor into lucid tech. That means they can continue to control you until you rid your systems of it."

"Sir..." Winterton said, trailing off. Husher looked at the tactical display, a knot tightening at the base of his throat.

All four of the affected capital starships that had survived till now remained protected by their formations, but the *Simon*'s defending ships had responded the slowest, and she was still positioned near the protective barrier of destroyers and missile cruisers.

Progenitor ships descended on that part of the formation now, no doubt spotting that all they needed to do was break through in order to take down their target. She was too close to the edge for the other ships to rally around her in time.

Ravagers rained on destroyer, missile cruiser, and capital starship alike, and particle beams struck home, warping and twisting hulls. Like dominoes, allied warships exploded one after another, until finally the *Simon* went up in an explosion that mimicked the *Artemis*'.

Husher's insides had turned to ice. *Four capital starships.* They'd begun this war with eight. *The fleet's spine, snapped in half.*

CHAPTER 50

Target-Rich Environments

The world seemed to contract, and the CIC's usual noises quieted, till Husher could hear only the sound of his heart beating.

"Tell the formations that were protecting *Simon* and *Artemis* to disperse and join those protecting the remaining capital starships, Coms," he heard himself say, though he felt like he was running completely on autopilot.

"Sir, the *Ceres* is going to crash into us," Winterton said.

With that, the world resumed its normal volume, snapping back into focus at the same time. "Transition out," he barked.

Noni did, just in time.

"Get us back as soon as you can. Winterton, what did the trajectory of the surviving capital starships look like?"

The sensor operator swallowed, clearly struggling to compose himself. Husher knew that he *would* get himself together. The ensign was among the most solid men he'd ever met, and Husher truly believed that nothing would break him down for long. But he needed the man to pull himself together right away.

"The capital starships were moving with full speed toward the planet, sir," Winterton said, his voice shaky. "If they're allowed to get much farther, the defense platforms will interfere with the spherical formations of ships accompanying them. I suspect the Brotherhood's aim is to crash our remaining supercarriers into the orbital platforms."

With an effort of will, Husher denied an urge to grip the command seat's armrests. "The Progenitors will probably strike as the capital ships reach those platforms. Noni, I need you to get us near one of them, to help defend."

"Aye, sir."

Minutes later, the *Vesta* appeared far above the planet Home. Below, rich greens and blues proclaimed the Kaithian homeworld's lushness. Above, the Progenitor forces were converging on the out-of-control capital starships, just as Husher had foreseen.

"Coms, put out a broadcast encoded to the Secret Service ships. The Progenitor forces guarding the Brotherhood ships appear to be breaking off to join the chase. If we can take out whatever ship is responsible for subverting the capital starships, maybe we can stop this. Tell the Secret Service captains to appear in formation behind the Brotherhood's thirty ships and blast them all to hell."

"Aye, sir."

"Winterton, where's our Air Group?"

"They're making their way toward us, sir. I think they see what we're aiming to do."

"Excellent. Tremaine, see that dense cluster of oncoming enemy ships? I'm sharing the designation with you now."

"I see them, sir."

"I hope you like target-rich environments. Those ships are so tightly packed and focused on the compromised capital starships, my guess is that Hydras would pay off in dividends for us. Load every missile tube with them, except for the Gorgons you'll scatter in."

"I like it, sir."

"So do I. Let's even this thing up."

He knew they wouldn't even up anything with this missile barrage, no matter how well it did, but he also knew an opportunity when he saw one.

"Nav, set a course for the middle of the enemy fleet, and Helm, be ready for evasive maneuvers at a moment's notice. Tremaine, fire only on my mark. In the meantime, answer any ships that oppose our advance with a dispersed spray of kinetic impactors, and ready tertiary lasers to supplement point defense. The impactors will keep the enemy off-balance, unable to train a particle beam on us, and laser-supplemented point defense should handle whatever Ravagers they throw at us."

On the tactical display, Progenitor ships sailed past the *Vesta*—above, below, and on both sides. Some did take potshots as they passed, but as Husher had predicted, they were hungry for the prey that had been made lame by the Brotherhood's trickery. A few Ravagers were sent the *Vesta*'s way, and particle beams flickered toward her, but the countermeasures he'd ordered were enough to keep those paltry efforts at bay.

"Mark," Husher said to Tremaine.

Missiles exploded from the *Vesta* in all directions. The closest Progenitor ships barely had time to react, and warhead-bearing Hydra segments slammed into hulls nearly unopposed, neutralizing twenty-three ships in spectacular explosions.

Other targets had more time, their point defense systems coming online to fend off some of the incoming ordnance. But each Hydra that came under fire split into eight, and the barrage those segments formed soon proved overwhelming.

Several Progenitor ships transitioned out, abandoning their pursuit of the crippled capital starships, but many remained, and the *Vesta*'s expanding barrage continued on. Hydra segments fell like hail on Progenitor hulls, and the missiles' numbers effectively concealed the Gorgons peppered in, which took down still more ships.

In response, enemy ships began transitioning out all around the *Vesta*, and others broke off, turning to head away from the planet. There were still plenty of Progenitors pursuing the wayward capital starships from other directions, but the *Vesta* had singlehandedly broken the largest, densest charge.

Hopefully it will buy enough time.

"Sir, the Secret Service ships have appeared behind the Brotherhood and are hitting them with everything they've got," Winterton said, sounding as satisfied as Husher felt.

Husher monitored the unfolding engagement on the tactical display. He might have been seeing things, but it seemed to him that two of the six ships capable of interdimensional travel were fighting with particular vigor: the ones whose capital starships had fallen because of the Brotherhood's treachery.

The Secret Service ships had no lasers. With their smaller size, they needed their entire capacitor charge for multiverse travel. But they carried plenty of missiles and plenty of impactors. Combined with the element of surprise, their arsenals were packing an outsized punch against the turncoat IGF ships: five had gone down already, and as Husher turned his attention to the battle, six more fell.

It wasn't enough. The Brotherhood formation broke apart, scattering in every direction, and the capital starships continued their suicide run for the defense platforms.

"We're getting a transmission request from one of the Brotherhood ships, sir," Ensign Fry said. "Should I accept? Do you think they're trying to compromise us, too?"

Husher shook his head. "No, I don't. The other ships didn't accept and were still compromised. Besides, we removed lucid from our ship, so we're not vulnerable in the same way. Accept the transmission."

The face that appeared on the main display was one Husher hadn't seen for twenty years. It was just as bald as it had been, and the white handlebar mustache it bore was just as flamboyant. But the skin sagged now, and the eyes were even deader.

"Bronson," Husher spat. "Who let you crawl back into the galaxy?"

"No one *lets* me do anything. Don't you remember that? You should have killed me during the Second Galactic War, Husher. When you had the chance."

"I agree. But there's no time like the present."

"Are you kidding? This is over, and it's thanks to *me*. If there's anything left of you after we're finished wiping the floor with you, I'm gonna take a piss on it."

Winterton went rigid at his console. "Sir, Teth's destroyer has appeared directly behind us with eight destroyers accompanying. They're hitting us with particle beams!"

Eyes drawn to the tactical display, Husher realized the purpose of Bronson's taunting. It had been meant to anger and distract him, so that Teth could get into position. And it had worked.

"Helm, full lateral thrust!"

"Sir, shouldn't we transition out?" Noni said, twisting to face him, fear painting her face.

"Negative," Husher said. "We're finishing this."

CHAPTER 51

Military History

There was no time to think. Only to react.

"Tremaine, fire a spray of dispersed kinetic impactors to disrupt the attack, and fire Hydras from rear tubes as quick as you can."

"Yes, sir," the Tactical officer answered, his words clipped.

"Coms, order the Arrowwood Pythons we kept in reserve to scramble at once and target Teth's destroyer."

"Aye."

A part of Husher told him it was irresponsible not to have transitioned out in response to Teth's appearance. But a much louder part pointed out that Teth wouldn't stick around either, unless he thought he could destroy Husher.

Taking a risk like this is the only way we'll get a shot at him.

"Impactors away, sir," Tremaine said. "Hydras will be ready momentarily."

Winterton spoke: "Our lateral movement threw the enemy's targeting off, but our stern took massive damage from superheating, Captain. Dangerously close to a main reactor. They appear to be refocusing on that reactor now."

"Acknowledged. Helm, bring us about, as quickly as she can handle. Tremaine?" If those missiles didn't launch now, the rear launch tubes would be out of position.

"Launching Hydras!" Tremaine said. "This doesn't leave us with many left, sir."

"Order a forward Banshee barrage prepared, with Gorgons mixed in."

"Aye, Captain."

"Winterton? Status?"

"They've broken off their attack to deal with our reserve Pythons, sir. The bad news is the Arrowwood pilots don't seem very experienced with dodging Ravagers. Combined with the Progenitor point defense systems, the enemy is cutting down their numbers rapidly." Winterton leaned closer to his console. "Hydras are nearing their targets, however. They—" The sensor operator blinked.

"What?"

"All nine destroyers have vanished, sir."

"I don't trust that. Tremaine, keep a close eye on the Tactical display. Helm, don't slow our rotation. If they appear behind us again, I don't want them there for long."

"They have, sir," Winterton exclaimed. "The destroyers have appeared behind us!"

Husher suppressed a wince. That confirmed that every Hydra they'd launched had been wasted.

"They're hitting us with particle beams again," Winterton said. "Our rotation is preventing them from focusing on any part of our hull for long, but the energy transfer is still immense. I don't think we can withstand it much longer."

"Can the Pythons reach the enemy ships in time to make a difference?" Thanks to the destroyers' abrupt relocation, the starfighters were now out of position.

"I don't think so," the sensor operator answered.

"Tremaine, spray impactors. Do we have enough charge to both fire our primary and transition out?"

"Negative, sir."

Winterton's eyes were fixed on Husher's face. "The destroyers' formation is much more spread out this time, sir. I don't know that impactors will be enough to throw them off."

Husher drew a deep breath, racking his brain, but knowing it was futile. He was beaten. He opened his mouth to give the order to transition out.

Then, something caught his eye on the tactical display: Ayam's subspace squadron dropped into reality from nowhere, executing an alpha strike that connected cleanly with one of Teth's main capacitor banks, which blew out into the void.

Instantly, the other destroyers broke off their attack on the *Vesta*, desperately trying to neutralize the subspace-capable Pythons.

As well they might. After deploying its particle beam for so long, and with one of her main capacitors destroyed, Teth likely didn't have the energy to transition out.

"Winterton, where are those Arrowwood Pythons?"

"They're closing in, but they'll still need another minute."

"Let's buy them that time. Our nose will soon be in line with Teth's ship, Tremaine. Unleash the entire barrage of Banshees at it, and follow up with several tight bursts of kinetic impactors, along firing solutions designed to anticipate the ship's trajectory."

Teth's destroyer would still be able to maneuver under thrusters, but she could only move so fast.

I've got you right where I want you, you bastard.

Dozens of Banshees left their tubes, and the Arrowwood Pythons followed soon after, flying past the *Vesta* toward Teth's ship. The eight destroyers accompanying Teth had clearly been ordered to divert everything they had to protecting him. They mowed down Banshees as they approached, but they couldn't get them all—not while picking off every Python. Not only that, defending against kinetic impactors was much trickier, and Ayam's squadron continued to harry Teth's destroyer.

Husher could see that the writing was on the wall. Then he remembered his battle with Teth over Klaxon's moon, when he'd destroyed the Ixan's ship but his enemy had still escaped.

"All ahead, Helm, right now."

Tremaine shot a concerned glance at Husher. "Sir, is that wise?"

"I said all ahead," Husher barked, and the *Vesta* surged forward.

Two Banshees connected with Teth's hull, and then an Arrowwood squadron got in an alpha strike, followed by one from Ayam's fighters. Finally, a burst of impactors achieved a direct hit, and Teth's ship burst apart.

"Watch for the escape pod, Winterton, and send the designation to Tremaine the moment you have it."

Even as he nodded, Winterton made the flicking motion atop his console that would transfer the data to Tremaine. "It's done."

"Impactors, Tremaine."

The tactical officer only had one shot, and no time to whip up a firing solution. He'd have to free-hand it, something rarely done in space combat.

Tremaine took the shot.

He scored a hit. Teth's shuttle burst apart—a brief flash against the void, and the Ixan was gone.

"Fantastic work, Chief Tremaine," Husher said, and the Tactical officer nodded. "Let's turn our attention to the remaining destroyers."

But those destroyers were already transitioning out, eager to escape Ayam's subspace squadron, not to mention the rest of the *Vesta*'s non-Arrowwood fighters, which were finally about to reach the engagement.

Husher didn't feel nearly as satisfied by Teth's demise as he'd expected to. He'd battled the Ixan across vast stretches of space and time. Teth was responsible for the deaths of millions of innocent beings. And yet Husher felt...nothing.

He didn't regret what he'd done. Teth had deserved to die, and he would have killed him again if he'd needed to, a thousand times over. But the battle still raged all around him, and the allied forces were just as desperate. They were almost as outnumbered as before, too—they'd whittled things down to three-to-one, perhaps. As for the remaining Progenitor ships, it was difficult to tell whether they'd even realized their commander had died.

You barely need a commander, with numbers like those. You just need to continue attacking in waves until your enemy is defeated.

Killing Teth had been a personal victory, nothing more. The galaxy was still in just as much danger.

His CIC crew seemed to take no pleasure in Teth's destruction, either. In fact, their hearts hadn't seemed in this battle from the outset. It was as though they were simply going through the motions, and now that Husher considered it, the rest of the allied fleet seemed much the same.

Would we have lost those two capital ships if morale was higher?

As though reading his thoughts, Winterton said, "The capital starships appear to have regained control, sir. They're pulling away from the defense platforms to reengage the enemy forces."

Husher nodded distractedly. "Thank you, Ensign."

Why should anyone's hearts be in this? What are we supposed to be fighting for? A society that's given in to its own jealousy and resentment, so that its members tear each other down for scraps?

"Chief Noni," he said.

"Sir?"

"It's time to pay the Progenitors a visit in their home." *It's the only way to end this.* "Coms, while the chief calibrates our interdimensional course, I want you to recall our entire Air Group."

"Aye, Captain."

Within ten minutes, the *Vesta*'s Pythons had all returned to their flight decks, and Noni's course was prepared. "Transition out, Chief," he said, and they did.

Husher sat in silence for the duration of the interdimensional voyage: this time, over ten minutes. He spent part of the time wondering why it took longer to reach the Progenitors' dimension than it did to loop through the multiverse and return to a different place in their own dimension. *I suppose it makes sense.*

"We've arrived, sir," Noni said.

Husher nodded. "Winterton? What do you see?"

The sensor operator frowned at his display, no doubt waiting for more sensor data to populate. "I—" He shook his head.

"What is it, Ensign?"

"This system...it's an exact match for the Corydalis System, sir."

Corydalis. That was the system just outside the Concord System—formerly the Baxa System, the home of the Ixa.

"Do you see any Progenitor ships?" Husher asked. "Structures? Anything?"

"There are many ships," Winterton said. "Two large fleets, fighting on the opposite side of the system. One of them much larger than the other. Sir...I minored in military history, with a focus on the Second Galactic War."

Husher raised his eyebrows. "And?"

"One of these fleets is comprised of Ixan ships from that era. The other fleet...unless I'm grossly mistaken, this appears to be the final battle of the Second Galactic War. The other fleet is led by the *Providence*."

CHAPTER 52

Death Struggle

Ochrim was in the CIC once more, head joined with Noni's as they attempted to figure out whether there was an error with either her course or his calculations...or whether this was truly where the coordinates for the Progenitor home dimension had taken them.

If so, then nothing about it made sense. What they were seeing certainly didn't cohere with what Sato had told him. It was possible she'd lied, but if that was the case then she'd concocted a pretty elaborate fiction, for no reason Husher could discern.

The fleets battling on the other side of the system showed no sign they'd noticed the *Vesta*'s arrival. Locked in their death struggle, they fought on, the allied fleet dwindling, just as it had twenty years before, in Husher's native dimension.

The idea that his old mentor, his personal hero, was about to die before him...he had no idea how to process that. There certainly wasn't anything he could do about it. If he joined his supercarrier with Keyes's, he would merely share his fate. The Ixa's numbers were too great, and besides, Husher knew that soon a wormhole would rupture, destroying almost every ship participating in the battle.

Stranger and more unsettling still was the notion that in the next system over, a younger version of himself fought to reach the Ixan superintelligence named Baxa, and to destroy him.

He had expected to encounter another version of himself today. Sato had told him about his double's importance to the Progenitor command structure. Husher had managed to start thinking of that other self as a demonic, false version, but given that whatever universe they'd landed in seemed to mirror his native universe, he had to assume that it was basically him fighting through the Baxa System, completely unaware of what was about to happen.

"I believe this may indeed have been an error in my calculations," Ochrim said from the Nav station. "Which makes it very fortunate that my error didn't affect our interdimensional transitions as we fought the Progenitors around Home." The Ixan's eyes met Husher's. "Now that I've identified the problem, I should be able to fix it in minutes. Just a matter of altering the algorithm so that it emphasizes the *Vesta*'s mass during certain transitions along the path integral."

Husher nodded. "Do it."

He continued to watch the tactical display as more and more allied ships fell. Victory seemed impossible, but Husher knew what was coming: Keyes's sacrifice. Admiral Keyes and his CIC crew, having emptied the rest of their ship, would fight to hold the Ixa at bay while the Tumbran Piper would use the *Constellation* to generate a wormhole under Keyes's orders. Then, also under Keyes's orders, he would let it collapse, resulting in a catastrophic release of energy that would destroy most of the Ixan fleet. Teth would survive. Husher knew that, now. But the enemy fleet would be decimated.

He watched as the allied ships fought with a level of valor Husher hadn't beheld for a long time. *What makes them so determined to give their lives in battle, when IGF members seem like robots going through the motions, even as their defeat draws ever nearer?*

He thought about what shape Milky Way society had taken, twenty years ago—and in this dimension's present. They'd just fought a revolution against a corrupt Commonwealth, and against all odds, they'd brought down the government that had sold the public good to the highest bidder. Then, they'd set about building something new. Something they could be proud of.

These people are fighting for a society they believe in.

Everything seemed to fall into place for Husher, then, and a great calm fell over him. During the entire war with the Progenitors, he'd been plagued with self-doubt over whether he would be able to protect the galaxy.

And now he realized he was completely right to doubt himself.

I can't protect the galaxy. No one can. If the galaxy is going to survive, it has to protect itself. It has to want *to protect itself.*

On the tactical display, fewer than a hundred allied ships remained. Abruptly, they began to retreat, heading for the Corydalis-Baxa darkgate. Keyes had ordered them to flee, and soon he would deploy his final gambit.

Beating the Progenitors isn't about preserving galactic society so that it can one day become just. It's about becoming a good and just society so that we can *beat them.*

He doubted there was enough time to do that, with the IU's defeat already well underway. But he also knew that doubt no longer factored in. He needed to strive for what he knew was right. It was better to die striving than to take the coward's way out.

On the tactical display, both of Piper's wormhole ends collapsed, bracketing the Ixan fleet. A surge of energy washed across the system.

"It's done," Ochrim said. "We can continue on to the Progenitor dimension."

"Transition out," Husher told Noni. "But not to the Progenitor's universe. Take us home again."

CHAPTER 53

The Old Way

The *Vesta* reappeared in the Kaithian home system, well away from the warring fleets. If any enemy ships decided to transition out to attack her, then Husher would deal with them.

But he didn't believe they would. The *Vesta* had reentered the system far enough away that he would be finished broadcasting his message before it reached its first recipients, and the Progenitors would likely view the *Vesta*'s removal from the battle as an advantage not to be challenged.

And it clearly was an advantage. A simple glance at the tactical display told him that the allied fleet was losing ships at a faster rate than before—that the odds against them grew even more overwhelming with every passing second.

"Broadcast my words, and my face," he told his Coms officer. "No encryption. I don't care about preventing the enemy from listening. It's far more important that every being in the system hears, soldier and civilian alike."

"You're on, Captain Husher," Ensign Fry said.

He stared into the visual sensor below the main display, which would be the one to capture his likeness.

"As you know, I've been given command of the allied fleet," he began, "and so you may think it's my job to save you. It isn't. And yes, I'm talking to you. Whether you're a starship captain, a marine, a Python pilot, or a civilian—a father, a mother, a brother, a sister, a son, a daughter.

"Today is the first chance I've had to speak to everyone who dwells in this galaxy, and I've realized that I have to take advantage of that. The horrors of war have forced us to come together in a single system. That's a sign of our desperation, but we've been desperate for a long time. Long before the Progenitors showed up to finish us off.

"We've allowed ourselves to be reduced to animals. Frightened rabbits, to be specific: huddling together with our families and staying silent, because we're afraid to draw attention to ourselves by saying what we really think."

Husher shook his head, lips pressed tightly together. "I thought I could save this galaxy, but I can't. All I can do is try to help you understand that you need to become the sort of galaxy that saves itself.

"We've gone backward. Twenty years ago, humanity fought and defeated a corporation who'd corrupted our government and knocked down every policy designed to help the people. Now, the IU flirts with another corporation—Invigor Technologies, whose lucid tech we have to thank for losing two capital starships today. It doesn't matter whether we win or lose, if all we're going to do afterward is let our government get in bed with another corporation bent on milking us all for profit. Businesses are vital to our society, but we can't let any corporation grow its power so much that it's able to influence public policy.

"At the same time, we've let galactic society rot from the inside out. We've let resentment seep in everywhere, and I'm not just talking about the government. The only reason the IU has been able to do what it's done is because we frightened rabbits have allowed it to. We let it push policies driven by the resentment of those unwilling to take responsibility for their relative lack of success—and I say relative, because more often than not the policies I'm talking about are pushed by middle class intellectuals who have no actual interest in helping the poor. They're only interested in tearing down those above them, and the main way they try to do that is to divide everyone by group identity and attack those with identities they see as privileged.

"I happen to believe that it *is* possible for inequality to grow so much that it destabilizes a society. That happened when Darkstream perverted the democracy of the old Commonwealth. But the answer isn't to take from those who've worked hard, or even from those who've simply been fortunate. The answer is to work to lift up everyone in poverty, a rising tide that doesn't pick and choose based on identity.

"Our society's downfall isn't the government's fault. Not really. It isn't even the Progenitors' fault. It's your fault. Yours. If you deny that, then you're no better than the ones filled with resentment, who refuse to take any responsibility for their lives. This society is dying because you refused to speak up when you saw your neighbor cast low. It's because you wouldn't say anything to oppose the things you knew were wrong, the things that sprang out of a poisonous ideology.

"During this war, we've learned the true identity of the Progenitors. They are humanity, a version of humanity that let themselves fall into darkness. In their universe, Darkstream's power was never broken, and it almost destroyed them. Except, they survived the universe-shattering cataclysm that followed, and their ordeal left their souls drenched in bitterness and resentment. But the Progenitors could just as easily have turned out to be Wingers, or Tumbra, or Kaithe, or Fins, or Gok, or Quatro. In one sense, we *are* the Progenitors. All of us. Because each one of us is capable of letting resentment take over and drive our actions. Even if you think you've been doing good—even if you believe you fight for the less fortunate—you need to take a hard look at yourself. Take out your ideological lenses and ask yourself: what are my motives? Am I truly acting to help the poor, or am I letting resentment steer my ship so that I end up attacking the very people whose productivity gives us everything we love about our society? We can continue fragmenting, continue tearing each other down, and we can die. Right here, today. Or we can turn inward, confront our true motives, and then devote ourselves to what truly matters.

"For the first time, we're all gathered together in one place. That offers a unique opportunity, if we're willing to take it. As I said, I can't save you. I can't help you. Whether you live or die depends on you. I *can* tell you that you have very little time left. Stop being a frightened rabbit. Instead, become someone who stands up for themselves, for their neighbors, for their community. It's up to you. Goodbye."

Husher nodded at Fry, who cut off the broadcast.

"Nav, set a course for the Progenitor home dimension," he said. "But before we transition out, I have one last order. Everyone, take out your Oculenses."

His CIC crew looked at him wearing expressions of confusion and concern. None of them moved to comply with his order.

"How will we perform our duties?" Winterton said at last.

"The old way. This CIC's main display *was* designed so that it retains all the old viewscreen functionality from older warships, was it not?"

"Yes..." Winterton answered.

"And your consoles are able to revert to the old mode as well."

"They are, Captain."

"Then that's how we'll control this ship. Not by each of us peering at something different, but with all of us seeing the same thing. We'll all see the same reality. And we'll contend with it together." Another pause. "I gave an order, people."

Slowly, each CIC officer reached into their eyes and plucked out their Oculenses, most placing them on consoles, though Tremaine dropped his onto the deck. Husher did the same—he used his thumb and forefinger to pinch the Oculens in his right eye so that it buckled, allowing him to remove it. Then he did the same for the left, and cast both to the deck.

Nodding to himself, he glanced at Chief Noni. "Take us out, Nav."

CHAPTER 54

A Proper Talking-To

The crowd had almost managed to upend the truck whose bed Wanda cowered inside. To prevent it, her security detail had had to disobey her order not to shoot their guns. They fired them into the air, and the staccato reports seemed to have some effect on the mob. The rioters drew back briefly, before regrouping and pressing forward. Gunshots sounded in the distance, too, and that only seemed to agitate them further. Soon, the truck was rocking back and forth again, as the rioters seemed to realize that the guards protecting it weren't going to shoot them.

Wanda clutched her robe tightly around her. She'd become convinced that soon, she would be in the hands of the mob. *I need to make peace with it,* she told herself, but she couldn't stop her imagination from speculating wildly about what they might do to her once they had her.

"Stop this," a magnified voice rang out. At first, the crowd didn't react, and its members continued attacking the truck. Fingertips brushed Wanda's side, and she recoiled, screaming.

"I said stop, or we will stop you," the voice said again, and the pounding and thumping and shoving seemed to lessen.

"You've done enough damage," the voice said. "More than enough. And the rest of us have sat back and watched you throw your tantrums for too long. Leave that poor woman be."

Gathering her courage, Wanda did what might have been the bravest thing she'd ever done: she stood up.

Another crowd surrounded the mob pressed against her truck—one that encircled the mob completely, dwarfing it in number, many times over. It had members of just as many species in it: all of the Union species, and some Gok as well.

Wanda's eyes fell on the woman holding the bullhorn, just as she spoke again. "Ma'am, my name is Cath Morrissey, and we all owe you a big apology. It might seem like everyone's against you, lately, but they're not. Most of us are with you. We're just scared. Scared of being called out by these maniacs. Scared of being accused of prejudice, scared of being singled out for even mentioning the crazy things we see people doing every day. Scared of losing our jobs, and our voices, because we've seen others lose theirs.

"But if we stick together, and we decide to stop letting this happen, then no one has to be torn down by them again." Morrissey gestured at the mob around the truck, which had stopped their agitating altogether. Most of them now looked pretty nervous. "Their view of the world is ass-backward, and we've always known it, but we've let them overrun everything that makes this galaxy worth living in. Well, we're not scared anymore. We just got a proper talking-to from that Captain Husher, and I think we're finally ready to step up and speak for the things we should have been speaking for all along. Get away from that truck, you lot, or we'll drag you away from it. While you're at it, why don't you grow the hell up?"

The silence that followed held sway for a long moment, and Wanda was afraid of how the mob might react. Would they take her hostage? Would someone else pull a gun?

But at last, the mob around the truck began to slink away. The encircling crowd parted to let them pass.

Then, Cath Morrissey was at the back of the truck, hand extended to help Wanda down. She took it.

"Thank you," Wanda said.

"No thanks necessary. I bet you'd have done the same for me, and someday, maybe you'll have to. It's high time we all started watching out for each other, instead of tearing each other down. It's time we started taking some risks again, and using our voices. The galaxy's changed, sure, but it hasn't changed so much that we're gonna let tyrants like those push us around any more."

Wanda nodded, but stopped herself. "I—I think I might have been one of those tyrants, actually. Until very recently. At the very least, I cheered them on."

"Well at least you're seeing clearer now. I hope you are, anyway."

"I think I am."

Morrissey smiled. "No need to write anyone off, then. Not nearly as quickly as we have been writing them off, anyway. Everyone has something to contribute, provided they can get out of their own way to contribute it."

"Agreed."

Morrissey stuck out her hand, and Wanda shook it.

CHAPTER 55

Orbital Fortress

The *Vesta* transitioned inside of a dense asteroid belt.

"Any immediate threats, Winterton?" Husher said. "Or signs our arrival was detected?"

"Not yet, Captain," Winterton said, his tone betraying his confusion.

"What do you see?"

"Sensor data is still populating, but...sir, what I have so far is very odd."

"Tell me."

"Just beyond the asteroid belt, space seems to just...end. There are no visible stars beyond it. There doesn't seem to be anything there." Winterton squinted at his console, frowning. "An asteroid just connected with the barrier and was vaporized. I'm tracking another on a similar course. Should I...?"

Husher nodded. "Put a zoomed-in visual on the viewscreen." What his sensor operator described was consistent with Sato's account of the state of her universe. He hadn't distributed that intel very widely. The fewer people knew, the less likely it would be for the Progenitors to find out what he knew.

Winterton did as instructed, and when the asteroid connected with what seemed to be the border of space, it disintegrated, sending blue ripples of energy spreading from the point of impact.

"Its properties seem similar to the forcefield Teth erected around Klaxon's moon," Winterton said. "But that's not all."

"What else?"

"Sir, this system...it's the Sol System."

Husher squinted at the tactical display he'd called up on his console, which showed the system's planets in their slow, majestic orbits around a familiar-looking sun. *Humanity's home, burgeoning with life. Unlike the version of it that the Ixa scoured clean.*

At the Nav station, Noni twisted to face him. "Sir, should I reinspect our interdimensional trajectory for anomalies?"

"No. This is all consistent with intel you haven't had access to. Set a course down-system. Send it to Helm the moment you have it."

"Aye."

At his console, Winterton tensed. "Captain, the surfaces of several surrounding asteroids are opening to reveal mounted guns. They're firing on us—kinetic impactors."

That, I didn't anticipate. "Helm, punch it," he barked. "Full ahead. Noni, adjust your course so that it avoids the densest regions of the asteroid belt."

"More asteroids opening, sir," Winterton said. "They're deploying missiles as well as impactors. The computer's detected ninety-three missiles already in play."

"Coms, have Commander Ayam scramble the entire Air Group. They're on missile defense until further notice."

"Yes, Captain."

On the tactical display, Pythons streamed out of their launch tubes, moving immediately to engage the incoming ordnance. Winterton was still staring intently at his console, as well he might be. But Husher sensed there was something there that amounted to more than the usual situational awareness. "Do you have something for me, Ensign?"

Before answering, the sensor operator tapped at his console a couple of times, as though finishing off a calculation. "I think so, sir. Using gravimetric analysis, I can tell which asteroids have been modified and which are still in their natural state. The weapon-mounted asteroids have a distinct profile, but there are many other asteroids scattered throughout the belt that appear to have been hollowed out, and their innards replaced with artificial constructs."

"I see." It made perfect sense to Husher, in fact, and if the weaponized asteroids hadn't been confirmation enough that they were in the Progenitors' home dimension, then the ones hollowed out for nonmilitary purposes did seem to confirm it.

He'd seen something similar down Pirate's Path, months before the start of the Second Galactic War. Back then, pirates had been using hollowed-out asteroids to conceal shipbuilding facilities. But if the Progenitor universe was down to one system thanks to their misuse of dark tech, then they would have had to get creative in order to sustain themselves. Those asteroids were more likely to contain hydroponic farms than shipbuilding facilities, especially given how large Progenitor ships tended to be.

A tremor ran through the *Vesta*. Then another.

"We're taking hits, sir," Winterton said, though Husher had already figured that out.

"Ensign, I want you to have the computer use the gravimetric data to compile a map of every asteroid likely to contain automated weapons, then send that map to Chief Noni. Send a copy to Chief Tremaine as well, and to Ensign Fry, for forwarding to our entire Air Group."

"I will, sir." The sensor operator bent to his work.

"Noni, once you have that map, use it to inform our course out of the belt. That done, send the course over to Tactical as well as Helm. Tremaine, prepare to launch Banshees in groups of three at any weaponized asteroid you deem likely to threaten us along the course Noni sends you. Monitor our missiles' success, and be ready to follow up with kinetic impactors if necessary. It often won't be, I think. The asteroids aren't likely to have point defense systems of any kind. Assuming they've been programmed to try to defend themselves at all, each asteroid will have to use its only gun to pick off our Banshees one-by-one, which I doubt will prove very effective."

With the computer's assistance, Winterton soon completed his map, as Husher had known he would. That changed everything about their passage through what Husher had begun to think of as the Kuiper Belt.

His analysis of the asteroids' lack of defenses proved out, and by proactively targeting any asteroids well-positioned to damage the *Vesta*, they reduced them from existential threats to minor annoyances.

That taken care of, Husher turned his attention to collecting intel as they neared the belt's inner edge. "Winterton, what can you tell me about the system's planets? I'm particularly interested in their defenses, along with whatever you can give me about how heavily settled they are."

Winterton's hands hovered over his console, tapping and sliding assets as he shuffled information. "Heavy colonization all across the system, sir," he said. "Most of Jupiter's moons show signs of terraforming and settlement. All of the settled moons have formidable-looking orbital defense platforms. Cursory visual analysis suggests the platforms have guns capable of firing down as well as up."

"Ah. They're prepared to defend against ships with interdimensional capabilities." *Ships like theirs. Ships like the* Vesta, *too.* "What about the other planets?"

"Very similar. Even Venus appears colonized, with heat-shielded balloon colonies floating in the thick CO_2 atmosphere. It also has its own defense platforms."

"And Earth?"

"It looks about as populated as you'd expect it to be, if it hadn't been destroyed in our universe twenty years ago. The planet's temperature seems to have risen considerably. Heavy fortifications, part of which appears to be an orbital station that dwarfs every other artificial construct in the galaxy."

"Put a zoomed-in visual of that station on the viewscreen."

"Aye."

Husher studied it for several long moments. *It has the look of a fortress.* "Any other artificial structures in the system?"

"Various space stations and orbital facilities. There are also at least four large constructs in close heliocentric orbit. Their form is unlike anything I'm familiar with, but if they have any computerized systems aboard then they must also have massive cooling systems, that close to the sun."

As Husher considered the meaning of what Winterton had told him, he caught himself drumming his fingers against his seat's armrest, and stopped.

They left the asteroid belt at last, and Winterton spoke again: "A sizable battle group is moving out from Earth orbit on an intercept course. Seven destroyers and eleven carriers."

Husher knew who would be in command of that battle group: *he* would. Or at least, a darker version of himself.

Still, it *was* himself. Yes, what the Progenitor Lisa Sato had told him about this Husher had made his stomach churn and cost him sleep. It had haunted him, refusing to leave him alone until he took a hard look, deep inside himself.

How could any version of Vin Husher do the things this Husher has done? What would cause me to act so ruthlessly?

He thought he knew the answer. And soon, he would have the opportunity to test his theory.

"Coms, get me Commander Ayam."

CHAPTER 56

Warpath

"We're getting a transmission request, sir," Ensign Fry said. "It's from the destroyer that appears to be serving as their flagship."

"Accept, and put it on the viewscreen. I want a split-screen: the transmission on the left and a tactical display on the right, focused on the approaching ships."

"Aye, sir."

The fact that there were only eighteen defending ships meant Husher's greatest hope had been realized: the Progenitors had sent almost everything they had to attack Home. In fact, he'd considered this the most likely scenario. After Fesky's appearance here, they would have been motivated to stamp out the IU as quickly as possible, before a viable attack on this dimension could be marshaled.

And the *Vesta* was that attack—almost certainly the only attack the Milky Way would ever launch against the Progenitor system. Whether it was viable or not would be determined over the next handful of hours.

Husher's own face appeared on the part of the viewscreen he'd designated for the transmission. Even though he'd tried to prepare himself for this moment as best could, he now realized that nothing could have prepared him.

An angry scar divided his face, running from temple to chin, and the corner of his mouth was misshapen as a result. Even more disturbing was the man's gaze: colder and more hollow than Husher could have imagined possible, even during his most personal, most doubt-filled moments of staring into the mirror.

"I'm genuinely shocked," the other Husher said.

"Are you?" Husher said, managing to moderate his tone so he sounded only mildly interested.

"I'm shocked you'd abandon your galaxy to come here, at the very moment it's about to fall. I honestly didn't expect it, and I *am* you. So congratulations on that. It's obviously futile for you to come here, of course. Your lone ship can't challenge our defenses. But you have surprised me, even if you did it by exhibiting incredible stupidity."

"I'm betting it won't be the first time you surprise yourself today." He motioned to his Coms officer to cut the transmission. "All ahead, Helm."

"Aye, sir."

Given the *Vesta*'s present course, "all ahead" would take them straight at the enemy's right flank. Some might have called that a dangerous maneuver, when faced with eighteen warships, seven of which wielded particle beams.

"Tremaine, open with our missile barrage."

"Yes, sir."

A great wave of Banshees, Gorgons, and the remaining Hydras left the *Vesta*, spreading out as they screamed across the void toward the flank the supercarrier was already barreling toward.

"Coms, tell Ayam to scramble Pythons."

"Aye."

The deadly starfighters leapt from their launch tubes, hard on the missiles' heels, ready to engage whatever the missiles failed to clear away. Ayam's subspace squadron disappeared from the tactical display, adding even more menace to the attack.

As the parade of missiles, fighters, and supercarrier reached the targeted flank, Progenitor ships began to vanish, transitioning out of this dimension to avoid getting hit. Then, at the *Vesta*'s top speed, Husher gave another order: "Coms, tell Major Gamble that he is clear to launch."

"Aye."

Seconds later, a host of shuttles surged from the *Vesta*, surrounded by dozens of mechs.

The last of the Progenitor ships was now transitioning out of the universe to remove themselves from the missiles' and Pythons' warpath. "Transmit the deactivation signal to our missiles," Husher said, eyes on Ensign Fry.

"Doing so now, sir."

The Air Group sailed past the enemy formation without attempting to engage them, and the shuttles' and mechs' greater speed soon allowed them to catch up with the Pythons. As for the missiles, they would sail on, their destructive power neutralized. Husher hadn't wanted to risk the missiles hitting this version of Earth, even if the version of humanity it housed had allowed all this to happen. He also hadn't wanted to destroy the great space station that orbited the planet. The station where he expected his marines would find his old friend.

"The enemy ships that didn't transition out are overreacting, just as you predicted, Captain," Winterton said. "I think they've realized we never planned to actually engage them."

"What are they sending at us?"

"Particle beams, though they're unlikely to be able to focus them properly, given our speed. They have however already launched nearly a thousand Ravagers, along an arc wide enough to intercept us, even if we accelerate. A few more Progenitor ships have transitioned out."

Husher nodded. He'd expected that, too. They would likely try to intercept the shuttles carrying *Vesta* marines, which was why he'd sent his entire Air Group as escort.

"Let's see how the Progenitors like being made to waste massive amounts of ordnance," he said. "Noni, transition us out."

CHAPTER 57

Merging

A destroyer and two carriers appeared directly in the marine shuttles' path, in an attempt to stop them from reaching the huge station orbiting the Progenitor version of Earth.

But Captain Husher had anticipated it. Ayam's subspace squadron dropped back into realspace to execute a drive-by alpha strike on the destroyer before transitioning out again. The missiles slammed into the ship's hull, and then the rest of the Air Group began descending on all three ships, squadron by squadron, heedless of the Ravagers and point defense fire tearing them up.

Jake had rarely beheld such a willingness to die in battle, and it reaffirmed for him what he'd already realized: everyone who'd come with Husher to the Progenitor's home system had known they were embarking on a suicide mission. Clearly, they'd embraced that fact. At least, these Python pilots had. They fell by the dozens, but they were getting the job done, one way or another.

Even from inside his alien mech, Jake felt a strange and uncomfortable kinship with the dying pilots. In some real sense, he *was* them, and as they died, so did parts of him.

This was something he'd been contending with since the *Vesta* had arrived in the Kaithian home system. He began to feel like humanity wasn't just his species, but his soul. And after Husher's speech to everyone who'd gathered together in that system, Jake had even begun to identify with the IU as a whole, despite their corruption and folly.

I guess this is exactly how you want to feel, when the chips are down. Each fighter wasn't just part of the whole, they *were* the whole, and they fought hard for base survival.

When he drew near enough, Jake formed his arms into a single, massive energy cannon and began blasting away at the hull of the nearest carrier. Moments later, the rest of Oneiri Force added their fire.

At last, the destroyer exploded, flinging shrapnel in all directions. Then so did both carriers, all in quick succession. The ensuing shrapnel took out a few more Pythons, along with two shuttles and even a MIMAS.

But they were through.

Jake kept the energy cannon intact, and several minutes later he drew close enough to the station to use it. He blasted away at the broad hull on approach, working to open an area large enough for the shuttles and the mechs to pour in.

But the station wasn't taking this lying down. Dozens upon dozens of point defense turrets blazed all across its surface, and lasers flashed from myriad projectors. The remainder of the

Vesta's Air Group engaged them all, destroying as many as they could while providing cover for the massive boarding party. Husher had held three marine platoons back to guard against any Ravagers that penetrated his supercarrier's hull. The rest were on shuttles about to enter this station.

Jake hit the station's deck running. He was inside what looked to be a cavernous, multi-tiered storage bay, with elevators, escalators, and floor-crawlers hauling freight up and down and across the station's various levels.

Gunfire followed that realization: turrets directing high-velocity rounds at his mech, and pressure-suited human and Ixan soldiers sending all manner of ordnance from positions on multiple levels. Assault rifle fire, sniper fire, rockets, grenades—Jake sprinted to the left to escape the heat, fearful of his mech getting compromised, despite its extreme durability.

MIMAS mechs started entering the station through the opening Jake had created, and right away three were neutralized by the concentrated enemy fire.

Jake dove behind a stack of sturdy-looking metal crates, turning to level his energy cannon at the interior bulkhead of the station's hull. Several energy blasts later, he'd created a second point of ingress. That done, he got on a wide channel: "I want half of you to start coming through the breach I just made. The enemy's giving us hell, and we need to start establishing a position."

As he finished the transmission, he split the single energy cannon into two and sprang from hiding, aiming at two targets at once and opening fire. He swept the cannons across multiple hostiles.

Two more Oneiri mechs went down, but Jake's covering fire allowed several more to reach the deck and run to safety behind crates, vehicles, terminals, and whatever other cover the huge facility had to offer.

Finally, the tide of battle began to turn. As Oneiri Force established a foothold, the marines began to arrive, their shuttles' outer airlocks already open. *Vesta* marines in pressure suits leapt out, rushing to the combat shuttle's fold-out barriers and increasing the pressure on the enemy.

At last, they neutralized enough enemy soldiers to gain some breathing room. "I'm sure they'll send more at us," Jake said to Major Gamble over a two-way channel. The major was positioned behind a barrier two shuttles over, peering through a sniper scope and scanning the station's levels for more targets. "Can I make a suggestion, Major?"

"Please do."

"We need to get out of this storage area. We're way too vulnerable here. If you and your marines take a couple freight elevators, we can start using them to deploy to different levels and find a way deeper into the station."

Gamble tilted his head to one side. "We'll be even more vulnerable inside the elevators."

"That's where my mechs come in. We'll rocket from level to level and cover you."

"All right. I like it. We'd better start moving—I'm sure you're right that more company is on the way."

The prediction soon proved out: enemy fire picked up a few seconds after the first marines piled into an elevator, Gamble among them.

A rocket sailed toward the elevator from one of the upper levels, but Jake managed to pick it off well before it reached its target. He jumped on an Oneiri-wide channel: "We need to make sure no explosive ordnance makes it to those elevators while marines are inside. Make good use of the mech dream, people. Listen to it like I've been training you to listen. Do that, and you'll be shooting grenades out of the air with ease."

The remaining thirty-one MIMAS mechs performed admirably, though Jake, Ash, Rug, and Maura did most of the work. Even with all the drama they'd suffered through recently, they still operated as a seamless unit, with each pilot's strengths compensating for the weaknesses of the next.

At last, they located two entrances that appeared to lead deeper into the station, separated by several levels from each other.

"We'll split up," Gamble said. "Cut down on our chances of going the wrong way. We're not long on time."

"Sounds good, Major."

"I want you to take half the battalion with you, under your direct command. I'll take the other."

"Acknowledged, Major. God speed."

"And you."

The station's corridors were broad and tall, larger than any Jake had seen inside a space-based structure. It gave his forces lots of room to spread out, but it also gave the station defenders plenty of attack angles. Each intersection was a potential battle, and as they fought through the station, most of the time that potential was realized.

Jake charged in with his mechs first, engaging the defenders with as much shock and awe as they could bring to bear. Then the marines would charge in, to plug the gaps.

The approach worked well. For a time.

As he charged into yet another intersection, the world went black, as though every one of the station's lights had blown out at once.

He felt himself crash to his knees, felt the gunfire that peppered his mech's skin. Ash's voice came through the dream: "Jake, what's going on?"

Then even her voice was gone, along with the sensation of the metal deck beneath him. The din of battle faded to nothing.

You will yield to me, came the whispers. *Here, in my homeland, you will yield. You have refused to merge willingly, and so you will be enslaved.*

"No," Jake said, but with a creeping horror, he realized that the process had already begun. He felt his mind and nervous system being probed, scanned. It took only a few seconds, and when it finished, he began to dissolve.

"No!" he screamed, even as his fingertips were eaten away by whatever acidic solution the mech had deployed.

With a titanic effort of will, he made reality slam back into place, and he forced the mech to surge to his feet. All around him, marines and mechs were cleaning up the defending force that had attempted to outflank them using the intersection.

"Let's go!" Jake yelled over a wide channel. "We have to go now!"

Both his arms became broadswords, and relying on only his instincts and internal compass, he began charging through the station. Someone stumbled out of a hatch a couple meters ahead of him, and Jake cleaved him in two without thinking to check whether he was armed or not.

Desperation drove him. Nothing could impede him before he reached his goal.

Before he reached Lisa.

At the next intersection, the defenders attempted the same pincering tactic, just with more firepower. Jake threw himself into a roll, though he wasn't able to avoid all the gunfire, and it bit into his shifting metal flesh. Then he was through the intersection, barreling through the ranks trying to hold this corridor. Broadswords flashed in the overhead halogens, and blood sprayed. He cut a swath through the defenders and continued on, their bullets eating into his back. The pain was immense, but when a bullet dug deep enough to enter his human body's back, he barely felt it at all.

Relinquish your human form, the mech commanded. *It is done.*

And so it was. Jake's hands had dissolved past the wrists, now, leaving only the nerve endings. His feet and ankles were gone, too. The merging process showed no sign of stopping.

His mad charge brought him to what had to be the center of the station, based on the data the mech had compiled on his trajectory since entering it.

A hatch bigger than any he'd seen greeted him at the end of the corridor, and he blasted it open with energy cannons.

Inside, he found a cavernous chamber whose ceiling wasn't visible through the dimness overhead. Only the floor was lit, though Jake couldn't see any lights. Such a chamber seemed odd aboard an orbital station, especially since its only purpose was apparently to house the single chair in its very center.

Strapped to that chair was a Winger, though barely recognizable as one. Blood stained the wings, which looked tattered and flayed open in parts. As Jake drew closer, he saw that the Winger's beak was cracked, and that several of its talons had been sheared off.

"Commander Fesky," he said, standing over her. She was trembling.

Her eyes locked onto his mech's face, with a fervor that took him aback. "I said nothing," she said, her voice a faint rasp. "I said nothing."

"I'll take you out," he replied, converting his energy cannons into thin blades. She winced away as he lowered them to flick apart the straps binding her. He wanted to tell her that his mech was consuming him. He wanted to tell *someone.* But he barely dared to speak to Fesky at all, in her current condition. She looked as though an errant breeze would break her.

According to what she'd just said, though, she *hadn't* broken.

Jake carried Fesky out into the corridor, with her nestled in one arm while he used the other in energy-cannon form, blasting apart hatches one by one.

At last, he found the one he was looking for. It led to a single chamber, which was divided in half by metal bars. On the other side of the bars, dozens of prisoners were being held. Most species were represented—humans, Kaithe, Wingers, and even a Quatro that looked just like the Eldest. The chamber's temperature was that of a sauna, and it took a moment for him to grasp the purpose: to prevent the Quatro from using its superconducting ability to bend the bars.

Then, Jake's gaze fell on her. Lisa Sato sat with her back against the wall, eyes wide and unfocused.

"Lisa," he called. She didn't respond.

Anger flooded him, and adrenaline, and he set Fesky down to grip a pair of metal bars, wrenching them apart. They buckled outward, and he stepped back to allow the prisoners to start climbing out.

"Take her with you," he commanded, pointing at Lisa. A Winger bent to scoop her into its arms.

As rage continued to course through him, Jake noticed something else: the merging process had stopped. He'd regained control of the mech, it seemed, though it had cost him dearly.

CHAPTER 58

Ordnance in Play

The *Vesta* reemerged into the Progenitor home system, at the coordinates Husher had judged most likely to yield results: near Earth's hulking orbital station.

As he'd expected, the enemy ships had displaced themselves to engage the Pythons attacking the station, which was clearly important to the system's defense—probably to the entire Progenitor military.

"Missiles, Tremaine," Husher said.

The Tactical officer nodded, then executed the sequence that would launch the barrage they'd already discussed: mostly Banshees, though Gorgons were overrepresented.

He hadn't bothered ordering his Tactical officer to calculate firing solutions that avoided the orbital station. In fact, many of the missiles *would* hit it, if they missed their initial targets and were allowed to continue on.

But Husher was counting on the station being important enough that the Progenitors wouldn't allow it to be hit.

On the tactical display, he watched as his gamble quickly paid off: the enemy seemed to realize just how many stealth missiles he'd included in the barrage, and twelve of the fifteen remaining Progenitor ships converged on them, attempting to neutralize the Banshees while combing space with their sensors to locate and destroy the Gorgons.

Husher permitted himself a smile. *No transitioning out to dodge my missiles this time. Not with your most valuable asset behind you.* "Tremaine, sweep them with kinetic impactors."

"Aye, Captain."

A slight tremor ran through the *Vesta* as every forward gun opened up, spraying kinetic impactors across the battle space.

Ravagers poured hastily from launch tubes, but there was too much ordnance in play, along too many randomized trajectories.

Explosions soon lit up enemy hulls, and moments later, they began to appear on the station behind as well.

A carrier exploded, followed by another, then a destroyer.

"Follow up with our primary laser. Direct it at the closest carrier." *No need to conserve capacitor charge. We won't be transitioning out again.* Husher tapped his console to indicate the ship he meant on the main viewscreen, since he could no longer share an Oculens overlay with his Tactical officer.

"Firing primary," Tremaine said, and seconds later, the immense energy transfer ripped apart the carrier in question.

The three enemy warships who hadn't moved to clean up missiles—two destroyers and a carrier—had already transitioned out, and now they appeared behind the *Vesta*, unleashing a missile barrage of their own as both destroyers targeted the supercarrier with particle beams.

"Helm, activate starboard thrusters at full power," Husher ordered. "Coms, call three Python squadrons off the station."

Even with those squadrons backing them up, Husher wasn't confident they would survive the next attack. Most of the Air Group had been destroyed since attacking the station. There were barely two hundred fighters left. Destroying four enemy ships in one fell swoop had been gratifying, but he'd known it couldn't last.

An explosion rocked the *Vesta*, jostling Husher violently in his seat. "Damage report."

"Particle beam just blew out a secondary engine, sir," Winterton said.

Another explosion. "That was a main battery of point defense turrets. They blew inward, killing at least five crew."

Husher stared bleakly at the Tactical display. *We just need to hold on a little longer.* But he wasn't sure they could.

"Tremaine, let's use up the rest of our Banshees. For starters, lob them at the ships targeting us with particle beams—see does that throw them off."

"Aye," the Tactical officer said, though he didn't sound hopeful.

Husher's eyes were glued to the tactical display shown by his console, which wasn't limited to the immediate engagement. Instead, it showed an expanded view of the entire system.

"The enemy is targeting our starboard main reactor, sir."

"Spin us around, Helm. Coms, order that reactor shut down as fast as safely possible."

"Aye, Captain."

Then, Husher saw it: thirteen icons appeared on his display at the center of the system, near the sun. They were speeding toward one of the four strange structures Winterton had identified during their initial trip down-system.

He made it in time. Ayam made it.

A wave of missiles poured out of that structure, toward the subspace-capable Python squadron, but they transitioned out at the last second.

When they transitioned back in, another wave of missiles was there to greet them, and they lost a fighter before they could transition out again.

With their third appearance, they delivered an alpha strike, which connected solidly with the structure. It burst apart.

The forcefield surrounding the system lurched inward, swallowing the Kuiper Belt whole.

CHAPTER 59

Alpha Strike in Parting

"Transmission request incoming, Captain," Ensign Fry said.

Husher nodded. "Put it on the main screen."

His double appeared, his face flushed with rage, which didn't come as a surprise. If Husher was right about what the hollowed-out asteroids in the Kuiper Belt had contained, then he'd likely just taken out the majority of the system's agricultural base. Clearly, the Progenitors were capable of bringing in resources from other dimensions, but coming up with a replacement for a food system designed to feed billions was hard to do on short notice.

"What in Sol are you doing?" the other Husher demanded. "You'll kill us all. All of your people will die!"

"And yours." On the tactical display, Husher saw that Ayam and his fighters were already engaging the second forcefield generator, weaving in and out of reality to dodge the missiles it deployed. "As for my people, they're soldiers, and they knew they would likely die here."

His double's scar had turned an angry red, much redder than the rest of his face. On the tactical display, Husher noticed three destroyers and two carriers disappear, and he felt like he had a pretty good idea where they were headed. "What about the civilians aboard your ship?" his double said. "I know they're there. My intel is extensive."

"Not extensive enough. I offloaded the population of Cybele before I left the Kaithian system."

Other Husher's lips peeled back, baring his teeth. "Quit trying to bluff me, all right? You went to a lot of trouble to get your forces to Ragnarok Station, and I know it's because you expect to find prisoners there. Besides, this system is littered with civilians, too. Earth alone has twelve billion of them. You're not about to let them die."

The second generator exploded, and the forcefield contracted again, eating Pluto, Neptune, Uranus, and Saturn.

The color was beginning to drain from other Husher's face, now. "You just killed millions of humans."

"Then my soul is blackened by it," Husher said, surprised at how cold and bitter his own voice sounded. "But I will kill billions more. Yes, I sent forces to your station—because I always play to the best possible outcome, and if we win here, then I'll take those prisoners home. But I always prepare for the worst outcome, too. Let me tell you the worst outcome I'm willing to tolerate, since apparently you don't already know. You've killed hundreds of billions of my people, and I include all Union species in that. You've forced the survivors to flee their homes, and even now, your forces attack them with the aim to exterminate. Yes, my soul is blackened. But you forced my hand, you bastard, and I'll annihilate this wretched system before I'll ever stand by while you murder my society—my family."

As Ayam's fighters neared the third generator, five Progenitor ships appeared in their path, just a handful of kilometers out from the structure. They unleashed everything they had at the incoming Pythons, but the fighters simply dropped back into subspace.

Even so, the Progenitors had left as little space between them and the generator as possible: not enough for Ayam to pop in and destroy it. Not at the speed they were traveling at.

Husher held his breath until the subspace squadron reentered realspace once more...*beyond* the generator. The instant they returned, they loosed their alpha strike in parting.

Their timing was immaculate. They'd fired their missiles too close-in to the generator for the five Progenitor ships to react. The precision of Ayam and his pilots was such that the resulting explosion came close to engulfing their fighters.

The system's forcefield collapsed down until the border of this universe lay a couple light seconds away, just outside Earth's orbit.

"Please," the other Husher said. "Please. My son is on Earth."

Husher grimaced, his stomach churning as he paused to contemplate what twisted creature this version of himself might have produced as a son.

Then, he nodded at his Coms officer—the signal for her to send Ayam the order to hold.

Turning back to his double, he said, "Fifteen minutes. That's how long you have to call your ships here and have their crews abandon them. You will all present yourselves on the *Vesta*'s Flight Deck Epsilon, where you'll turn yourselves over to my custody. If you haven't vacated your ships within fifteen minutes, you will die, since that's when I intend to burn them from space."

"It'll be done."

"I suggest you hurry."

CHAPTER 60

Old Friend

Husher strode onto Flight Deck Epsilon. At his back were all three marine platoons who'd remained on the *Vesta*.

Normally he did his best to dodge marine escorts, but with the thousands and thousands of enemy prisoners now arriving on his ship, he wasn't going to take any chances.

Thankfully, Major Gamble and the rest of what remained of the *Vesta* marine battalion was returning at the same time. That was good. They'd need all hands on deck in order to properly search their new prisoners, escort them to Cybele, and figure out where to put them.

Before long, Husher came face to face with himself, the other's scar the only feature to distinguish them for others, apart from their uniforms. He wondered whether even the man's soulless stare might not be reflected in his own face, after what had happened with the forcefield—after what he'd done.

Millions of civilians, gone. History won't look kindly on me for that. He doubted the IU would, either. He'd followed the only path to victory open to him. His choice had been between allowing the Progenitors to win and doing what he'd done.

Even so, his mind reeled at it, trying to disassociate itself from his actions. He told himself that if the Progenitors had been allowed to win, they would have gone on to wreak untold carnage, not only in his native universe but across the multiverse as well.

What if my government goes on to wreak similar carnage? I must not allow that, either. I must use whatever influence I have left to prevent it.

He reminded himself of Ochrim, in that moment, whose reasoning he had once denounced. Husher had just killed millions to save billions—possibly trillions or more, if you counted what the Progenitors would surely have gone on to do.

Even so, the blood on his hands was no less red.

"Are you going to say anything?" his double asked.

Husher realized he'd allowed himself to become lost in thought while staring vacantly at his double's face. "I expect full cooperation from you and your people," he said at last. "I can return to this system at any time to destroy the last generator. Never forget that, and never doubt my willingness to do it if you push me."

The other Husher gave a curt nod, adding nothing else.

Husher continued: "For now, we're taking you back to the Kaithian home system, where you will order your forces to stand—"

"You'll need me to deactivate the AIs," his double broke in.

Husher narrowed his eyes. "You can do that?"

"I can, using the kill codes."

"Why would they give you kill codes for AIs in a universe you've never been to?"

"As a last line of defense," the other Husher said. "The AIs were programmed never to interface with technology that allowed travel between the dimensions, but in the event they managed to circumvent that programming and travel here, my orders were to broadcast the kill codes and shut them down."

"Right." Husher shook his head. "The AIs you set loose on us are what brought your side such success. I still don't get why you're this eager to deactivate them."

His double's eyes locked onto his, burning with a mix of anger and frustration. "Don't you get it? I *have* to deactivate them. I expect to be a prisoner going forward, meaning I won't be here to protect what you've left of this system. If I don't stop them, there's a chance they'll make it here someday, to threaten my son or his children. I won't allow that. Besides, I also expect you'll take me to your dimension, and if that's the case then I have just as much incentive to stop them as you do. No one is safe sharing a universe with superintelligences, not even their creators. Why do you think all of our warships are crewed by Ixa? Other than a few select agents, most Progenitors have avoided your universe at all costs."

Slowly, Husher nodded. "Okay."

"I'll provide you with their locations throughout your local galactic cluster."

"Very well. What about the ships you sent against us—were they built in this system?"

The double frowned. "No. They were constructed in facilities also scattered across your galactic cluster."

"Then were they installed with deactivations codes, too? Surely you have little trust for the Ixa."

A pause. Then: "Yes. Individual codes, as well as a master code."

"Give me the master code. I intend to broadcast it the moment we return to the Kaithian home system. If it doesn't work, I won't consult you about it. I'll just return here and finish destroying this system. So do not lie, and do not make a mistake as you recite it."

At that moment, Jake Price's mech rocketed down from an airlock overhead, landing beside the two Hushers.

Husher expected some pithy remark, but Price gave none. Instead, he lifted a great metal hand to indicate a shuttle that was touching down fifty meters off.

"There's someone you may want to see."

Price's mech opened up, then, its front extending to the floor as a ramp. Price tumbled out of the tight cockpit, trailing blood all down the ramp until he came to a stop on the deck.

Husher's eyes went wide. Past the elbows, the petty officer's arms no longer existed, and his legs were gone past the knees. The wounds looked partially cauterized, but he was still bleeding profusely. A patch of blood was spreading across his back, as well.

"Medic!" Husher barked.

Soon, Price was surrounded by medical personnel, who worked to staunch the bleeding and to stabilize him.

Before they took Price to sick bay, Husher bent down toward him where he lay on the collapsible gurney.

"Good work, son," he said.

Price's eyes fluttered open, which Husher hadn't been expecting. He spoke, but his voice was too weak to hear, so Husher bent lower.

"Launch my mech into the sun," Price rasped.

Slowly, Husher nodded. Then the medics took the petty officer away.

When he turned, he came face to face with Fesky, who was flanked by two more medics supporting her.

"Old friend," Husher said softly, approaching to embrace her. But as he neared, Fesky flinched away.

Turning slowly, Husher's gaze locked onto his double's. "What did you do to her?"

The other Husher's expression didn't change, but Husher thought he detected satisfaction lurking beneath it—satisfaction at the deep bond he'd managed to destroy.

"You'd better get back to your galaxy, Captain," the other Husher said, "while there's something left to return to."

CHAPTER 61

The Moment I Return

The IGS *Vesta* transitioned back into the Milky Way. As close to Home as they could get.

Husher turned to the tactical display. As expected, most of the Progenitor ships still clustered around the planet.

But that was where reality stopped conforming with his expectations.

"Winterton," he said. "Are you seeing what I'm seeing?"

"I believe so, sir," the sensor operator said, his tone one of wonder.

The attacking Progenitor fleet had taken heavy losses…but the defending forces had taken far fewer than he'd expected, having regrouped around Home in tight formations. And, apparently, having given the enemy absolute hell.

Ek spoke up. "While the allied fleet's performance is remarkable, the Progenitors still have far greater numbers. If the battle is allowed to progress, our fleet will surely fall."

Husher shook his head, feeling slightly annoyed at the Fin's analysis. "The fact we came back to find the allied fleet intact at all is a near miracle."

But then, as though to underscore Ek's words, Husher witnessed the destruction of three IGF destroyers, in quick succession. A Quatro warship followed seconds later, then another, and then a Gok missile cruiser.

"Broadcast the code," Husher ordered.

"Aye, sir," Ensign Amy Fry replied.

He'd ordered the *Vesta* to transition as close to the planet as possible, which he'd expected would shut down the most enemy ships the quickest.

He was right. The *Vesta*'s broadcast spread throughout the system, and enemy ships stopped shooting, stopped maneuvering. They drifted along their previous courses instead, and Husher saw that there was now a risk of collisions between the Progenitor ships and allied ships—or worse, between enemy ships and the planet.

"Coms, put me on the fleetwide."

"Aye. You're on, sir."

"Beings of the Milky Way, the battle is over, and you have done your galaxy proud. I might have returned to find only ruin, but instead I found an intact fleet, fighting fiercely. I've returned with a master code designed to deactivate every Progenitor vessel. I'm ordering you to stop attacking them, as they can't shoot back. In time, we will secure each ship's surrender, but for now we have to prevent any of their ships drifting into ours, into orbital defense platforms, or into the planet's gravity well. Board the vessels in danger of doing so, take control, and steer them to safety. The war is won, and we must start putting things back together at once."

He gestured at Ensign Fry to end the transmission. She spoke up again almost immediately: "Incoming transmission request, Captain. It's from President Chiba."

Husher suppressed a sigh. Speaking to a politician was perhaps the last thing he felt like doing right now—but probably, it was exactly what needed to be done.

The Kaithian appeared on the CIC's main viewscreen. "Captain Husher. You've saved us. I can hardly believe it. The IU is left with a fleet intact, which isn't an outcome I expected. I expected to die. On behalf of every citizen of the galaxy, I thank you, and I thank your crew."

"We accept," Husher said. "But our job isn't over. I have my double aboard. He was in charge of the Progenitor home system's defense, and he has kill codes for every AI they sent against us. He seems just as incentivized to stop them as we are, now that I've brought him to this universe."

The Kaithian hesitated. "Are you sure it's wise for you to leave, Captain? How do we know that this was the final attack?"

"The beings of this galaxy just proved they can take care of themselves, President Chiba. I'll give you the master code in case any more Progenitor ships come, but I don't think they will. Even if they did, and even if you had no deactivation code, my faith in the galaxy has been restored. Either way, you'll have the kill code. I think you'll be all right."

Chiba didn't sound so sure. "All right, Captain."

"The Progenitor threat will end when the AIs are deactivated. I expect the mission will take a few months. In the meantime, you have no shortage of work to do here. People need to be returned to their homes. The galaxy needs to be recolonized. Oh—and the Eldest needs to be removed from office."

The Kaithian blinked rapidly. "Removed? Why?"

"He's a Progenitor puppet. We found the real Eldest held prisoner in their system."

"But how is that possible?"

"I have to assume they cloned him. They destroyed their universe, so the Quatro there would have been wiped out."

"How am I going to remove him from power without starting another battle with the entire Quatro fleet?" Chiba said, his voice rising in pitch. Husher began to wonder whether the Kaithian was nearing his breaking point. *That's not good.* But if the president broke under the pressure, a new one would simply have to be found.

"It should be fairly straightforward," Husher said. "Present the Quatro with their true leader, and tell them they've been manipulated by a fraud."

The Kaithian nodded, seeming to calm a little, now that Husher had laid out the path before him. "You'll be greeted to a hero's welcome when you return."

Husher drew a deep breath. "I'm not sure I'm entitled to one. Before you start planning it, I'd suggest you review the *Vesta*'s recorded logs of the events in the Progenitor home system. I'll transmit them to you the moment our conversation has ended. It's possible you'll want to start planning a trial instead. If so, I'll submit to it...the moment I return from destroying the AIs."

That made the Kaithian fall silent once more. At last, he said, "Even so. I thank you, Captain."

For the first time that Husher could remember, he felt a twinge of admiration for the president. It seemed he'd just said something he truly felt, despite the political cost that might come with it.

"Thank me by never repeating what you allowed to happen," Husher said. "Thank me by making sure the Interstellar Union scrutinizes its own motives with a truly critical eye, every day, and never stops doing so. Never stop looking in the mirror. And take out your damned Oculenses every now and then."

The president nodded. "Very well, Captain Husher."

"Very well. Goodbye for now, President Chiba."

"Farewell."

Husher indicated that Ensign Fry should cut off the transmission. Then, he gave her another order: "Have Major Gamble delegate a squad of marines to escort my double to the CIC, so that he can provide us with the first set of coordinates. Nav, begin preliminary preparations to transition us out."

"Aye, Captain."

EPILOGUE 1

Nostalgia

Bob Bronson sat in his jail cell and bided his time. They'd taken everything from him, again. His rank, his ship, his connections.

But it didn't matter. He would rise again. *I'll find a way.*

Once they'd realized what had happened to every Progenitor ship, the Sapient Brotherhood captains had attempted to sneak theirs out of the system, but of course they'd been noticed. At once, the IGF had dispatched a small fleet to chase them through Pirate's Path—to hunt them down.

The allied ships had caught up with the Brotherhood well before the Dooryard System, and the battle that ensued had been swift and one-sided. It had ended with the unconditional surrender of those Brotherhood vessels that survived.

Bronson's trial had followed soon after. The IU was making a big show of cleaning up its act, even though it had been their plans to spy on and control their own populace that had allowed him to do the damage he'd done.

He'd pointed that out at the trial, loudly, at every opportunity. But it hadn't mattered. Everyone had been quite content to make

Bob Bronson into a convenient scapegoat for all the galaxy's ills. And now they'd stuck him in here.

Doesn't matter. He was patient, and the universe was strange. No one could predict what would surface from the flows of time. Anomalies tended to manifest themselves. Chaos took root with extreme subtlety. Bronson knew it when he saw it, and he knew how to exploit it.

Footsteps echoed down the corridor outside his cell, and part of him expected Eve Quinn to appear at his bars, to taunt him. *I still need to make her pay. Someday, I will.*

Instead of Quinn, Vin Husher came into view.

"Bronson," he said with a wry smile. "Face to face again, for the first time in decades. Not counting our recent transmission."

"*You,*" Bronson spat. "You're responsible for more civilian deaths than I ever managed. Yet you walk free while I'm in here."

Husher's smile fell away. "You would have helped kill billions if you succeeded."

"If you're looking to soothe your conscience, you've come to the wrong place. We both know you're just as monstrous as I am. Take it from me, it's far simpler to dispense with your conscience entirely."

"Maybe that's why we've dispensed with *you* entirely. Why the universe has."

Husher's words echoed Bronson's thoughts from earlier, and that made his stomach twist. "I'm going to get out of here, Husher. And when I do, I'll kill you."

With that, Husher threw back his head and laughed, loud and long.

"What?" Bronson said. "What is it? What are you laughing at, you bastard?"

"I have no doubt," Husher said, still mirthful, "that you or someone like you will become a player again, at some point. Threats never cease, and I'm not talking about the empty ones you've leveled at me today. Real threats. Danger, from without and from within. That's life. But there will always be people like Leonard Keyes—remember him?—and people like me, to oppose you. As for you, Bronson, you're getting pretty old for this stuff. And so am I, for that matter."

Husher turned to leave, then, still smiling.

"Is that it?" Bronson called after him, suddenly loath to be alone. "That's all you came to say?"

Husher paused. "That's it. I thought that maybe seeing you in that cell, just as you spent so many weeks in the *Providence* brig...I thought it might bring me back to the old days. We did serve together, after all, Bronson. For better or worse. And this conversation *has* helped me remember."

Bronson cursed Husher in the vilest way he knew how, but the man was already walking away, laughing again.

EPILOGUE 2

Right to Business

Jake sat next to Lisa Sato, who occupied a chair next to her bed in the *Vesta*'s sick bay. He held her hand in his new prosthetic, though hers hung limply, and he knew that if he let go, it would flop to her side.

Occupying her chair, staring vacantly into nothing, was one of the three things Lisa did. The second was to lie in her bed—sleeping, or staring at the ceiling if she was awake. And the other thing Lisa did was get led around the *Vesta*'s corridors by the hand.

"What did they do to you?" he asked, but as usual, she gave no indication he'd spoken. He expected Lisa had endured treatment similar to that of Fesky, except for much longer. So long that her spirit had not only been broken, but eradicated entirely.

He sighed and gently lowered her hand to her lap. Then, he got to his prosthetic feet and walked through sick bay toward the exit.

In function and appearance, the prosthetics were just like his old limbs, though he could turn up the grip strength if he wanted, and there were spaces inside the fingers to house a variety of tools, if he decided to have them installed.

He wasn't sure whether he wanted that, yet…wasn't sure that he desired anything beyond a regular hand, a regular foot. The reminder that he had become partly mechanical led him to memories of the alien mech's attempt to consume him. To turn him into itself.

After deactivating the first superintelligent AI, Husher had taken Jake's advice and jettisoned the alien mech into the sun. With that, the withdrawals had begun. Worse than losing his limbs, worse than the phantom sensations that haunted him until he was fitted with prosthetics, was realizing just how addicted he'd become to the mech. It had already become a huge part of him, and he of it. Looking back, he realized that physically merging would have been little more than a formality. He'd already given himself to the machine, and if Husher hadn't destroyed it, he would have only tried to access it again. To *become* it again.

He still became the mech, every night, in his dreams.

Rug had dealt with addiction to her mech in a different way. The stoic alien had never let on that she was struggling, but when the war ended, it became clear she had been. She asked President Chiba if he could arrange for her to be given a shuttle capable of interdimensional travel, which he did, on the condition she only use it to travel to other parts of this universe—and not to visit other universes for longer than it took to travel through them. With that, she'd departed the Milky Way, leaving behind her Progenitor-made mech. *Along with her friends. Those left alive, anyway.* No doubt seeing Lisa's condition had taken a toll on her, too. Jake missed the Quatro already. *I wonder if I'll see her again.*

Iris waited in the corridor outside sick bay, hands clasped before her while she waited. "Hey," she said, falling into step with him.

"Hey," he said.

As they walked she glanced over her shoulder, back toward the sick bay hatch. "Do you still love her?" she asked.

Jake glanced at Iris, eyebrows raised. "Wow. Getting right to business, hey?"

"Just answer the question."

"Yes," he said. "I do."

A long silence followed, into which their footstep echoed between the bulkheads.

"Do you love me?" she asked at last.

"I do," Jake said, suddenly feeling very tired.

Iris reached out and took his prosthetic hand. They walked in that manner for a long time, hand in hand through corridor after corridor. They didn't encounter a single person. The *Vesta* was mostly empty.

EPILOGUE 3

The Things That Keep Us Sane

Husher strolled through Home's emerald fields, trying his best to relax. Even now, days after returning, the strain of war rested heavily upon him. His throat felt dry and tight, and constant tension headaches assaulted his skull.

He'd been acquitted of what some still called war crimes—the killing of millions of civilians in the Progenitor home system. But that didn't mean he'd been acquitted by his conscience.

Spending time with Ochrim helped, some. The Ixan was the only being capable of understanding what he was going through. The only one alive who'd also brought himself to pay such a terrible price, out of the conviction that it served the greater good.

Husher knew, now, that the decision still haunted Ochrim, even all these years hence. *And that doesn't bode well for me.* But he had shouldered massive burdens before. He would shoulder this one, too. He would do it for his daughter, whose relationship with Price seemed to be solidifying—a union Husher had played a part in helping to form, by pretending to forbid it. The heart always wanted what it thought it couldn't have.

He'll be good for her, Husher reflected. *He's a good kid.*

Up ahead, fifty meters away and well out of earshot, Ek and Fesky walked together through the towering green grass, along the same cobbled path Husher and Ochrim were on. The path cut whip-straight across the landscape, so that they rarely lost view of the pair ahead.

"If Fesky didn't have such a deep bond with Ek, I'm not sure she ever would have come out of her trance," he said.

Ochrim glanced at him. "Fesky had a deep bond with you, too, Vin." They were on a first-name basis, now. Husher saw no need to insist that the Ixan address him by his rank.

"Not anymore, she doesn't. Not after what that bastard did to her." He shook his head, trying to ward off the sadness that weighed heavily on him whenever he spoke or thought of the Winger. "No, I think the only sort of bond that could have saved Fesky was the one Wingers establish with Fins: the one between members of two species who evolved together, who grew up together. Fesky still can't look at me without flinching, Ochrim. She treats me with fear and revulsion. I doubt our friendship will ever be the same." Husher sucked the warm summer air through his nostrils, in another attempt to stay his emotions.

"She may surprise you," the Ixan said. "I think you ought to have more faith in her. She withstood the Progenitor's torture for a long time, with no real hope of rescue. She never divulged any intel, and she kept herself together. Enough that she could pass on information to *us*. It's quite remarkable."

"I know." It was only thanks to Fesky that they'd learned how the Progenitors had been able to send their AIs to a time thousands of years prior, along this universe's timeline. According to what Husher's double had let slip to Fesky, this was the first form of interdimensional travel they'd discovered. "Have you made a start on figuring out how they sent AIs back along our timeline?"

Ochrim nodded. "I've spoken to Fesky about it, though very sparingly. We don't want to push her too much, in her present state."

"I agree," Husher said. "In fact, I'm not sure we should be pushing her at all."

"In a sense, I'm glad I did. I felt it was important to learn why the Progenitors didn't simply continue sending AIs into our past until one succeeded in completely dominating us. It seems the explanation is that, in addition to only being able to send small amounts of matter and information, the technique also involves a heavy element of randomness. The Progenitors discovered they could only aim their 'injection' of AIs at a region of the path integral, not at a single universe. Hitting a precise spot along a dimension's timeline also proved exceedingly difficult. According to Fesky, they injected their low-level, self-improving AIs into hundreds of universes before successfully hitting ours, and they would have preferred to send their AIs millions of years into our past rather than the thousands they achieved."

Husher felt his eyes widen slightly. "So there are hundreds of other universes with AIs equally as powerful as the ones we just shut down."

Ochrim shrugged. "We still have the kill codes. And the Progenitors will have programmed them never to attempt interdimensional travel."

"Isn't it possible that at least some of the AIs figured out how to circumvent both the kill codes and the strictures against leaving their universes?"

"It's difficult to say, especially if we're talking about an intelligence with potentially an entire universe to harvest for additional processing power."

"Right. And even assuming those AIs are never able to escape their universes, there's still the suffering they'll inflict, or are inflicting, on whatever beings happen to live in those universes."

Turning toward Husher, Ochrim smiled grimly. "I recognize that tone, Captain Husher."

He used my rank. Only to make a point, I'm sure. "Until they're dealt with, those AIs pose existential risks, Ochrim. Especially if we're going to continue traveling the multiverse. Supposing an AI managed to turn its entire dimension into one big trap for ships passing through..." Husher shook his head. "There's also always the danger of a species within our own dimension creating an unbridled AI. I'm assuming the rest of this universe is as teeming with life as our local galactic cluster, so we need to get our own house in order too, so to speak. In the meantime, I want you to stop researching that Progenitor tech, Ochrim. At once. The ability to alter another dimension's timeline...that's something we should keep a lid on for as long as we possibly can."

The Ixan's face expanded, the scaled area around his eyes going wide. "I must be dreaming. You're telling me *not* to pursue tech with military applications? Have we switched roles entirely?"

"It seems so. I'm impressed with the IU's reform efforts, but even if they succeed in changing, who's to say they won't become corrupted again? That's how these things go, in my experience. The people forget their responsibility to keep their government in check, and the powerful start trying to increase control. The thing is, we can't afford for it to happen again, Ochrim. Now that the Progenitors are defeated, interdimensional travel has granted the IU the same godhood that dark tech once gave humanity, but without the universe-destroying qualities of dark tech. If we allow our government to become corrupted again, I'm not sure we'll be able to stop it. It will be too strong to rein in."

"Interdimensional travel may not make us as godlike as you're thinking. The multiverse is vast, and my research has given me good reason to think the quantum engine only gives us access to a tiny corner of it, as colossal as that corner may be. We have no idea what the entire vastness could contain."

Husher's lips tightened, though he knew Ochrim was right. "We don't even know what our own *universe* contains."

"Precisely. But I see your point. There may never be a noble reason to exercise the ability to influence another dimension's history. I will cease my research."

"Good," Husher said, relieved that Ochrim agreed. Unfortunately, he knew that someone would likely stumble on the tech someday, and even if they didn't, the galaxy still faced a host of other problems. The Quatro had broken away from negotiations to join the IU soon after the Battle for Home. Rocked by the revelation that their Eldest had been replaced by a fraud, they'd retreated into the systems they'd been given. No one had heard from them since.

Then there was the issue of how to humanely deal with the billions of civilians still alive in the Progenitor dimension—as well as the millions of Ixan clones the allies had taken prisoner.

The Gok still had their problems, and the general tension surrounding interspecies relations certainly hadn't resolved itself overnight. There was still plenty of room for the Interstellar Union to regress into the tyranny and madness that had seized it in recent years.

And even if *that* didn't happen, there was this new matter of the hundreds of AIs scattered throughout the multiverse, burgeoning inside their own universal fiefdoms, committing who knew what unholy acts.

It's never been so vital to protect the things that keep us sane. With that thought, Husher's gaze settled on Fesky's feathered back, ranging far ahead along the cobbled path. At the same moment, he thought of his daughter, Iris, and his ex-wife, Sera.

And he resolved to do better. Just as he so often had.

Acknowledgments

Thank you to Rex Bain, Sheila Beitler, Bruce A. Brandt, Maikel Hölzel, and Jeff Rudolph for offering insightful editorial input and helping to make this book as strong as it could be.

Thank you to Tom Edwards for creating such stunning cover art.

Thank you to my family - your support means everything.

Thank you to Cecily, my heart.

Thank you to the people who read my stories, write reviews, and help spread the word. I couldn't do this without you.

About the Author

Scott Bartlett was born in St. John's, Newfoundland – the easternmost province of Canada. During his decade-long journey to become a full-time author, he supported himself by working a number of different jobs: salmon hatchery technician, grocery clerk, youth care worker, ghostwriter, research assistant, pita maker, and freelance editor.

In 2014, he succeeded in becoming a full-time novelist, and he's been writing science fiction at light speed ever since.

Visit scottplots.com to learn about Scott's other books.

Printed in Great Britain
by Amazon